25
YEARS TO
LIFE

JOHN SCHRAUB

Publishing Coordinator – Sharon Kizziah-Holmes
Cover Design – Jaycee DeLorenzo

Paperback-Press
an imprint of A & S Publishing
A & S Holmes, Inc.

ISBN -13: 978-1-956806-20-5

DEDICATION

For the first 25 years of my life some very special people gave me much of their time and much of themselves to help me build the foundation I would need to live a good, successful life. Nothing I've accomplished, no matter how big or small, would have been possible without their love.

Thank you Frantisek, Anna, Joseph, Georgiana, Wally, Helen, and Frank.

And to the one person who was just always present in my life … my mentor, my protector, my friend, Artie.

ACKNOWLEDGMENTS

Special thanks go out to Jola and Sarah, who comprise my team, a much better team than I deserve. They encourage me, help me smooth out my rough ideas, and lend an ear on those days I need to talk about the story. I don't pass page one without them.

And finally thank you to my publisher, Sharon. She taught me so much more than I could ever list here, but two of the most valuable gifts she gave me were, every word I use is important, choose it wisely, and be sure I am enjoying my writing journey. I not only remember those words as I write, but lean on them as I go through life.

PROLOGUE

Jack Spencer

Jack Spencer didn't really want to make this trip, or at least 98% of him didn't. If they were merely closing the old school and turning the building into lofts or specialty shops, well, he could live with that. But they're going to level the building and bury every dark tale that occurred there twenty-five years ago.

He had spent the last twenty-five years throwing dust on those memories and he's learned that there is just no amount of dust in this world that can cover some wrongs - this wrong. He has covered, twisted, and denied, but he still carries the pain of loss with him every day. This is his last chance for peace. "If I let my regrets get buried before I exorcise them, they will carry me to my grave and I'll be buried as deeply and as silently as those two innocent girls who were murdered there that night."

CHAPTER 1

Jack stood at the hotel window looking toward the mountain peaks well in the distance. Pyrite, Colorado lay in a valley surrounded by those peaks. When he lived there, the population was enough to support a high school, a few stores, a movie house, and even a couple restaurants. Not any longer.

Most people had left Pyrite; many settled here in Greenleaf. Greenleaf had become a real tourist destination complete with hiking trails, outdoor bars, backcountry jeep tours, and the three-story hotel he was staying in, said to be haunted. They even offered tours of the hotel a few times a year when they claimed that the spirits were most active. The tour included cheese and spirits of a different sort, so nobody left disappointed. But he wasn't here for haunted tours; he was haunted enough for a lifetime.

He was here because it was the closest hotel to Pyrite and his old town was holding a sort of 'Farewell Pyrite' get-together in the hotel banquet hall. His old friends would be staying here also and he hoped they too were still searching for peace.

Tomorrow, Friday, he would know where their thoughts were. They'd all arrive early, attend the party tomorrow night, and Saturday meet at the old high school in Pyrite. By Sunday night, he'd be back home in New York, hopefully at peace with all his demons buried in Pyrite. Monday the bulldozers would level and haul the school and half the town away. *"Should have happened long ago"* he thought.

He turned from the window with a few tears running from his eyes and looked around the room. He couldn't remember entering the room or even checking into the hotel. "I hate everything about this area," Jack admitted to himself.

He sat on the edge of the bed and let the memories of his long-gone friends run through his mind and heart. Sylvia Kean and Rachel Morgan were more his friends than the rest of the group. The three of them made up their own inner circle along with Sylvia's boyfriend, Paul Winston. Sylvia liked him a lot, no doubt about that, but with most of the town thinking Paul was more than a little weird, she kept their relationship pretty secretive. Jack and Rachel went along with the act.

As old memories filled his head, the good thoughts soon turned to the night of the murders. Sylvia was strangled in her new apartment and although they found Rachel's blood just about everywhere in the apartment, her body was never found. The police looked, her friends didn't. Whatever fears they had then about finding the body were still here today.

Overcome with grief, guilt, and exhaustion he collapsed onto the bed and had one last thought, *"this is a bad idea, a very bad idea."*

Nightmares invaded his sleep while he rolled around in the strange bed over and over. Visions of blood and knives, kisses from a girl who morphed into a killer, a car speeding toward him with a familiar figure behind the wheel. Just before the car hit him, Jack was awakened by the ringing phone.

His body still shaking from his bad dreams; cold sweat on his head, he picked up the phone with his clammy hand and it slipped to the floor. The clock read 4:00. "Who would be calling me?" He fumbled for the object in the dark then placed it to his ear. "Hello."

"You've got a lot of nerve showing up here; more nerve than I thought you had."

It was a woman's voice he didn't recognize "Who is this?"

A long silence followed, then he heard heavy breathing so he waited. Before he could repeat his question he got his answer.

"Rachel Morgan."

His breath caught in his throat. He tried to repeat the name, but he couldn't speak. The phone went dead and all he could do was stare at it. He walked over to the mini-bar and with his trembling hand grabbed a couple small bottles of whiskey.

Too shaken to go back to bed, he sat in the recliner in the corner. "This couldn't be! Rachel was dead. Wasn't she? You must have heard wrong," he said to himself. He sipped the alcohol until he fell asleep in the chair.

When Jack woke later that morning, the 4:00 am phone call was temporarily forgotten. He didn't know why he was in the chair and fought the morning sun to get his eyes to focus. He saw the two empty whiskey bottles and his memory flooded back.

"Rachel? Oh my god, it had to have been another nightmare." He tried to put the pieces together to understand what was real and what was a warped dream. With his head hanging low, the bottles Jack stared at were putting him into a trance. He jumped a few feet when the phone rang. He gawked at it and after four or five rings, he hesitantly picked up. "Hello."

"Hey Jack, its Shelby. Did I wake you?"

"No, I'm up. Where are you?"

"In my room. I just got in. I want to see you before everyone else arrives."

"Room 301. Give me half an hour."

"See you then".

"Hey Shel, did you call me last night?"

"Call you? You know darn well I didn't. See you in a bit. Oh, order a pot of coffee. What room did you say?"

"301. I'll leave it unlocked. No need to knock."

CHAPTER 2

Shelby Runnert

Jack didn't remember a time in his life when he didn't know Shelby. They grew up together, as did their entire circle of eight friends. all of whom said that they'd be back in Pyrite this weekend. Jack and Shelby dated throughout high school, but Jack left her without a word shortly after graduation which was also shortly after the murders.

He didn't know what to expect from Shelby as he nervously straightened an already tidy room. Two little bottles in the trash and the room was ready. 15 minutes in the shower and Jack was ready too. As if on cue, the knock on the door followed a final fluff of his pillow. Jack opened the door slowly almost hiding his face behind it as he looked at Shelby. "Hi, come on in Shel. You haven't changed a bit."

Shelby walked into the room and took a quick look around. It was pretty similar to her room, but much larger.

"Look out the window, Shel. Pyrite is in the middle of those peaks somewhere."

"I lived there for almost 30 years. I think I know where Pyrite is."

"I'm sorry Shel. Of course you do."

The uneasiness between the two was palpable. In earlier times, when lovers ended their relationship, they just walked away from one another and started new phases of their lives. Jack and Shelby did that. But in today's world, finding old friends and lovers was all too easy. They did that too.

"So you found us all Jack, and we're coming back here. Was it worth it?"

"I hope so Shel, guess I'll know by Monday."

"I guess I know how you found us Jack … internet, Facebook, school records. Easy enough. But I don't know why. Not one bit. And I have to be honest with you, standing here seeing you again, I think maybe I made a big mistake coming back."

Jack's stomach flipped. If Shelby didn't want to be here it was all for naught. "I felt the same way last night, but I want to come to grips with the past."

"The past? Your e-mails never mentioned the past. This is supposed to be a simple get together weekend. You blew up our past long ago. And where's the coffee?"

"Oh man, I forgot the coffee, what with straightening up and everything. Let's go downstairs for a cup."

While they walked down the three floors, Jack put his pains aside and recalled some of the good times he shared with Shelby. He knew her about as well as he knew any person and probably better than he knew any female. They came from a time and place where people tended to stay put. Everyone in and around Pyrite worked on one end of the spectrum or the other and Jack and Shelby's families fit right into that.

One set of families worked the fields trying to raise cattle and always fighting drought and rising grain prices; the other side was old third generation miners who, over time, started pulling more dust out of the ground than any worthwhile minerals. The town grew to over 5,000 for a while then a slow parade of 4900 marched out of town in rustic floats and deflated cartoon dreams. While the exodus was gaining momentum, Jack and Shelby attended Pyrite High School and moved their grade school friendship into a high school romance.

Shelby loved skiing and hanging out with her closest friends, Nancy Braxton, Lynn Mitchell, and Rita Tanner. They weren't big on music. The radio reception was terrible in Pyrite and the one or two stations that did come in did so quite badly, if at all. They weren't that big on Hollywood types, the movie house ran mainly old movies. But they made it work - kind of.

"If it's new to you, it's new," Shelby would say. It was a great town for the 1950s the girls thought, the only problem was that it was the 1990s. Ski trips to the Denver or Salt Lake areas were the key winter activity and drink became the summer sport. By age 16, most kids in town believed if you couldn't escape these times, you could at least drink enough to not know what day it was. Shelby walked that line too, but not overly so. She was more likely to be seen with a bag of licorice than a bag with a bottle hidden inside. Jack felt something looked different about her - something not caused by the passing of 25 years, but he couldn't quite put his finger on it. They got their coffee from the front counter and found a quiet table to be alone.

"It's been a long time, Jack. You found me easily enough when you wanted to, but never a word before this. Not even a Christmas card."

"I heard you were married, Shel."

"I was never so married I couldn't appreciate a hello from an old friend. You disappeared to some college out east without a word. I think I saw you once after that and you not only disappeared that day, but you made that one for good. Now welcome home, stranger."

"Don't call me that please."

"You're more a stranger than a friend aren't you," she paused and stared then added, "stranger."

"I had to get out of Pyrite, I told you that back then. I came to hate it there. Things were closing in and I was sick to my stomach every day."

"Is this about the past you mentioned? What the hell's on your mind Jack?"

"Sylvia and Rachel. Come on Shel, you know damn well we never did them right. Their blood is on my hands - our hands."

The mood changed instantly. Jack's forehead broke out in a sweat and Shelby's eyes fought to hold back the tears. She looked at Jack with an anger he'd never before seen. Her breath deepened and her eyes narrowed like a laser ready to fire. She wiped the tears away and spoke.

"I didn't come here for this Jack and your e-mail, your damn e-mail to all of us, said we should get together one last night and live like it was yesterday. Some dancing, some laughs, a tour of the school for a long overdue goodbye. Sound about right? You begged and now we're all going to be here. For what? No laughs, no dance, no fond memories. None of us had anything to do with those murders. At least I know I didn't." Shelby paused and shot a look of confusion at Jack. "Are you trying to tell me something? Those girls were more your friends than anybody else's in our group. That last time I saw you before you disappeared in the crowd was at crazy Paul's trial for their murder. You were there. What are you stirring up here, Jack?"

"Nothing bad like that. Just hear me out."

Before he could start, two people walked up to the table. The 'Oh my Gods' were followed with the hugs and cheek kisses. He looked into Shelby's eyes and nodded his head to acknowledge that their talk would have to wait. The floor belonged to Artie and Rita now.

CHAPTER 3

Artie Paychek and Rita Tanner

Jack considered Artie his best friend back in the day when people made such distinctions. Jack's family money came from cattle and Artie and Rita's came from mining. The Paychek and Tanner families both made a fair living in Pyrite as the mine struggled to make a profit through its changes. Artie and Rita worked in the office there, strictly white collar, and although their livelihood came out of the mine, they never bothered to step into it.

Working together was completely natural to them. They hung around together so much that they were almost always viewed as one entity. Kids who played together while their parents got together; high school students who took all the same classes; a dating couple who went everywhere together and just about anything else one could imagine. They even went away to college together, studying mines of course, and eventually got married, adding the legal paperwork to what was already a given by everyone else.

Their wedding was small and rather private and even though it came well after the murder trial, getting the group together to party without Sylvia and Rachel seemed wrong to Artie and Rita. That was in keeping with their personalities … always soft spoken, always thinking of others … they were a little more on the right side of things than the rest of the group. They drank a little less, in fact, Rita almost not at all, and partied less and more quietly than most others. If one of them ever let loose, it was Artie. He would take part in some town hazing's with Jack, Bill Addison, and Steve Connor.

Today it's called bullying and the guilt from those days may bother the others, but it haunts Artie. He tries to rid himself of the past with volunteer work and donating money. Even today, he still feels he is falling short of balancing his scales. When the mine closed for good, Artie and Rita enrolled in a cooking school, together, in Denver.

Their parents bought them a decent restaurant in Greenleaf, an old stone building that could easily pass for a castle. As the town of Greenleaf prospered, so did their restaurant. Today Artie and Rita are two of the most respected people in town. The four old friends sat down to catch up on the missing years.

"You two aren't together are you?" Artie jumped right in. "Shelby, I saw you a few times after high-school and I remember you told me that this old son-of-gun," Artie motioned at Jack, "just took off."

"Artie stop," Rita said sternly.

"It's been over 25 years Rita, there's no feelings left to bruise. Right, Jack?"

"There's always feelings, Artie. Some things never completely die."

The words dropped a damper on the four as though they were all waiting for it. Silence followed for a very long few seconds and Rita tried to salvage the morning.

"Hey, you two haven't seen our restaurant. It's our home too, full second and third floor for living above the restaurant. Let's take a walk and I can give you the tour. We can catch up on things, it's more relaxed that way."

"Good idea." Artie added. "You girls go ahead. We'll catch up. Let Jack finish his coffee and I'll apologize to him for my big mouth."

The girls headed to the Paychek's restaurant and Jack and Artie moved sugar grains around the table.

"You've been gone a long time Jack, and there's not one question I have about the time you've been gone. I do want to know one thing about today however. Why'd you come back? That letter you sent out begging all of us to come home for the leveling of the school and to have one last great time, that was all BS wasn't it?"

"No Artie, I want that. It's going to be a great time. I hear 200 people might show up."

"That's what they're saying. The hall downstairs is going to be packed. My restaurant turned down the request to cook. Too many people and me and Rita wanted to enjoy ourselves. Going to be people from every graduating class imaginable. Thought it would be fun, but you have other goals, don't you?"

"No, not a goal. I just need to put the murders behind me. It's been 25 years and instead of memories and guilt fading away, they've gotten worse. I thought if we walked through the old school and recalled the good times, they would rise to the main part of my brain. If that school gets leveled, my last chance of peace in my lifetime goes with it. It's that simple and nobody else needs to know what I'm dealing with. Dinner and party tonight, laughs, memories, and school tour tomorrow, remember the good old days, and home on Sunday. Then they can level that god-awful building and you'll never hear from me again. I promise."

"We shouldn't be feeling any guilt Jack. We all know crazy Paul killed Sylvia and Rachel. Nothing we could have said or done would ever change that."

"Paul wasn't crazy, Artie. He stuttered a bit and looked at life in an odd way. Oh, and he liked predicting the weather. For that we picked on him and drove him out of school. I think Sylvia really liked him, but kept it quiet."

"And you were running around with Rachel while you were dating Shelby. Feel guilty about that, not murder."

"I wasn't running around with Rachel. The more I got to know her the more I liked her, as a friend. She was probably the funniest person I've ever met. Life was fun with her and we went out a couple times with Sylvia and Paul. But my heart was always with Shelby. Everything changed between me and Shelby after the murders and I had to get away from here. I went to the trial for a day or two in the beginning. They called Paul a madman. They said that he took a sledge hammer to the janitor's closet and busted the hell out of it for no reason. They said that that proved him a lunatic. I tucked my tail between my legs after that and went back to New York for good, I said nothing."

"So, what? Keep your voice down. We didn't do anything wrong."

"We locked Paul in that closet, Artie. I have to see why he freaked out in there. I have nightmares it's me locked in there."

Artie looked around the room to see who was there and who might have been listening. This was his town. The place he called home and where he made his living. To him and Rita, this was their entire world. "Just shut-up man. They locked up the right man."

"Boy, I had you all wrong Artie. The good guy, the giver, the volunteer. The one of us with the big heart. Are you just a big fake Artie?" Jack's temperature was reaching a boiling point. The long dormant volcano was about to explode.

"If any of what you're saying made any difference I'd shout it from the rooftops. We know crazy Paul committed those murders. Anything we could offer would only be to give false hope to a guilty man. I won't do that. That is part of my good guy behavior. Sorry if you can't handle that."

The argument continued in muffled tones.

"I'm not saying that we go anywhere with a 25-year-old story. I just want us to go to the school tomorrow and look at that damn closet. See why Paul freaked out. All he had to do was turn on the light and bang on the door. Someone would have let him out. If I see that closet is no big deal, I think I can rest easy. Finally."

"You go without me, but let me know what you find. I'm not going anywhere near there. If I get mixed up in anything questionable, if Rita and I get mixed up in anything, we could lose our business. A small town like this, people get shunned quickly. I don't think that busted door had anything to do with Paul's conviction. He was crazy, Jack. Talk to the others tonight, but don't let them suspect anything. Get them to go with you. I'll say that Rita and I have to work or we would love to go. You'll have your company and find peace too."

"If that's the best you can do, then so be it. Not a big deal if you're there. Let's go meet the girls. I think I've had about enough of you."

"One last thing Jack. Did you mail me a package to nudge me into going tomorrow?"

"Package? No. I sent you an e-mail, that's it. What kind of package?"

"It's at my place. I'll show you, but it's not going to make your journey any easier."

Artie and Jack left the hotel coffee shop and walked over to Artie's Place. The exterior definitely resembled a castle. The first-floor terrace was a series of glass oriel windows straight out of the Elizabethan age filled with stuffed local animals. It looked like a taxidermist's display window. A giant brown bear filled the window over the main entrance and a mountain lion, moose, lynx, and bighorn sheep filled the others. The main door itself was an old dark oak door with iron trimming and handles. All that the building was missing was a moat. They entered through the restaurant door and saw the women sitting at the bar talking over a mimosa. Before joining them, Artie offered to show Jack around the restaurant and the living area upstairs. It was just an excuse to get upstairs and show him the package. Crawling far back in his bedroom closet, Artie resurfaced with an opened, ratty looking cardboard box about a foot long and three or four inches wide and tall. He handed the box to Jack and waited for a reaction. Jack took the package, but hesitated before putting his hand inside.

"Is that blood on the newspapers?"

"I don't know", Artie said. "The box came in the mail a couple weeks ago. I opened it and reached under the papers. I was more than a little shocked. You can look under there too. It's dry, just packing."

Jack reached in the box and pulled out a pretty old carving knife with a busted handle and discolored blade. The knife was big and thick enough to bring down a bear.

Artie continued. "I don't know why someone would send something like that to me. I thought about calling the sheriff, but with the past were all living with, I didn't want to start anything. I just put the knife back in the box and shoved it in the closet. I didn't even mention it to Rita; no reason to scare her."

Jack put the knife back in the box and closed the flaps. He studied the box and got a quizzical look on his face. "You say this came in the mail? Where does your mail get delivered?"

"Mailman just drops it at the end of the bar. Why?"

"There's no stamp here Artie, no postmark either. Whoever wanted you to have this, walked it right into your building. Was the knife the only thing in here?"

"That's all I saw, but like I said, I looked at it for about 2 seconds and shoved it in the closet. Look through it now."

Jack took out the newspapers that covered the knife and put them on the side. The knife was all that remained in the box.

"Yeah, just the knife, Artie. This could be blood on the papers. Some of these papers are real old, look how yellow they are."

"Yeah," Artie replied, "but most of the papers look new. Real white."

"Odd," Jack mumbled and started unrolling the wrapping. "This old paper's from 1993." Jack scanned the stories on the page. "There's a story here about Sylvia's car accident. Just a blurb, but it blames the town. Says that Rachel was the only other passenger in her car. You got this for a reason Artie. Something's going on, something bad."

"What's the newer paper say? Just packing?"

"Yeah, it's world news, nothing local. Mentions a hurricane heading for Morgan County, Florida."

"Morgan as in Rachel Morgan?"

"Damn it Artie, I think someone just gave you a warning."

Before Jack and Artie dissected the meaning, the girls called from downstairs. They repacked the package and returned it to its hiding place. They agreed to keep the package a secret from them and went down to the bar.

"What were you two doing up there? It's almost noon and we've been waiting to have a mimosa with you." The glasses were full and sitting on the bar. "Let's drink up," Shelby said, "I want to get back to the hotel and see if anyone else has shown up yet."

"Well Nancy Braxton is staying here tonight", Rita said, "we've stayed in touch over the years, we even get together every once and while. She lives a few hours from here, small mountain town this side of Denver. She was shocked to get your e-mail Jack. Asked me if it was on the up and up. We expect her late, but she'll be at the party. I did have to twist her arm a bit. Strange thing, with all of us saying how great it will be to come home again and get together, nobody was happy about actually doing it. Why you think that is Jack? You started this reunion."

"Your imagination Rita. We're all tickled pink to be getting back together even if it's only for one or two nights. It will be a great party, you'll see. Save me a dance. You want to head back to the hotel Shel? I'm ready and I need to call home."

The foursome parted company for the afternoon and had mixed feelings about the evening. Jack wanted to calm things down with Shelby about what he hoped for and Shelby only wanted to feel 18 again. It was a toss-up who had the more unobtainable wish, but neither was comfortable now.

They no sooner started their walk and Shelby jumped on Jack's words again. "So who do you need to call at home? Wife?"

"I don't have to call anybody. I just wanted a minute to pick up where we left off this morning. You misunderstood me and I think you were getting mad."

"I didn't say anything that you could twist and call a misunderstanding. I asked what you are up to. You brought up Rachel. You think I never knew that you were seeing her while you were wasting my nights telling me how much you loved me? You didn't fool anybody. I thought maybe, just maybe, you wanted to get us back here together to make amends with me. Amends for cheating on me, amends for lying to me, amends for disappearing on me without so much as a note saying goodbye. But that's not your hope. You want to make amends for a murder you didn't prevent. Your heart is still with Rachel isn't it? Do you even remember that Sylvia was murdered too? I'll ask you again stranger, what are you up to?"

As they neared the hotel, Jack just wanted to wrap up this conversation and cool Shelby down. He didn't know how she could still find anything to be mad at him about after all these years.

"Look Shel, the real reason I'm here, the only reason I'm here and the reason I begged everyone to come was just to get you here and see you again. I knew you were married so I couldn't just ask you, but believe me, you're why I'm here. As for that other stuff, I do have pains inside me, but not guilt, only some feeling that's becoming all-consuming as time passes. You'd think it would fade in time, but it's killing me. When I got that notice about this party and the school tour, I thought that if I went through the old school one more time I could get some good memories back, memories that belong to you and me. It's that simple Shel. And when I talked to Artie, he panicked. He said if one word came out about how we treated Paul and then kept quiet about it during his trial, we'd be all be run out town and with him living here and running a business, he and Rita would never recover. If I get mixed up in anything in the press or with the law it will hit the internet, everything today does Shel, it's not 1993 anymore. My life in New York would be ruined and my firm would run me off. I'd be dead Shel. Please just let me walk through the school, let me quiet down my thoughts and don't mention a word of this to anyone. You know the last good time we had together was at that party at your house senior year. At least when the party started. By the time that party ended, our lives were changed forever."

"Don't bring that up. I never want to think about that party ever again."

Standing on the hotel steps, they were about to pull open the door when a voice from right behind them startled them both.

"What party guys? Was I there?"

Standing there in a wrinkled shirt that was fighting a losing battle to hide a large belly stood Bill Addison. His bald head helped make him look 10 years older than his classmates.

"No party," Shelby said as Jack opened the hotel door.

"Guys! It's me. Bill."

"They stared hard and unknowingly for a second. Finally Jack said, "Bill Addison? I'll be damned.""

CHAPTER 4

Bill Addison

Bill Addison, born and raised in Pyrite, was perhaps Jack's longest known friend. They met in grade school but knew one another from town events well before that. Jack didn't really understand why he tolerated so much shadiness from Bill, but it was just a lifelong decision that Jack preferred to not overanalyze.

Bill's entire life seemed to be covered in the dust that replaced the silver and the iron ore of the Pyrite mines. Jack viewed him as one of those individuals who spent – no, wasted - twenty plus years in school and exited with little knowledge to help him succeed in the world. Looking back, his childhood problem that laid the foundation for his adult problems was clear, his physical size was far larger than his mental size.

From the very beginning of school, Bill surrounded himself with smaller kids whom he could constantly boss around. He was the leader in grade school of getting his group to torment Paul Winston with his endless pranks.

By high school, the people Bill picked on grew in numbers as did the pranks he pulled on Paul. Finally, about junior year, Bill lost interest in the meanness game and turned his attention to the girls. He was good looking enough and possessed enough of the gift of gab to attract a fair number of girlfriends. Predictably, none ever stuck around very long.

By graduation, Bill's reputation was completely shot as he was labeled a player and pretty much viewed as poison by most girls in Pyrite and Greenleaf. Bill's dad got him a manual labor job at the mine after graduation. He worked just long enough to get together enough money to buy a newer used car and he hit the road.

Bill's travels mirrored his life up to that point. Some east, some west, into the wind, over and around the Rocky Mountains. Near Albuquerque, Bill settled down and signed on with a construction company building mainly casinos in the area. It was hard work under a hot sun nearly every day and was definitely the zenith of his life. He was tanned from the sun and lean and muscular from the hard work. He was making a good living and still cherished his skirt chasing lifestyle. He met and dated a pretty girl named Naomi whom he met in a district called 'Old Albuquerque' just off Route 66.

A short time after they met, they were married. If Bill's story ended there you could slap a 'they lived happily ever after' sticker on it and be happy for him. But his story didn't end there because his skirt chasing didn't end there.

After marriage, Bill ate more, drank more, and chased more women. Within 2 years, Naomi filed for divorce and never saw Bill again. She lived happily ever after. Bill drank his way out of the construction field and headed southwest, landing a job dealing blackjack in a casino near Phoenix. There he met a middle aged woman at one of his tables and enjoyed many booze filled evenings. When money ran tight and then out, Bill and his lady friend tried to scam the casino with Bill paying her for winning when she didn't and slipping her some stolen 25 dollar chips. This worked for about 20 minutes and Bill felt the wrath of the casino. Bruised and battered, Bill returned to New Mexico and has spent the better part of two decades dealing cards in casino after casino in the Albuquerque area. This was Bill's first trip back to Colorado in 25 years. Nobody had any idea why Jack's e-mails brought him back.

"No hugs for your best friend guys? Come on, give it up!"

"Here you go Bill, a handshake will have to do."

"I know you got a hug for me Shelby," a smiling Bill said.

"Sure." A loose hug followed from Shelby.

"We didn't recognize you Bill. Sorry."

"Don't rub it in. Time's been cruel. You two look great though. Living a different life than me, that's obvious."

A dejected Bill Addison hung his head low and followed Jack and Shelby into the hotel lobby. There was an air of tension among the three of them, but nothing anyone could put a finger on. Bill's appearance was somewhat shocking. He was about 43 or 44, like the rest of the group, but he looked closer to 65. He said that his room wasn't ready yet so they sat on the sofa on the far side of the lobby. Small chit-chat started the conversation and things got around to life today rather quickly.

"You know I was real happy to get your e-mails Jack. I was thinking for a long time about coming back here and starting over. Every once and awhile I bump into someone from around here down in Albuquerque, usually Coloradoans flying out. They all mention Pyrite going under so I didn't see any reason to come back. But lately I've been reading about Greenleaf hitting it big as a tourist destination. Talk about a switch of fortunes huh. Anyway, I figured I'm owed some of the gravy from here, I paid my dues and got forced out of here with nothing. Know what I mean Jack?"

"No, I don't Bill. Nobody forced you out. I hope you aren't here for the wrong reason. Let's just have a good visit alright, a few drinks and some laughs. I don't know anything about how this town works anyway, I've been in New York for over 20 years."

"Well I think you can help me, buddy. And I bet you know more about this area than you think. Perhaps you've just forgotten some things and need me to jog your memory. I'm more than happy to do that, after all, what are old friends for. But we'll talk later. I need to check if my room's ready. I'm in 211 if they ever get it cleaned. I could use a few cold drinks and some rest before the party tonight. It was a long drive to get here and to be honest with you I'm a little tired of spinning my wheels. I'll see you guys later."

Bill walked over to the front desk leaving Jack and Shelby standing confused and concerned.

"What's his problem, Jack?"

"I have no idea. Let's go up to my room before he comes back.

I can't take another second of him right now. You would think that in 25 years a person would change for the better, but it seems like Bill's still playing some angle. He was my cross to bear for a large chuck of my life and now I feel like he expects me to pick him up again. Guess I sent one too many e-mails Shel, but let's give him a chance."

CHAPTER 5

Favors

Jack and Shelby went up to Jack's room to relax and have a drink. Shelby chose a coke, Jack a bourbon. He wanted to make sure that Shelby was comfortable with his actions now so he tried to make the conversation revolve around her.

"So how's married life Shel? Does it make you happy?"

"It's making me feel old, I'll tell you that."

"How so?"

The tv watching, visiting with his family every weekend, the endless small talk. Exciting right?"

Jack tried to fill the role of savior. "You were never bored when we were together. Maybe you need a warm hug. Let me hold you a second, just for old time's sake."

They started in a warm embrace and soon their lips were locked in a kiss that they both had been missing for way too long. They then looked into one another's eyes and smiles crossed their faces. Jack was about to kiss Shelby again when a loud knock on the door startled them both.

"Shh, Shel. That's got to be Bill. Keep quiet. He'll go away."

They stood in the middle of the floor staring at the door. Holding back laughter, Jack held a finger in front of his lips. The handle on the door started moving.

"That son-of-a-bitch is trying to break in."

The phone rang and Jack left Shelby to answer it. "Don't go near the door. I'll take care of him in a minute."

"Hello."

"Hey Jack I just saw Steve and Lynn come in to the hotel, man she's still a looker."

"Bill?"

Shelby looked at Jack with confusion in her eyes and then looked back at the door. "Bill? Then who's trying to get in here."

"I gotta go," Jack said as he threw down the phone. He ran to the door and looked through the peephole. Nobody was in view. "Lock yourself in the bathroom Shel." As soon as she closed the bathroom door Jack ripped open the entrance door. Whoever was there was gone now. Jack ran to the stairs and didn't see anyone heading down. He opened the fire exit door and thought he heard a door close on a lower level. He went down a level and again saw nobody. His heart pounding, his pulse racing he hurried back to his room to check on Shelby. He got her out of the bathroom and held the trembling woman in his arms.

"I'm scared, Jack. Who would want to break in on you?"

"Or you Shel. I better walk you to your room. I'll see about getting a different room. Great weekend so far."

He walked Shelby down to her room, number 208. He told her to be sure to use the deadbolt safety lock. He convincingly explained that that would keep her safe. To further make his point, he held Shelby tightly and caressed her back. He lightly touched her under her chin and raised her face to kiss her once again. Shelby pulled back quickly.

"What's wrong, Shel?"

"I can't do this, I shouldn't have kissed you. My husband deserves better from me."

"Does he Shel? He's aging and boring you when he should be making you feel young and happy. I only want what's best for you."

"There's a line a lady doesn't hear a thousand times in her life."

"OK, I deserved that. But know that I am here for you, that's honest. Lock your door. I can pick you up at 6:00 and we can head down to the party together. If you want."

"I'll meet you down there. My head needs to cool."

Shelby went inside and threw the safety latch. She sat in the large easy chair and dreamed of the past. Jack made her feel young for 10 seconds, but he didn't do her any favors. She knew he would be high tailing it back to his Wall Street investment job as soon as he figured out what he was really here for. She didn't feel like being a notch on his belt. The thought put a sad frown on her face. The frown gradually straightened and finally became a smile as she exhaled the smallest of laughter. "Nothing wrong with him being a notch on my belt!" She drifted into the shower.

Jack went downstairs and asked for another room without telling the desk clerk why he was making the request. He wasn't sure why he didn't mention the attempted break in. It could have been a total stranger or it could have been one of his former friends. At any rate, it was Jack's problem to deal with. The hotel was over booked already and it was room 301 or the back seat of his rental car.

"I guess the room will be fine. I understand my friends Steve Conner and Lynn Mitchell checked in. Could you tell me what rooms they're in?"

The desk clerk checked his computer. "Yes sir, they're in adjoining rooms 215 and 217."

Jack thanked him and started to walk away, but quickly returned. "Hey, do you always tell people what rooms your guests are staying in? We'd never do that in New York."

"Well you obviously don't know this area very well, we're not New York. You're safe here sir."

"Right, or maybe you don't know this area very well. Did anybody just ask what room I was staying in?"

"Not of me. Is there anything else, sir?"

Jack nodded an unhappy yes and headed to 215.

CHAPTER 6

Steve and Lynn

Jack always thought that Steve and Lynn were an interesting couple. They weren't a couple at all in the general sense, emotional or physical, but were a couple in the business and inseparable friends sense. They currently co-owned a cattle ranch in Wyoming just a bit north of Laramie. Their road there was long and like everything else that left Pyrite, dusty.

They grew up as close together as two kids from different families could. Their playground was their parents' cattle ranches in Pyrite. Before their teenage years, they were both adept at driving the farm equipment and helping with the heavy lifting; in spite of Lynn's natural beauty, she always did more than her fair share of the heavy work.

The Connor and Mitchell families were neighbors and their ranch properties ran alongside one another's. This was never a problem as they were good friends and having the extra acreage for the stock was a good thing. When the rains were good and the soil rich, the profits were good. There was always some hired help working with both families to relieve some of the burden from aging parents and children growing up. When high school started for Steve and Lynn, they remained close friends, but both started distancing themselves from farm and cattle work.

Steve played a little basketball in high school; he would have preferred baseball or football, but there weren't enough boys in school to field one of those teams. His parents bought him a new 1990 Silverado pick-up truck when he gave his word that he would stay and work the ranch for at least two years after graduation. The truck was perfect for Steve. It had a sliding window at the back of the cab that Steve and his buddies could open and reach into the bed of the truck for their stashed liquor. Drinking and driving, not considered the worst thing in the world in the 90s, was a way of life for Pyrite teens. With Lynn living so close to Steve, she became a regular passenger and drinking partner; they even dated a bit, but were much too close friendship-wise to ever get too serious. As with most of the boys in Pyrite High, Steve preferred a night of screwing around, as he called it, with his buddies than a night out with Lynn. On one summer night before senior year while out cruising with Bill Addison, a tipsy Steve ran over a skunk a few miles out of town. The drunken boys bagged the skunk and threw it into the movie house which promptly emptied out in a mild panic. Steve and Bill sat in the bed of the truck laughing and finishing their beers, not realizing just how bad they smelled. A little immature for 17 year olds, but as bad they got up until that time.

Lynn thought about college quite a bit during high school and if there had been a good school for her to attend near Pyrite, she would have enrolled. Things around town and on the ranch were starting to get a little tough in her high school years and she knew that she would probably be relegated to working at home. She became resigned to her fate and just tried to enjoy those years as best she could. Winter weekend ski trips were her favorite. She and Shelby always seemed to have a trip planned to somewhere and one or two of the other girls often went along. For spring break during senior year, the four girls went to Aspen for a week and invited Sylvia and Rachel up for couple days during their stay. They got the fringe friends pretty drunk and paraded the girls from bar to bar. It wasn't a big deal but it might have been a little mean. While Sylvia and Rachel returned home a little sick, they were unaware that they were the butt of a joke. The other girls laughed about the night for a bit, but they also felt a little bad. They swore to make it up to them and invite the girls to Shelby's senior party that was coming up.

As time passed and making a living in Pyrite became too difficult, the Connors and Mitchells sold their ranches for a dime on the dollar and became business partners on a cattle ranch in northern Wyoming. Both families had their own home site on the edge of a shared 300 acre cattle ranch. Steve and Lynn eventually took over the business as their parents retired and are very successful cattle partners to this day. Still best of friends, still best of partners, there is no romantic link between them. Steve has claimed, perhaps a little jokingly, that Lynn is far too tough for him to ever have an affair with much less marry. Lynn counters with an accusation that Steve is far too weak. To their acquaintances in Wyoming, it sure sounds like love.

They drove down together in Steve's 2015 Silverado with no booze in the truck bed and looking forward, for the most part, to seeing every one of their old group. However as Lynn walked into her room she said to Steve, "It won't be pretty if I hear so much as one word about the murders."

Steve was sitting on the edge of his bed with a beer in his hand. He was tired from the long drive and was hoping to get his blood flowing through his body again. He brought the beer up to his mouth for a sip, but never moved his head. His head held still his eyes glued on the door. Then a knock. Steve flew off the bed dropping his beer and ripped open the door.

"Jack?"

"Yeah, calm down buddy. You scared the hell out of me opening the door like that."

Steve poked his head out the door and looked down the hallway. "I'm sorry. Come in."

"Good to see you Steve, something bothering you?"

"No, no. I swear someone was trying to get in my room. I was waiting for the door knob to move again and then grab em. Turned out to be you this time." Steve hesitated. "It wasn't you last time was it?"

"No, I just got here, but the same thing happened to me and Shelby. Could it have been housekeeping?"

Yeah, that's it. But keep the door locked just for the hell of it. So hey, big guy, how about a big hello for your old buddy. Grab a beer and a seat, let's shoot the breeze."

"I just stopped by for a quick hello. We'll have all night at the party tonight. I want everyone to hear about everyone else. Wouldn't be fair to just share your life story with only me. But I have read that you and Lynn are pretty big time cattle tycoons."

"Not really. We probably owe more money than we'll ever have, it's that kind of business, always borrowing to buy things you need, never selling enough cattle to pay off the loan. If and when we sell the business, then we'll have money. But hey, I hear you're a big time Wall Street broker. Why don't you invest the money I don't have and make me a fellow millionaire."

"If I had a million, it'd be yours. You know I'm really glad you're in for the party. You going on the school tour tomorrow?"

"I doubt it, I think tonight will be enough. Just put those years back in line with the universe, salvage our best."

"I know this is weird Steve, but I have to see the closet we locked Paul in. Why'd he freak out?"

"He was crazy Jack, we all know that. Let it go. You mention crazy Paul to Lynn and she'll bite your head off. I had a hard time getting her to come back home. Drop it; she's right next door."

"Wow, I think you're afraid of your business partner."

Steve didn't think the too-close-to-home joke was very funny.

"I'm kidding buddy. No more Paul talk, I promise, but think about going tomorrow. I'll see you and Lynn downstairs at 6:00. We'll all catch up then."

CHAPTER 7

Nervous Anticipation

Jack walked back down to his room and heard his phone ringing as he fumbled with his key card. He was in no hurry to answer the phone and probably wouldn't have except that it wouldn't stop ringing.

"All right, all right, I'm coming. Hello."

"Hey Jack, its Bill. Why didn't you call me back? I've been waiting."

"I just got back. I walked Shelby to her room."

"That took a long time. Must have gone well, right?"

"Just old friends, Bill. What do you want?"

"Relax kid. Simple request. You guys are all making money from your life here. I want a fresh start and I think, no, I want, one of my dear old friends to give a helping hand. I'll work hard for whoever does. I read that you were a big investor with a Wall Street firm. You can hook me up if you wanted to."

"Come on Bill, what do you know about investing and retirement funds, tax shelters, overseas investments? If you knew that, you'd be doing it already. I can't help you."

"I see your point kid, I'm reasonable. But Artie and Steve run businesses that I can handle. Put in the word for me buddy. You guys owe me."

"Nobody owes you anything. You know you were a jerk in grade school; you were bigger than us and you thought that that made you king. It didn't then and it doesn't now. What the hell do you know about the restaurant business or the cattle industry? You want to ask them for work go ahead, leave me out of it. Why don't you just relax and have a nice visit with all of us tonight and then head home? You'll be glad you did."

There was a long pause on the other end of the line and Jack's stomach twisted as he waited for a reply.

"I'll talk to them, all of them. You want to know what I bring to the table Jack? With money coming in, I know how to keep quiet." The line went dead.

Jack boiled instantly and tore the phone cord out of the socket. He picked up the phone and flung it against the wall. "I'll kill him," he shouted.

He sat on the bed shaking, glad no one else was in the room to get hurt when he snapped.

Bill paced back and forth in his room wondering how to force his former friends into giving him a new start in life with some much-needed cash.

Artie stood nervous at the back door of his restaurant and watched as his wife drove up to the garage.

Shelby laid out the clothes she brought for the evening on her bed and opened her new bottle of perfume. She dialed her husband's number then hung up the phone.

Steve sat with the local paper on his lap reconsidering going back to the high school tomorrow.

Lynn looked in the mirror and cussed at herself for being here. There was anger in her eyes and pain in her stomach. The memory of 'why' was the only thing fading.

Rita helped her friend out of the car and a tear ran down her face as she now believed bringing her here might have been a bad idea.

The friend kept her eyes on the ground and leaned on Rita for strength. It was a big moment for Nancy Braxton.

CHAPTER 8

Nancy Braxton

Back to the earliest days of school, Jack believed that there was no sweeter girl in Pyrite, perhaps in all of Colorado, than Nancy Braxton. Light hair, fair skin, always a smile on her face, shy beyond shy. Every single day throughout grade school, Nancy's mother met her after school and the two walked home together. All the kids saw the two of them meet every day from kindergarten on, so it wasn't anything out of the ordinary. Everyone liked Nancy so much so that nobody would ever had made fun of her daily pick up. Nancy was sort of an enigma within the group. If any one of the group didn't seem to belong, it was Nancy. She didn't drink, didn't stay out late, didn't tease or pick on other classmates, and didn't even seem to ever resort to an argument to make a point. And yet this outsider was the one who kept the group together. When the boys argued, which they often did, Nancy played peacemaker and always put the cars back on the rails. When the girls needed advice, they turned to Nancy more often than to their own mothers.

Her role grew in high school and she became the matriarch of the group. She skied with the girls and made sure that they used some common sense on their drinking outings. Nancy was the one who invited Sylvia and Rachel to Aspen on their spring break. Late in the winter of their senior year, the four girls were sitting at a booth in a coffee shop discussing their plans for the week. Sylvia and Rachel stopped by to say hello and Nancy put the invitation out there for a day or two in the middle of the week. Their acceptance of the invitation didn't sit too well with the other girls, but Nancy sold them on the merits. She got pretty aggravated when they got the girls drunk and sick and insisted that Shelby make it up to them by inviting them to her party a month later. The thought was good, the result not so much so, but she tried. Nancy's parents didn't work mine or cattle ranches either. Her father drove a propane truck and filled tanks all around town and her mother waitressed in a town café working similar hours to Nancy's school hours. This helped keep mother and daughter close and when Nancy's father died of natural causes before she was out of high school, their bond grew necessarily close.

Nancy and her mother moved to a small town about two hours east of Pyrite soon after high school. Nancy was done with school and had no desire for college. She did eventually meet a good guy whom she married and with whom she started a family. Nancy's mother lived with the family and in hindsight, that relationship might have been a little too close. A short time after the marriage began Nancy's mother passed away and that began the slow downward spiral of Nancy's life. Perhaps her old Pyrite friends or a minor reunion at that time may have helped. But it wasn't to be. Despite staying in touch with Rita, her life and then her mind slowly unraveled. For the first time in nearly twenty years, Nancy was going back to Pyrite. Memories were about to be tested.

CHAPTER 9

All Together Now

Jack took the long walk downstairs and stopped at the registration table outside the banquet hall. He said hello to a few people he casually knew back in the day and added a 'name tag' to his thousand dollar suit. He stood in the doorway looking around the room and spotted Artie, Rita, and Nancy sitting at one of the round tables. He hurried on over excitedly and offered his hellos. Nancy said nothing and when Jack finally focused his eyes on her, he was taken aback by her appearance. He needed to talk to Artie and suggested they go to the bar for drinks. He grabbed Artie's arm hard and pulled him away from the table.

"What's wrong with Nancy? She looks terrible. You never mentioned a damn thing."

"Let's go upstairs and find a quiet place. We can't talk here."

Across the lobby from the front desk Artie opened up.

"Number one, we brought Nancy here today because we thought, and her doctor agreed, that it just might be a good thing for her, so that's what we're hoping for. She doesn't have any interest right now in how she looks, doesn't do make-up, and doesn't pay much attention to her hair. Rita tried a few things before we came over, but she had to be careful to not make her uncomfortable. And just so you know, she looks okay for what she's going through and has even talked a bit more today than she has in a while."

"What do mean what she's going through?"

"I'll explain as best I can and then we'd better hurry back downstairs. Nancy moved away from here shortly after high school like most of you guys did. She moved with her mom a bit east of here and settled in a small town pretty much like Pyrite. Rita stayed in touch with her by snail mail mostly and an occasional phone call. Nancy eventually got married and had a child and they all lived together with Nancy's mom until she passed about fifteen years ago … I'm making a wild guess on the years. Anyway, Nancy took it real hard and her husband called Rita and asked for help. He said that she was way too depressed and quiet even for her."

"She and her mother were always kind of weird close," Jack said.

"Yeah, too close. We drove out there after the mom died and Nancy was awfully quiet and distant, but nothing that we were that worried about. About 5, maybe 6 years after that, Nancy's husband and daughter got killed in a car accident."

"Oh my God. That's not something anyone can handle, much less Nancy."

"Right, well Nancy then withdrew further and I don't know if it was right away and sometime after, but Nancy had a complete breakdown. I don't know what they call it, but it was some sort of mental or physical breakdown. She ended up in a hospital. They tried all sorts of medicine on her, counseling, you name it, but she was pretty far gone for a number of years. At some point, they said something else was happening in her head. I can't think of the word, psych something or other. Psychosis, that's it. She started talking to her daughter, maybe seeing her too. Well they obviously had to put her in a state run home and she's been there a number of years now. For the last year or so, and we think because of some new drugs, she's been doing a lot better. When this reunion thing you started came up, we mentioned it to her doctor and we all thought there was a chance this could have a positive effect on her and that this trip was worth the gamble. We love Nancy, so you have to do your best to be normal around her."

"What's normal to her."

"I guess nobody knows that. Just be yourself. The doctor thinks she may actually do better remembering all of us, her old close friends, rather than a lot of other people. We're all pre-accident memories. Try to be yourself. To be honest with you, if it wasn't for Nancy, I don't think Rita and I would be here tonight."

"Didn't anyone want to be here tonight? I guess I'm not the only one with nightmares."

They went back down to the banquet room and Jack stopped Artie again. "We'd better bring some drinks back, that's what we said we went for. Our tables full now, the whole group back here."

"Hope you're happy. You pay for the drinks."

"Sure, I got the first round. You carry me the rest of the night. Oh, before I forget, Bill may hit you up for a job, he says we owe it to him."

"Right, I want that loser in my restaurant. Same old Bill Addison, everyone owes him something."

"He wanted me to hire him for investments in New York. I passed him down to you I guess. You can pass him to Steve, cow crap seems right up Bill's alley."

"No, over-qualified."

"Bill?"

"No, the cow crap."

The two got the drinks and laughed their way to the table.

CHAPTER 10

A Loud Dark Night

By the time Jack and Artie arrived back at their table, the entire group was talking up a storm. They moved the flowers from the center of the table and placed the drinks there. A couple soft drinks, a couple screwdrivers, three bourbon and cokes, and Jack brought a martini for himself. Everyone chose their drink of choice, Bill grabbed a bourbon and coke then went to the bar for a straight whiskey. "Smoother", he said.

A DJ played music from the 90s as small talk filled the room. The tragic story of Nancy quickly and quietly made it to everyone's ears and they treated her extra special in light of it. They posed together for pictures with the event photographer, the photographer from the local paper, posing in all sorts of various combinations of people. The pictures would be posted online for purchase. Amid the talk and photos, the friends took time out to dance with each other and did their share of gimmick dances like the hokey-pokey and chicken dance. Corny as could be, but since they were all too cool to do these dances when they lived here it was a good time to finally capture their corny side. They all shared laughs on the dance floor and shared some tender moments too. A couple guys danced with Nancy and everyone thought that her distant look was actually softening. It may have just been wishful thinking.

Jack danced with Shelby and complimented her on everything, her clothes, her hair, her perfume, her dancing, and everything Shelby in general. Bill corralled Artie at one point and asked him for a manager's job at the restaurant. Artie was ready, said that that was his job, but suggested he talk to Steve. Bill mumbled something and returned to his whiskey and seat at the table. Rita thought it would be a good idea for everyone to exchange cell phone numbers and this began a comical 30 minutes of everyone calling everyone else and saving and editing numbers. By the end of this foray, they all believed that they had the right number to the right name. Over two hours into the party everyone was having a great time. Jack was smiling a wide grin at Shelby and Bill felt it his duty to point that out.

"Hey Jack, you and Shelby look pretty happy. Did you get to finish that discussion you were having at the hotel this afternoon?"

"Yeah we're all set, thanks."

"Share guys, I think it was about your senior party Shelby, right?"

"Why don't you shut up Bill, and put the whiskey down."

"That party got ugly didn't it Shel?" Lynn said.

"What party Rita?" Nancy asked, "was I there?"

"Oh yes Nancy," Bill was all too eager to answer. "We were all there."

"Tell me about it," Nancy whispered.

"Sure. You want to tell what you remember Shel?"

"No, but feel free if you want Rita; it's vague to me."

Rita decided it wouldn't hurt to talk about it, it wasn't that big of a bomb, and it might help Nancy deal with some memory issues. She took the floor.

"Anyone jump in if they remember something different than what I say."

"I'll jump in now," said Lynn, "limit the story to the people here. That's plenty."

"Well after we girls got home from our April Aspen spring break, we decided to throw a senior party. With class night set for mid-May and graduation at the end of the month, we set our party early May, whatever Friday or Saturday that was. Shelby, you had the bright idea to bring in a fortune teller."

"Right," Shelby said, "a harmless palm reader."

"Well, maybe not so harmless. Records played, some of us played cards, and drinking was out of control. We were 18 going on 25 in our minds, we were the big tough adults that night. The fortune teller set up in a bedroom and one by one we went in to have our palm read. She was seeing ghosts and dead people in everyone's palm. She was talking about guardian angels and grandparents weeping for some of us because how we are living life. As the night went on, more and more of us were crying, upset over our dead relatives. It got very ugly and more than one argument broke out. That's really the gist of it. Sound familiar?" Rita asked Nancy.

"When we lose people, they do become our guardian angels. I've seen them" Nancy said.

"You forgot to mention crazy Paul and his meltdown," Bill added, "running all around yelling with that stutter, you, you, you, you, you; he was scary."

"He's not here Bill," Lynn said quite loudly. "We agreed to leave those not here alone."

"I didn't agree to that. You guys stole his truck that night and he went off on all of us."

"Drop it Bill." Lynn jumped him again. "This isn't the goddamn place for this talk, and there isn't any reason to go through that again."

"They brought it up at his trial, and none of you said a word."

Everyone was getting testy now and the loud voices were drawing attention from the other tables. Artie tried to calm things.

"You want to do this now, then let's go over to my restaurant. We closed at 7:00 tonight for this wonderful party. We can argue in the bar."

"And I can let Nancy have some peace in her bedroom. She doesn't deserve this fight."

"To the restaurant it is," an instigating Bill Addison said.

"You're such an ass, Bill," Lynn said as mad as she ever has been.

"Totally," Rita added, "if you hurt Nancy, I'll scratch your eyes out."

"Hear me out ladies, then if you still want to you can scratch my eyes out. Or if either of you got a good paying job for me, we can drop this whole thing now."

"Let's go have our talk."

The group headed out the door not sure what discussion they were headed for. Jack and Steve were at the back of the pack and were stopped by the party organizer, Frank Koonce, whom Jack knew vaguely from Pyrite and his years there.

"I take it your friend found you. Great crowd, but nowhere to hide. Oh, I didn't mean to imply that you'd hide."

"Understood, but I don't know which friend you mean."

"A lady about your age, held a scarf in front of her face. Asked if Jack Spencer was here, said she was going to surprise you."

A lady at the table jumped into the conversation. "Shock you. She said she was going to shock you."

"And she held a scarf?" Jack asked.

"I think her face was scarred. Looked like it around her eye above where she held the scarf. She was trying to hide something."

Frank was looking around the banquet room. "I don't see her. She must have gone."

"Come on Jack, probably some younger girl who had a crush on you in high school. We need to catch up to the others."

"Right." And off the group walked to Artie's Place.

Once in the restaurant Rita took Nancy up to bed and got her comfortable in the strange quarters. Artie offered drinks to everyone, but they were all out of party spirit. Lynn asked for a Coke. Rita came down and told everyone to make it quick, she was heading back up to be with Nancy as soon as she could.

Lynn, still fuming, started in on Bill. "What were you referring to that they brought up at crazy Paul's trial."

"Can we stop calling him crazy?" Jack asked.

"They brought up that we stole his car?" Lynn wondered aloud.

"I doubt that Lynn," Jack said, "I'm guessing that they brought up how wild he became and wanted to fight all of us. Remember him screaming for his car keys and saying his old man was going to kill him if anything happened to the truck."

"Man, that was a hideous truck," Artie said. "But you weren't at the trial, were you Jack?"

"A few days here and there."

"You took off for New York during the trial," Shelby said,

"kind of just disappeared."

"I was starting school in Columbia and had to go. I hardly disappeared."

"You never came back. That's disappearing in my book."

"Were getting off track here Shelby," Bill said, "this isn't about you. I only went to the trial a few days. The little I heard made me sick and I tried to forget it."

"Just get to it already."

Bill continued. "I'll get to it, but you guys are gonna have to fill in the blanks. Seems they found some lady who claimed she saw crazy - I'm sorry - claimed that she saw Paul's powder blue pick-up truck parked next to Sylvia's house and a man that she was sure was Paul was sneaking around looking in her windows. She said that this was about a month before the night of the murders. That would have been your party night Shelby. Now I don't know if any of you ladies went to the trial, but the few days I went, Artie and Steve were sitting arm in arm in the courtroom. You two knew damn well that you took Paul's truck and parked it by Sylvia's house and that Paul was only walking around to get to his truck. And you two sat there and never said a word. Reasonable doubt went out the window with your silence."

Steve jumped off the barstool and made a run at Bill. Jack and Artie held him back. Lynn looked at Steve with tears in her eyes, "Did you do that Steve? Did you hide the truth?"

"It wasn't like that, Lynn. We were eighteen years old and we all knew - we all know - that Paul killed those poor girls. There's nothing we could have added. That's why Bill and Jack were quiet too."

"I wasn't even here for that part of the trial," Jack said. "Don't put this on me. If you were here, you guys should have said something to someone."

Jack looked at his old friends and had an instant knot in his stomach. Whatever wish he came back to town with for ending his nightmares seemed to be quickly disappearing. He wondered if things were actually worse than he remembered and the deeper everyone dug, the deeper his nightmares would bury themselves in his mind. He found himself staring a hole through Bill when he started up again.

"You can't say that I was quiet, you have no idea what I told the police," Bill said. "They questioned me. I answered all of their questions as openly and honestly as anyone could. I have a clear conscience. If you have a clear conscience Jack, you wouldn't have begged all of us to return this weekend and you wouldn't be begging us to go to the school with you tomorrow."

"I have a clear conscience. The police never talked to me, I wouldn't have known who to talk to or why. We didn't steal Paul's truck, we hid the damn thing. If some lady saw him sneaking around, then he probably was. And if the police didn't talk to me, I doubt that they talked to you."

"They probably did," Rita said, "talk to Bill I mean. That old investigator questioned me too. I forget his name."

"Ken Anderson."

"Yeah, yeah, that's the guy. He told me that they had their guy, but just wanted to tie up some loose ends. He asked me about the evening ceremony and if I knew where everyone went afterwards. He said he knew all the cliques at the school and was only talking to one or two kids from each group. I don't remember everything I said, give me a minute. Let me look in on Nancy."

Rita was only gone for a couple minutes and appeared to be a little nervous when she returned. Looking in on Nancy and trying to recall class night, the night of the murders, and her meeting with Anderson, shook Rita up. She sat at a lounge table, all eyes on her, she began to talk slowly, but with conviction.

"Nancy's father had passed a few weeks before class night during our senior year. I remembered that as soon as I looked at her just now. He died before your party Shelby and the fortune teller really upset her. But I remember her mother met her after the class night ceremony and they walked home together. Pretty normal for them and the father's death made it hard for them to be alone. I told that to Anderson. We all knew that. I know I mentioned all of us to Anderson, I'll try to repeat my words that I said to him." Rita then retold a twenty-five year old story.

"I got a ride home from Artie. He walked me to the door and I was inside before he went back to his car."

"Artie, you dropped me off and drove home I guess. Pretty normal."

"Lynn, you got a ride home from Steve in the black pick-up."

"Steve, you dropped Lynn off at home and then you went

home."

"Jack and Shelby, you guys went into town and said that you were going for a pizza or fries or something."

"Bill, I didn't know where you went. I'm sorry but that's what I told Anderson."

"That's what I told Anderson about all of us."

"That's alright Rita," Bill said. "That's probably why he questioned me. I went straight home and was watching TV with the folks. They both confirmed that, my alibi, not that I ever needed one."

"Okay Bill. We all have alibis for a couple of murders we had nothing to do with and were never suspected of. What's your point?"

"Just a minute Jack; you don't exactly have an alibi, do you?" Shelby said. "We sat down at the café and ordered a couple Cokes. We were talking about college and you were all hyped up about getting out of Pyrite. We argued about how cold your decision was and you stormed out before we even ordered something to eat. The owner covered me on the Cokes, I had no money, and he even drove me home. I have no idea where you went, only that you were furious with me when you took off."

Jack was quiet now and he just stared at Shelby.

"Where did you go Jack?" Bill said, "I'm beginning to wonder about this guilty conscience of yours."

The words were infuriating and Artie and Steve were ready to hold Jack down, but Jack held back. "You're dirt Bill, no better now than 25 years ago."

"That's not a good alibi either Jack."

"He doesn't need an alibi Bill," Artie said, "Nobody here is under suspicion. Can we just drop this?"

"Soon. But let me ask Lynn a question. Where did Steve go after he took you home?"

"Home I guess."

"Right, you guess. And Rita, where did Artie go after he took you home?"

"I have no idea, is that what you want to hear?"

"That's what I want all of us to face. The night that Sylvia and Rachel were brutally murdered, there were three teens who were known to drink heavily, possibly driving around town looking for their kicks. And when these three drunks could have provided crazy Paul with the reasonable doubt he needed, they clammed up tighter than a bank vault. This gets out folks, we're going to have one giant problem here."

There was more anger than tension in the room now and most was directed at Bill with more than enough left over to cast shadows on most of them.

"What kind of problem, Bill?" Lynn asked. "If something needs to come out, then we're bringing it out, I don't care how many years it's been. I think we all agree on that."

"Slow down Lynn," Artie said. "There's a lot to lose here, Bill might be right. The story goes around that Rita and I covered something up, our business may go right down the drain. People in a town like this won't support that sort of thing, especially if gets blown all out of proportion."

"My company won't keep me on if I'm blamed for anything to do with a cover up. I have to have a clean record and people's trust. This could be bad, really bad." Jack looked at everyone and didn't see any support in anyone's eyes."

"Cover up?" Steve asked. "If I'm hearing this right, and we go to the police and say that 25 years ago we held back information about a double murder, we aren't going to get a wrist slap for a cover up. They may reopen the whole thing. We could all be suspects in the murders. Paul's probably sitting in prison somewhere and they'll have to at least look at the trial record. No, no, no. We have to stay quiet."

Lynn was getting sick. "Steve stop it. I won't stay quiet with a man sitting in jail. All you did up to now was hide a car and not talk about it. That can't go far."

"You got the closet thing at school too."

"What closet thing?" Lynn asked Steve.

He tried to explain. "We told Paul that there were old weather magazines in the back of the storage closet and the school said that he could have them if he wanted. Jack had an old skeleton key that fit the door."

"I actually saw it in the door lock and took it."

"So when Paul looked in there we shoved him back, slammed the door and locked him in. We thought he'd bang on the door until someone heard him and got him out, we all took off. So one of the things Paul found in the closet was a sledge hammer and he went absolutely crazy in there and busted down the door. When the teachers heard the racket, they came running down and Paul was out by this time. They assumed he busted down the door for no reason, just his anger. I heard that they started yelling at him, calling him crazy which set him off further, and he took off. He never came back to school, so I guess they mailed his diploma to him."

"So a couple pranks gone bad; we shouldn't let that ruin our lives, right?" Rita asked. "You guys had no reason to mention the closet."

There was a moment of silence and Steve motioned to Artie to talk. Artie shook his head and added some new details.

"Well one of the things they brought up at the trial was that there was a broken down door inside Sylvia's apartment that looked exactly like the broken down door in the school that Paul demolished."

"Please don't tell me you guys just sat there again and let them compare a door broken down by a pranked school kid and a door broken down by a murderer. Steve, I know you better than that, please say something." Lynn was crying harder now, her hands shaking.

"Why did Paul go crazy in the closet?" Rita asked, "maybe he really was the loose cannon they made him out to be."

"Jack thinks that if we check out the closet tomorrow we may get a clue, put our minds at peace that we didn't do anything wrong. It couldn't hurt to look." Artie was almost pleading Jack's case now.

"You came back to look at the crime scene Jack? All the things you said to me about walking the halls we walked together and seeing where we spent so much time together was just a pack of lies. You're not going to find peace that easy. Steve's right, this whole murder thing may land on you guys, us girls too just because we were too stupid to get away from you. And oh my god, they'll grill the hell out of Nancy. She can't take that. Now what? We should have never come back."

CHAPTER 11

Judging the Jury

After being called out by Shelby, Jack moved the conversation forward. "It's no wonder we all left Pyrite after graduation and the trial. Artie and Rita are the only ones who even stayed close and I'm guessing only because their parents got a screaming deal on the restaurant. But we're back now and we need to face up to what we did or didn't do. This is it guys."

"There's no question about what you need to do," an angry yet subdued Lynn persisted. "We tell somebody about the closet and Paul's truck or we girls become as guilty as you idiots. That clock starts ticking today and we won't sit on hard facts. You guys are haunted and want to drag us down too."

Shelby added her two cents. "If we stay quiet for a little while, we'll have to stay quiet forever. Is that what you want? Is our silence what you're trying to get this weekend? Are you guys hiding more secrets? What else did you do to Paul?"

"Nothing Shel. I swear," Jack said.

"Don't you dare swear to me. I don't believe a single word you're saying. I'm with Lynn, I say we go to the police."

"Hang on girls," Jack said, "Artie's livelihood, Rita's too for that matter, and my life are over if we go to the police. We know Paul did the crime and he's paying the price. Us boys, men I guess, have been paying the price ourselves for our silence. It's been twenty-five years and all's well. I say we leave it alone."

"I gotta think of myself here. What's best for one Bill Addison. I need to know which side of the bread my butter is on and up till now I'm not seeing any butter at all and what I really want to see is some bread."

Jack gave Bill a dirty look; his patience was wearing thin. It took all his inner strength to keep from pounding him, but he wanted the peace that had eluded him for too many years. "Come on guys, there's got to be a lot more from the trial that got Paul convicted. Steve, you and Artie were there, fill us in. We can figure out the right thing to do if we know a little more."

Artie wanted to do the right thing, but only up to a certain point; he had to protect his way of life. He figured he could tell about the trial in a way to push silence. "Hey sweetheart," he said to Rita, "maybe make a pot of coffee, we're all getting a little tired and could use a boost. Okay if I start, Steve?"

"Sure. My memories of the trial are pretty deeply buried, that's for sure."

"Well from what I remember, they ram-rodded the whole thing through. Anderson, the cop, had to be near 80 years old and his mind was going. He had to have turned his report in pretty damn quick because they went to trial in less than four months. That had to be a crappy investigation and I'm sure the prosecutor knew that too so he wasted none of his precious time looking into anything. They knew they had their guy and wanted this over and done with quickly. I don't think there was anything we could have said that they would have looked very deeply into. We know that Anderson talked to Rita and Bill so we did have our say, sort of."

Rita returned with a coffee pot and eight cups; everyone took a cup. All eyes were on Artie.

"If I remember correctly, the town prosecutor first tried to establish a motive of sorts. He said that Paul was infatuated with Sylvia and that's why he was lurking around her house and they had that witness to corroborate that. They said he was probably there peering through her windows a lot more than just that one time. They had no proof of that either so obviously we couldn't have gotten our story in."

Shelby was growing more agitated and turned on Jack again. "Jack you told me that you think Paul and Sylvia were into each other, an item that Sylvia wanted to keep quiet. And you were seeing Rachel while you were dating me, weren't you? So you knew that there was no infatuation there, they were an item and Paul had every right to be at her house. You sat on that too. How deep are you in Jack?"

"Let's bat all our questions around when I'm done, okay?" Artie said, "Maybe everything will be clear. Where was I?"

"The motive" someone whispered.

"So Paul's lust was his motive. They then went into his opportunity. The prosecutor said that Paul followed Sylvia's car to her new apartment. She just rented the house on Mineral Road where he believed Sylvia and Rachel were going to live after graduation."

"I never heard that theory," Jack said, "that's wrong, I'm pretty sure that's wrong."

"Did you hear different from Rachel herself Jack?" Shelby was beginning to become an entirely different person now, she was angry and everyone could see her face reddening even in the dimly lit restaurant. "Just where did you go when you walked out on me that night?"

"People, we'll be here all night if you don't let me finish. So they said that Paul parked outside and waited for his moment. He walked around the building looking in the windows and when he saw that the girls were in separate rooms he made his move. He broke in through the front door just like he did the door at the school."

"And you two assholes, our heroes," Lynn yelled at them, "sat there as quiet as little angels while a man's world was collapsing all around him. He broke the school door because of you guys. Do we need to hear more to know what the right thing to do is?"

"Let me try to tell their whole theory please." Artie continued. "So Paul's in the house and he knows from his peering where the girls are and he's lusting after Sylvia. He grabs a knife from a kitchen drawer and sneaks into Rachel's room. The prosecutor figured the girls were touching up their rooms before their move. Paul stabs Rachel and assumes she's dead or injured enough to not interfere with his plans. He goes to Sylvia's room and she must have heard the attack on Rachel. She's locked herself in her room. No problem for Paul - don't anyone say a word - but he breaks that door down. He starts fighting with Rachel for what he wants and has her by the throat. Autopsy records showed she was strangled."

Jack was engrossed as Bill paced the room. Rita turned her back on the group and stood teary eyed at the bar. Lynn sat in a chair, arms folded across her chest and felt her blood begin to boil. Steve and Shelby waited for Artie to continue. They were all finally quiet.

"While Paul is choking the life out of Sylvia, a badly injured Rachel has come to. She takes the knife she was stabbed with and uses whatever strength she has left and attempts to save Sylvia. She gets to Sylvia's room and weakly stabs Paul in the side; he has a wound when he's arrested. He gets off of Sylvia and gets the knife away from Rachel. He probably stabbed and slashed her according to the prosecutor, but her body was never found so that is just supposition. Paul leaves Sylvia on the floor or bed for now and carries the dead Rachel out to Sylvia's car and puts the body in the trunk. His pickup wouldn't have hidden the body as he drove to wherever it was he went to bury Rachel. He took a shovel out of his truck and put it in the trunk with Rachel, they find his shovel there when they found her car. So Paul buries Rachel somewhere close, leaves her car a short ways down the road and walks back to the house to have his way with Sylvia. The police in Pyrite got a call from someone; this was before we knew where each and every call came from - that a lot of noise was coming from Sylvia's house. They dispatched a car. What Paul didn't know when he went back was that he had already killed Sylvia. So he picked up the second dead body and was heading out to bury her with Rachel when the police arrived. They arrested him right then and there. They found Rachel's car the next day and found the shovel in the trunk. Anderson inspected the crime scene and sent the knife to the Denver FBI for blood analysis, he asked Paul if that was his shovel and Paul said yes. They showed the jury pictures of a dead Sylvia, pictures of Rachel, pictures of the knife, and they had the shovel in court. The FBI report said that the blood on the knife matched Paul's, they pulled his blood after his arrest, and some blood matched Rachel's. They had her blood report from some accident she and Sylvia got into years earlier. The report said that there was other blood on the knife, which is to be expected, but nobody else that they had on file. There's no reasonable doubt here, no reason to ruin our lives. They got Paul red-handed with the body, his shovel in the car, his blood on the knife. If we're here to put this nightmare behind us, I hope this does it."

A saddened Lynn now seemed satisfied and she whispered softly, "What did Paul say about all of this?"

"He knew he was caught," Artie said, "he never took the stand, never said a word."

"What did Paul's lawyer say? He had to offer some defense or why go to trial." Lynn's earlier aggression was returning.

"It just doesn't matter Lynn," Artie yelled at her, "let it go. I've got nothing else to say."

"You were there Steve, you better have more to say. What did Paul's lawyer say happened? Did he give Paul a fair trial that all of us kept from him?"

Steve feeling the discomfort of being under Lynn's thumb squirmed a bit. "He got a fair trial Lynn, his lawyer told a good story, but it didn't sway anyone. It was too far-fetched."

"Did we push Paul?" Jack asked Steve? "Was that the defense? I need to know."

"Hell no Jack. None of us were mentioned."

Artie walked over to get a cup of coffee, but the pot was empty. "Rita can you refill this," he said as he handed her the pot.

"It's after one, you sure?"

"If Steve's done talking, I'm fine without it."

"Steve hasn't started talking yet, Artie. Better fill it up Rita. Some people are too anxious to get out of here tonight." Lynn was back to demanding, she may well be the toughest one in the room. "Talk, Steve."

"I'm sure I'll get some of this story screwed up, but I'll try. Paul's lawyer kept him off the stand, I guess with Paul's stuttering and fidgeting he would have made an easy target to find guilty, not sympathetic. So his lawyer told the story by questioning Anderson and in his closing. Paul claimed that he got a phone call from someone, he didn't know who, that Sylvia was in trouble at her new apartment and needed his help and was told to hurry. Paul arrived and the house was dark; he was scared about what might be going on and walked quietly to the door which Paul says was opened, if he remembered correctly. He walked in, it was dark and he didn't know where the light switch was in the kitchen where he entered. He moved toward the bedroom and kicked something on the floor which he bent down to pick up, a knife. He held the knife and kept moving to the bedroom. When he reached there, he turned the doorknob and pushed but the door was locked. He said he took a big breath, feared someone was hurting Sylvia even though he didn't hear anything. So he busted down the door, crashed into an old wooden cabinet knocking himself out and he landed on the knife he was holding, stabbing himself in his side. He said that he didn't believe that he was out long and when he came to he was lying on the floor bleeding, next to Sylvia. He called out for help, but no one answered and he believed he was the only one in the house with Sylvia. He tried to wake her, but there was no movement so he picked her up and said he was going to put her in his truck and drive her for help. As soon as he walked out the front door he was facing a couple cops with drawn guns. He just froze and was standing there when the cops suddenly rushed him. They took Sylvia's body and knocked Paul to the ground in his own blood holding a fully loaded pistol to his head. An ambulance came from here, Greenleaf, and took Sylvia's dead body to the hospital leaving the bleeding Paul behind. The police took him for bandaging at the Pyrite clinic and then threw him in jail. Anderson started his investigation the next day and realized right away that Rachel was with Sylvia that night and was missing, most likely dead. Paul never said where the body was buried even with a vague promise of the town going easier on him if he told. The jury was out a couple hours tops, guilty. Judge gave him 25 years to life. I just realized that means he could get out this September; that's when he was sentenced. So there people, no reasonable doubt, no reason for us to doubt the verdict or ourselves. We stay silent. We all agree?"

The group looked at each other, nobody seemed committed to anything.

"I don't see a problem with either story," Shelby said. "I know that there was probably a lot more mentioned at the trial, but if you guys would have spoken up about the school door and stealing his truck, I think you would have added some doubt to the prosecutor's story. But yeah, Paul's shovel in Sylvia's car and a knife with Paul's and Rachel's blood on it is pretty incriminating. Imagine the lawyer waving that knife in front of your face if you were on the jury."

"Picture Shelby." Lynn corrected her. "He showed them a picture you said, Artie."

"Right," Artie said. "They only had a picture."

"Why was that?" A confused Lynn asked. "Steve?"

"If I remember correctly," Steve said to Lynn, "when they gave the picture to the jury they said that the FBI messengered the knife back to Pyrite from Denver and it hadn't arrived yet, but since they had the blood report, which was faxed down, you all remember faxes, they saw no point in holding things up for something that really didn't matter. Artie, do you remember what that guy sitting behind us said, it made us chuckle."

"Oh yeah, he said, *'that means they lost the knife'*. I think he was one of the cops that was at Sylvia's house that night."

"What the hell was funny about that that made you two idiots chuckle?" Lynn asked.

"We didn't chuckle from funny, we chuckled from *that's Pyrite for you*."

"Artie you said that the report listed unidentifiable blood on the knife. Maybe not identifiable in 1993 but if they had that knife today I bet they could lift DNA. They're doing it with stuff a lot older than that and a lot of innocent people are going free." Lynn was on a mission now.

"Well they don't have the knife, Lynn, and if Paul's getting out, he'll be out on his own soon." Shelby had reached exhaustion. "I'm heading to the hotel. This whole thing is as big a mess today as it was 25 years ago, and we contributed to it. But, I don't see a point in ruining your lives. I say we keep quiet and go back home with our guilt. But if you decide differently, I understand. I'm tired, I'm leaving."

"I'll walk you Shel," Jack offered.

"No thanks Jack, I don't really know you anymore do I?" With that, Shelby headed back to the hotel and her room.

Rita was visibly upset, protecting her and Artie's way of life was important, but these secrets didn't sit well with her. She searched her mind for an honest way out.

Lynn continued in her angry tone and made her beliefs known. "If anyone spends even one day longer in prison than they have to, that's a crime on us. Steve, I know you agree with me or I'm in business with the wrong partner. We need to tell the little we know. I'll go along with telling it anonymously if we can find a way, but we need to tell."

"Okay Lynn," said a beaten Steve, "anonymously."

"I say we march into the Pyrite police station right after the school tour tomorrow and tell every single detail we know." Bill was on one of his rants. "I have nothing to hide, I talked to the police 25 years ago and just because you guys turned chicken doesn't mean I have to take a fall. Not for free anyhow."

Rita felt sick and thought the anonymous telling would save everyone. Bill's comments worried her and she wanted to get out of the discussion. "Why don't you guys figure out what to do. You made the mess, you have to clean it up. Lynn will you look in on Nancy with me, maybe she's awake and we can talk about something else."

The men watched the two women walk upstairs. Artie got a bottle of bourbon from behind the bar and four glasses and they sat around a small round table sipping their bourbon and talking quietly.

Jack started in on Bill. "Why are you always trying to find a buck somewhere, Bill? You're coming across like a real ass and we're all really starting to hate you."

"Too damn bad, Jack. Three lives are maybe hanging in the balance here, You, Artie, and Rita and maybe more of us for all I know. I'm not playing dumb for free. I'll level with the three of you, I made some bad bets with some shady people in Nevada. I owe over 20 grand. If I don't come up with all of that, they're gonna beat me just this side of death until I do pay. And if I don't pay it all, the juice will get it right back to 20g in no time. So you see, you and your police don't scare me one bit, I'm a dead man walking. I need it all boys, $20,000 and I'm not only quiet, I'm gone. I'll pay the only people who'll be able to find me and I'll disappear for good."

"Oh Christ, you're poison Bill," Jack said. "Let's all sleep on this and figure out what to do at the school tomorrow. I need to get inside one more time, maybe hear if anyone else is talking about

Paul. Gauge the community, see if we need to talk. I need tomorrow guys."

Rita came into the bar alone and looked like she'd been crying.

Artie jumped up and hugged his wife. "You alright, dear?"

"Yes, Nancy upset us a little. Steve, Lynn is waiting for you at the back door, she wants to get some sleep and wants you to go with her back to the hotel. She said you two are done here."

"I better go fellas, it's pretty late," Steve said to the others.

"See you tomorrow; the tour's at noon," Jack said, "let's meet there at 11. I'm sure the building will be open and we were always able to break in anyhow. Unless you want to drive together, I'll be outside here at 10 if anyone wants to drive with me."

Steve left and met Lynn at the back door. While walking to the hotel, he asked her about the package she was now carrying.

Back at the restaurant Jack, Artie, and Bill continued their conversation and their attack on the now near empty bottle of bourbon.

"I'll meet you guys at the school," Bill said as he poured himself another drink, some bourbon even made it into his glass. "If you guys got a check for me, I'll hit the road right from there. It's the best deal you guys are gonna get tonight."

Artie and Jack were both irate and Artie spoke first. "None of us had anything to do with the murders and we had nothing to do with your gambling problem. But you'd combine those two things and use them against your old friends for money?"

Bill stared at his now ex-friends and the look in his eyes could have almost passed for concern. 'Well, when you put it that way Artie, I guess I have to say, yes. A thousand times yes. I'm planning on singing. I'll see you at our alma mater."

Jack leaped at Bill and pulled him up by his lapels. "I oughta beat your head in Bill; you're a no good bastard." Artie tried his best to peel Jack off Bill. The pushing and yelling continued until they heard a yell from the stairs.

"Stop it," Nancy shouted at all of them. "You have no idea the value of friends and the pain of losing someone you love. Stop."

"It's okay, Nancy," Rita said quietly to her, trying to be calming. "Go back upstairs, I'll be right there."

Nancy returned to her room and Rita turned back to the fighting fools.

"There's no reason to fight, no reason to pay for silence, no reason to talk or be silent. I saw that package you tried to hide upstairs Artie, I saw it the day you did on the end of the bar. When you took Jack upstairs and I heard you rustling in our closet I knew it was about the package, the box I guess. I looked in it the day it arrived and you tried to hide it. I saw the knife but I put the box back and didn't think any more about it until tonight when you said the knife from the murder was missing. I couldn't live with myself if I couldn't find a way to get it to the authorities. So I gave it to Lynn. She and Steve will take it to the police in Pyrite tomorrow and she'll try to keep our names out of it Artie. If it's the knife from the trial, they'll be able to find new DNA. If it isn't, they'll at least want to know why it was sent here. Either way the case will be open again."

"How could you do that honey?" Artie moaned. "I touched that knife, Jack touched that knife. Our fingerprints and DNA will be over it. What were you thinking? Call Lynn. Get that box back here."

"No. This must stop now. This is the only way. Paul served his time, he was found guilty of the two murders. They can't do anything more to him and we come clean by turning the knife over and giving the town a last chance to talk to us. We can all sleep again."

Jack stood watching the couple argue, he was so confused he almost passed out but didn't enter their argument. He listened intently to every word.

"Oh no Rita, you don't know what you've done. Neither Paul nor anyone else paid the price for Rachel. During the trial, the DA dropped the murder charges for Rachel. They said without a body they would have an impossible time to convict Paul. They put that murder on hold 25 years ago and that stupid knife could open everything back up. That stupid knife with Jack's and my DNA all over it. You're ruining us babe, you're ruining us." An angry Artie took off out the front door and sped off in his truck. The last three people standing in the room stood frozen.

"What's done is done fellas. You better go. It may be a hard day tomorrow. If you see Artie out there, send him home. Our love will get us through this."

Jack and Bill left through the back door and walked back to the hotel.

"You never mentioned the knife Jack."

"It has nothing to do with you. I think it was sent as a warning to Artie. You never touched it, you're clear."

"What makes you think it wasn't a warning to you Jack?"

"I got a different warning, maybe from Rachel herself."

Bill stopped dead in his tracks on the hotel stoop. "A warning from a dead girl? You've lost it buddy. You're crazier than crazy Paul."

"Yeah I know. Forget what I said, it's crazy."

"No way Jack, tell me what the warning was."

"Why, so you can ask me for more money? I'm going up to bed, be at Artie's place at 10:00 if you're riding with me. With all that's about to hit the fan, I think you'd better. Hey, I think that's Artie parked across the street, why don't you go send him home."

CHAPTER 12

Back to School

Jack was out of bed early Saturday. He was tired of spinning, rolling, thinking, cussing, and just about anything else you do in bed when you can't sleep. He had just enough liquor yesterday to prevent sleep for the night and enough crazy issues to prevent sleep for a year. He went down for breakfast at 7:00 and saw Shelby sitting alone at a table, looking as beat as he felt. He asked if he could join her and got a surprisingly friendly yes.

"Sorry if I seemed angry yesterday Jack, I'm not sure any more what I'm doing here and I seem to be getting that feeling from you too. I guess we all skipped the five stages of mourning when Sylvia and Rachel died and we're catching up with lost emotions now."

"You think that's possible?"

"Oh, don't ask me to think anymore. What time did the rest of you call it a night? I thought I saw Bill leaving here a little bit ago, heading to his room I guess. He looked cashed."

"I got back here by 3:00, Shel. For some reason, in my head in the weeks before we got here, I thought about walking home with you at 3:00 in morning, exhausted by a beautiful day of fun and long sought laughs. I never dreamed of the jousting we performed last night. It was quite the spectacle."

"Well, you're doing better than me. I don't remember my dreams being remotely associated with this place anymore and frankly I don't know why I'm still here. Sitting and watching TV in a food nook so I don't have to watch it in my room. Forcing down my fifth cup of coffee, seeing people pile so much free food on their plates that they drop most of it on the floor on the way to their table, and where it falls is where most people leave it. Lots of class Jack. And the more I watch that, the madder I get at myself, at me, Jack, and I'm only sitting here all alone and quiet. I'm mad at myself, I'm mad at the people in this room, and for some stupid reason I'll never understand. I'm already over being mad at you. I guess my world's gone upside down."

"Don't be so hard on yourself Shel. I still have hopes for the weekend. I'm driving to Pyrite at 10:00. If anyone wants to drive with me they'll be at Artie's by then. Why don't you come? Walk the halls with me, maybe hold my hand one more time."

"I am going to Pyrite today, I guess I'll drive with you. I want to see if going back makes anything more clear in my life. I don't really believe much of the things you're saying, but I came this far. I'll meet you down here before 10:00; I don't feel like walking to Artie's place. Now, if you'll excuse me, I'm going up to my room to have a good cry. Please don't ask me why because I have no idea."

Jack bit his lower lip to hold back his own tears, and why was he about to cry he asked himself; he had no idea either.

Jack went out for a walk in the cool mountain air. Greenleaf was starting to wake up and come alive with tourists and with the morning opening of the many coffee shops. The t-shirt shops would open later. Jack window-shopped absentmindedly and browsed the shelves of the few stores that opened this early. He made one purchase, made a quick stop in the local bank, and walked back to the hotel to think for an hour or so before heading out. A lot of words were exchanged last night, a few plans mentioned. Nothing concrete. As he sat in a corner chair, the room as dark as he could make it, no new ideas came. The only thing taking root was the giant headache building above his eyes. A little after 9:30 he went back downstairs to the breakfast room to wait for Shelby; she was already there when he entered.

"Surprise!" He shouted, handing Shelby a bag of licorice he bought this morning.

"You remembered. I don't eat hardly as many of these as I used to. I OD'd I guess, but I'll eat enough of these so you get your money's worth." Shelby giggled and put the bag in her purse.

"Just getting a smile from you makes it worth it; it would have been over 3 bucks squandered if you didn't smile. I couldn't have lived … oh never mind. Let's head to Artie's and see who shows up."

Jack and Shelby pulled up in front of Artie's Place well before 10:00 and almost immediately Artie came running out, alone.

"Morning buddy," Jack said, "no Rita or Nancy I guess."

"No, Rita's still shook and mad that I went for a ride last night. Nancy's just being Nancy. She makes a lot more sense than you'd think when you get her talking. They both should have come. How are you Shelby?"

"I'm on my roller coaster Artie. I laugh, I cry, I get sad, mad, happy in no particular order. But I'm good now."

"You figure no Bill?"

"You heard him last night Artie, he said he'll meet us at the school, get his money, and disappear forever. I'm sure he'll be there."

"We paying the bastard?"

"We can talk about it."

"Paying him for what?" Shelby asked.

"I'm sorry Shel, you left before Bill made his demand on us. He said he's into some bad people for $20,000 and they'll beat him pretty hard if he doesn't start paying. He wants the money from us, all $20,000 and he says that will buy his silence and he'll leave here. Claims he can go where nobody can find him."

"Buy his silence for what?" Shelby said, "a couple high-school pranks. He's gone mad fellas."

"It's more complicated Shel," Jack said. "But don't worry, whatever we decide, at least with Bill, the guys will take care of it without involving you girls. We made this mess."

Jack shifted his rented Cadillac into drive and they headed for Pyrite.

"Don't you want to wait and see if Steve and Lynn show up Jack?"

"They won't be coming."

"You can't say that, let's wait a few more minutes."

"I'm sorry guys," Jack quickly added, "of course we should wait."

Ten minutes later the three old friends gave up on Steve and Lynn and headed to Pyrite, pulling into the south end of town around 10:45.

"Drive by my folks' old house Jack. I want to see if it's still standing."

Jack made a right down Oak and slowed before coming to a stop in front of Shelby's old home.

"Pine trees are gone, but the house is still here. Needs a paint job." Jack said. "It looks empty. The windows are filthy"

"Let's go to the school Jack, you want to walk around inside before the people get there."

"No hurry Shel, we got time. Want to get out and have a better look at your house?"

"No."

"Let's go Jack," Artie said, "we've seen enough."

Jack drove up two streets and turned onto Elm. "The girls lived here, next door to one another. These houses look empty too."

Shelby was looking at the floor of the car and never lifted her head.

"Get going Jack. It's time." Artie felt Shelby's pain and knew Jack was missing the message. He shot him a detailed look.

"Sorry." Jack drove the few blocks to the high school; it was definitely empty. He pulled up next to Bill's car. Bill was standing by the school door.

"You got what I need boys?" Bill asked without hesitation. "I'd love to be on my way."

"Let's go inside," Jack said to all of them.

They got inside and Jack took Shelby's hand. They walked the halls looking into various rooms. They walked through the lunchroom and up a half flight of stairs stopping on the landing.

"We spent just about every morning here Shel. Our private world until that damn bell rang. There was a radiator here that we put our books on so we could hold each other. Got a few detentions as I recall for something called 'holding beyond acceptability'."

"Yeah, this town really wanted it to be the 50s didn't they?"

Artie asked.

"People will be getting here soon," Bill said. "Am I talking or leaving?"

"You got nothing to say Bill," Jack told him. "Let's go down a floor."

"You're messing with me fellas. I ain't happy."

They walked down a floor and to the south end of the building. They looked down the stairs that led to the maintenance room. Next to that was the small closet were they locked Paul Winston.

"I saw the key sticking in the lock one day so grabbed it, I had no idea why," Jack said. "When I told you guys I had it you said it was useless unless we locked someone in there."

"Yeah, I remember that," Bill said. "Then I think all of us blurted at once, 'Paul Winston'. And we did it, and he freaked and he never came back. And the rest is history."

"You need to look in the closet Jack?" Artie asked.

"We may as well."

The men walked down the stairs, Shelby wanted no part of it and wandered around to her old classrooms. Jack turned the knob on the closet door and pulled a bit.

"It's not locked," He opened it the rest of the way.

"Oh my god", he screamed, "there's a body in here, turn the light on."

The guys were tripping over themselves searching for a light.

"There's no light in here. Pull the body out, maybe he's alive."

They pulled the body out and rolled it onto its back.

Steve Conner. Dead.

CHAPTER 13

"911, What's Your Emergency"

Jack and Artie knelt over the body feeling for a pulse or any sign of life. Bill stood over them looking at the body and the blood stain on Steve's shirt.

"Call the police, Bill," Jack yelled in a panic. "Maybe they can save him."

"I'm getting out of here. I'm not calling the police. I don't know the number anyhow."

"911 you stupid asshole. Call em. You can't run from this."

"Wait, Jack," Artie said. "None of us know what happened here. Let Bill get Shelby and get the hell out of here. I'll phone it in. There might be over a hundred people here in a few minutes for that stupid tour. The cops will have to question everybody. They won't need Bill and Shelby."

"I don't know. Let me think."

"What about my money guys? I need to get the hell out of here. Steve was gonna go to the police today and talk, he said that. I agreed with him and said I would go. I might be next here. For all I know one of you guys did this."

"Get this bastard out of here, Jack."

"I guess you're right." Jack said. "Listen Bill, go find Shelby, high tail it back to Greenleaf. Don't say a word about this to her or Lynn. We have to tell Lynn in person and we'll tell Shelby and Rita after we talk to the police."

"And Nancy."

"Not Nancy. We have no idea what's happening in her head. Move it Bill. We'll give you 10 minutes and that's pushing it."

Bill took off and found Shelby on the first floor. He told her that Jack and Artie found something in the closet that they wanted to share with the police and they told him to get out of the school with her. She wanted to know what they found, but didn't push it, and she went with Bill.

Artie called 9-1-1 and told his story without prep or practice.

"9-1-1. What's your emergency?

"My name's Artie, I'm at the old high-school for the tour today. My friend and I got here early and were just walking around when we came upon a body. We're no experts, but we're pretty sure he's dead. Better send an ambulance in case he's alive, we don't really know."

"I'm sending a car right now, we don't have an ambulance in Pyrite. Is the body a man?"

"Yes."

"Is he breathing?"

"I just said that I think he's dead. How could he be breathing?"

The 911 operator was getting testy. "Calm down sir, a car's on the way. He'll have to go to the clinic and pick up our doctor. Can you tell me anything about the body?"

"His shirt is covered in blood."

"His own?"

"Now how would I know that. And why do you want to know that anyway?"

"Please stay calm sir. The most important thing is that you stay calm."

"Here Jack," Artie said as he handed Jack his cell phone. "This person's insane. I can't talk to her."

"Hello this is Jack Spencer, I helped find the body. I mean I also found the body. We both came across the body. Whatever. Please get the police here quickly. This is very bad."

"The car's on the way. They're going for a doctor."

"We need an ambulance." Jack was as frustrated as Artie now.

"The doctor will make that determination when he arrives. If you need an ambulance he will call the Greenleaf hospital. Stay calm sir, the police will be there shortly."

"I hear the car now, goodbye." Jack hung up and handed the phone back to Artie.

"I don't hear the police," Artie said.

"I just said that to get off the phone. That woman was insane, you were right. She hopes we're both calm as our goddamn friend lays here dead or dying."

One cop, Bob Mazer, Finally arrived and came down the stairs quickly along with the clinic doctor wearing his Saturday whites. The doctor knelt beside the body and touched Steve's hand. "This man's dead alright." The doctor opened Steve's shirt and examined his chest. "Shot in the chest."

"In a fight doc, close range? How long ago? Could the killer be close?"

"Hang on Bob. A kid comes into the clinic with an earache, I give em a shot. You come in with the flu, I give you a shot. I don't deal in dead bodies that have been shot. All I can tell is this guy was murdered. I know a little about rigor, every doctor gets versed in medical school. It's about noon now, rigor is setting almost completely in, means he got shot about 6 to, I'd say, 8 hours ago. Shot right by the front door."

"You're a lot better than you give yourself credit for doc, I'd have bet he was shot right here." Officer Bob Mazer said.

"You just didn't see the small puddle of blood we walked right passed on our way in."

Jack was shaking his head in disbelief. This level of stupidity can't possibly exist within a police department and a medical unit.

"Get me a ride back to the clinic, Bob," the doctor told the officer, "I have a lot of patients every Saturday and my work's done here. I'll call the coroner in Greenleaf to pick up the body and do an autopsy. You call the detective there, I'm guessing you've got a tough case on your hands. And Bob, it starts with these two. I'll wait upstairs for my ride."

"Don't mind him fellas, he's got an opinion on everything. I'm Officer Bob Mazer, I work out of Pyrite, there's a few of us left. I don't want to keep you long, but before I let you go do you have any idea who this is?"

Jack and Artie turned to look at one another and Jack thought that Artie was about say no, so he shouted quickly, "he's our friend Steve Conner, he came down for the farewell party in honor of this school, drove down from Wyoming."

"Holy crap. You know this guy? That means you gentlemen aren't going anywhere. Give me an ID."

They both handed the officer their driver's license. He read the names, "Jack Spencer; Arthur Paychek. You guys sit yourselves right here. I need to get the doc a ride to the clinic and check on my partner upstairs. Bunch of people milling around for your tour. Guess they'll be no tour today and if I don't get answers, they'll be no leveling of this building either. Who's running the show upstairs?"

"Frank Koonce," Jack said.

"Sit tight."

Bob Mazer walked off speaking into some kind of radio attached to his shoulder. He asked for a ride for the doctor and asked for another officer to be sent to sit with a body and wait for the county coroner to show up from Greenleaf. He then went to the north end of the school to talk to Frank Koonce. He took Frank off to the side and told him that the tour was canceled because of the body downstairs. Frank was more than a little shocked. Mazer asked if there was a record of the people attending the weekend affair. Frank was carrying a memorial book that he said everyone who attended the party last night signed. He said he brought it today for anyone coming into the school who wasn't in attendance yesterday to sign. Mazer told him to still get those names, give him the book, and then send everyone home.

Back downstairs Jack and Artie were discussing their strategy and immediately hit a disagreement.

"Why'd you say that we knew him?" Artie asked. "We could be on our way to Greenleaf right now if you'd have just dummied up."

"Hasn't dummying up got us into this mess?" Jack replied. "Besides this is our friend, we need to do better than we did for Paul. We wouldn't get 2 minutes out of town before that cop figured out that we knew Steve and we'd be in the slammer, so be careful what you hold back."

"Screw you. You be careful what you let out. And how can you call Steve your friend, you haven't seen him in a quarter century. If you had a deck of cards you'd play solitaire on his chest right now, so yeah, screw you."

Jack got up and clenched his fists in front of Artie's face. "I should beat some sense into you."

Artie stood up also and was very willing to confront Jack. "Any time you think you can, go for it.   You may find yourself laying with your great friend here."

Jack gave Artie a good shove forcing him hard against the wall. Artie took a run at Jack and tried to get him in a headlock. The grappling was about to turn more violent when Mazer came down the stairs.

"Knock it off you two before you feel my billy club." He stepped between them and pushed Jack back with his free hand, in his other was the signature book. "I got the names of everyone that attended your shindig, I'll get around to most of 'em, but obviously somethings going on right here, right now. You two are coming with me to the station as soon as one of my officers get here to watch the body. You stay right here," Mazer said to Jack, "you come upstairs with me," he told Artie. "My man will be here pronto."

Mazer and Artie went upstairs to wait, Jack opened the closet door and looked inside. He still wanted to know what made Paul snap. He looked into the dark room and fumbled for the light. "No light," he said to himself. He shut the door behind him. "Pitch black. Could it be that simple?" He pushed on the handle to get out and the handle didn't engage the lock. Jack panicked and feverishly kept pushing on the door handle. It finally grabbed and a nervous Jack emerged. "Of course it was that simple. Anyone would have panicked. Oh god, we should have said something."

Another cop came down the stairs and told Jack to get upstairs. "You're going for a ride."

CHAPTER 14

Time for the truth, but not the whole truth

A t the police station, Jack and Artie were searched for weapons, fingerprinted, shown to a conference room, and offered water or coffee. Jack accepted the coffee and while Officer Mazer waited for his assistant to take care of that, he read through the signature book. He knew a lot of the names, at least those of current Pyrite residents, but most were unknown to him. When his assistant, Judy Welch, brought in the coffee, he tossed the book aside and stared at the pair.

"We probably should interview you two separately," Mazer started, "but since I'll be the only one conducting the interview we'll at least start together. If I feel we need to separate later, we will."

"Do we need a lawyer?" Jack asked, very upset about being printed.

"A lawyer for what? I don't think you did anything, you're carrying no weapons, and you're not under arrest. But I do have a murder here so I have to run things by the book. I think you two can help, even if you don't know how, and I think you'll help more together. So let's talk."

Jack and Artie took a quick glance at one another and nodded their heads in agreement.

"Good. I see your three names in that book. I see a Rita Paychek too. She related to you Arthur?"

"My wife. Please call me Artie. I answer quicker to that."

"But no Rita here in Pyrite. You three decide to meet here on your own and have a boy's day out?"

"Something like that officer," Jack said, "but we found our friend dead before anything got under way. We called you right away."

"So you say. I left you two alone long enough to discuss this and all you did was end up fighting. Tells me you have conflicting opinions on what happened. Who wants to go first?"

"How about you Artie, you've been a bit quiet. Hey, Artie and Rita," the names suddenly registering with Officer Mazer, "are you the Artie from Artie's Place in Greenleaf?"

"Yeah that's me."

"Love your place, I've eaten there a few times. You're not the cheapest."

"Tourist town prices, Officer Mazer."

"Call me Bob; we're almost neighbors. Hey, let my assistant grab us some cold drinks, damn hot day." He called for three cokes which were immediately brought in. "Now tell me your theory, Artie." Mazer looked Artie in the eyes and started tapping his pencil on the desk. The repetitive tapping was meant to unnerve Artie.

"I don't have one. And our fight was stupid, I said that we were poor friends and not seeing Steve for 25 years proved it. Jack thinks he was a good friend and thought he could beat that opinion into me. The fight's over; let him believe what he wants."

Artie appeared to be done talking but the pencil tapping continued. He looked around the room focusing on the pictures hanging on the gray walls. Some wildlife, some buildings, an old portrait or two. No rhyme or reason he thought to himself, just like everything else in this dying town.

"What about you, Jack? You mystified too? You come here to meet a good friend that you're going to spend the day with, look at your old high school, and head out for a few beers. You find your friend dead and all you can think of to say is *aw, shucks*. You playing me for an idiot, Jack?"

The pencil tapping was louder now, slower but louder. Jack could feel Mazer's anger rise in every tap.

Tap, Tap, Tap. **"How about it Jack?"** Mazer screamed causing Jack to jump back in his chair.

"Alright officer, I have a theory and it's more than a wild guess, I'm pretty sure I know who killed Steve Conner."

Artie wanted to label Jack right now, not because of his theory, but because he didn't run his idea passed him first. He was scared of what words were going to pour out of Jack's mouth next. His stomach locked, he was getting sick. He worried about his wife, his restaurant, his livelihood. He put his head down on his arm and waited. Mazer stared at Artie and told Jack to wait a second, he wanted Judy to take some notes. He walked to the door and called out to her, he wouldn't leave these two alone now. He yelled for Judy to bring her pad and returned to his seat. Judy came in and sat at the table next to the fellas. Both she and Mazer were taking notes.

"It's time, Jack."

Jack took a few deep breaths, he was sweating from nervousness and shaking as if he was freezing at the same time. He passed his hand over his head from front to back a few times and then put his hand over his mouth. A last nervous breath and he offered his hunch.

"I'm sure this is all about the girls' murder. It fits too well to be anything else."

"What girls' murder?" Mazer's stare narrowed and his voice rose. "We're talking about Steve Connor's murder. What are you talking about, Jack?"

"I think Steve's murder was because of Sylvia and Rachel's murders 25 years ago. It has to be, it's all that makes sense. But to be honest, I don't know why Steve was killed."

"Who are Sylvia and Rachel?" Mazer asked.

Judy stopped her note taking which up to now she'd only written, *Steve Connor murder*, and provided Mazer with some information. "It happened long before you got here Bob. I was about 12 or 13 I think. A couple of the older girls got murdered after school. It was summer, I remember that because my parents wouldn't let me go out until they caught the murderers. I think they had somebody, but my parents thought that there could be more psychos going after young girls. They made me stay in all summer I think." Judy's voice trailed off and she looked at Jack. "You know I haven't thought of that in a long, long time. Guess our minds want to forget ugly memories."

"Connect the dots for me, Jack," Mazer said, "take me from two murdered girls to one murdered man. Same person killed them all?"

"Yes, I'm sure of it. Paul Winston. He got 25 to life almost exactly 25 years ago. He must have gotten his release, came back here, saw the school celebration, and it set him off again. He's settling grudges and I doubt he's done yet."

The room was silent, Artie looked at Jack and shook his head from side to side.

"You think that too, Artie?"

"I don't know, Bob," a nervous Artie said. "I would have never dreamed that up, but I guess it's possible. Just seems like a huge leap for Jack to make. I guess you'll look into Paul Winston though, right?"

"Easy enough. Judy, pull up what you can on Winston. Find the penitentiary where he was incarcerated, give them a call and see when he got out. If he's out on parole, see if they got an address for him. No con can hide in today's world."

Judy took her pad and headed for her computer. The story of the girls' murder came up instantly, but was pretty brief. She read it quickly and got the info she needed. Paul Winston sentenced 25 to life, sent to Colorado State Penitentiary. She switched to that website and got the phone number. Within minutes of Jack's accusation, she was speaking to a friendly gentleman in prison administration. They talked prison life and small town police work for a few minutes before Judy got around to the reason for her call. Her question was direct, "You got a Paul Winston there?"

The answer quick and just as direct, "I'll look him up and call you back."

Judy went back to the conference room to give Bob an update. He had returned to his pencil tapping and Jack waited anxiously for the info he was certain was accurate. Artie seemed to be lost and confused as to why Jack would open them up to suspicion.

"I got hold of the prison Winston was sent to, they're checking his records. Should hear back soon I hope."

"They say that Judy?"

"No, but that's what I expect. I guess it could be a while."

"Bob can we go?" Artie pleaded. "We gave you a lead. I got a timid wife at home and a restaurant to run."

"Give me a few more minutes; let's see if the Pen calls back. I'll have you out of here soon, just as long as you two know you can't leave Greenleaf. You're not suspects yet, but you're both on my watch list."

"Judy there's about 10 pages in this book that people signed and wrote their names and e-mails. Make a copy for me and you and lock this book in the evidence file. I'm guessing we'll have to contact these folks."

Judy left the office with the book as another officer entered. "County coroner just left with the body." The young cop looked at Steve's friends sitting there motionless. "Sorry guys, I didn't mean to be cold to your friend."

"I don't think you offended anybody." Mazer noted. "Is that everything you found on the body?"

"Yeah, not much. Room keys to the Peaks in Greenleaf, no room number on them, wallet with credit cards and some 50s, smaller bills and change from his pocket, and a comb. People still carry combs boss?"

"It looks like it. Go voucher that stuff, bring me the room keys, the hotel can tell us the room number, and have Judy lock the rest up in the evidence file."

"10-4 boss."

"10-4" Mazer repeated to Jack and Artie. "Kids. See what I have to work with. You guys want some lunch? I'm getting hungry. I can get us some bar food from right down the street."

"Aren't you letting us go, Bob," Artie asked again. "We'll be right in Greenleaf if you have any more questions."

"You two can leave whenever you want, you're not charged with anything ... yet."

Jack's thin skin was at the breaking point. He stood up, put his hands on the table in front of Mazer and got loud.

"What do you mean *yet*, Mazer. We didn't do a damn thing except try to help you. I am leaving, and yes, I'll stay in Greenleaf, for a short while. Anything else?"

"This guy a good friend of yours Artie? A little tightly wound.

Give me your driver's license Jack and you can go. Let's see you try to board a flight without it. In fact I may do the airlines a favor and get you on the no-fly list."

"You're a real S-O-B, kinda fitting B-O-B."

Judy walked into the conference carrying the signature pages which she handed to Mazer. "I got the Winston info."

"Read it."

"Paul Winston arrested for murder of Sylvia Kean and Rachel Morgan on Friday May 21st, 1993. Found guilty of murdering Sylvia Kean Tuesday September 14th, 1993. Sentenced to 25 years to life. Incarcerated at Colorado State Penitentiary on Friday October 1st, 1993. Died of cancer in prison March 20th, 2013, age 38."

"You knew that already didn't you, Jack? You keep playing me for an idiot. Why frame a dead guy for murder, Jack? Who you protecting?"

Jack was frozen in his chair. His skin was drawing tight and his mouth went dry. He looked around the room that was spinning like a carnival ride and he thought he would pass out. He mumbled to Bob Mazer.

"No sir, I didn't know. I thought he got out of prison an angry man and killed my friend. I had no reason to think that. I should have kept my mouth shut, but I really thought I was helping. I'm sorry. I'm sorry to you too, Artie."

Jack hung his head low and stared at the floor. He was playing his theory over and over in his head. Where did I go wrong? Did I base my whole theory on the 25 year sentence? Was I protecting myself by blaming the only person I could think of? I'm doing it again. I'm looking for a new suspect, a new scapegoat. Jack's mind drifted back to school.

"Jack!" Mazer shouted trying to get Jack's attention. "Look at me. I could hold you now, you've given me an obstruction charge to hold you on. But I still have a glimmer of a notion that you two are innocent." With those words the tapping started again. "Help me out before I let you head to Greenleaf. You two and Steve plan this trip for a long time, pretty important to get back here to Pyrite?"

"Actually no, officer," Jack said. "I got an e-mail from the committee and it sounded like fun. I hadn't been back here in a long time and I needed a break from New York finance. I didn't know who else was coming and was just lucky to bump into Steve and Artie."

"Not such a lucky bump for Steve, was it." Mazer was not buying much of what Jack said and he picked up the copies of the guest ledger. Something was bothering him and he looked hard at the sheets. He ruffled through them a couple times and lay them on his lap. He shook his head and looked at both of the men. They turned and looked at one another.

"Something wrong, Bob?" Artie asked.

"Maybe. I got over ten pages of names here fellas. You all signed in as you entered. People coming in all through the night just like you three guys did. Great crowd for your event."

"Right Bob, it was a great night." Artie answered.

Mazer sat silent again, just looking at the names. "Tell me Artie, or maybe better coming from you Jack, this seems more your area. Why are all of your three names, three guys who just happened to bump into one another, why are your three names all on page one?"

"I don't follow, officer," Jack said.

"I'm sorry Jack, I didn't mean to ask such a difficult question. Let me rephrase it. I got a guy from New York, a guy from Wyoming, a guy from right down the street, friends who haven't seen each other in years, and lo and behold, as their signatures clearly show, they all arrive at a party at just about the exact same time. Another accident guys?"

"C'mon officer. I was hanging in the lobby to see if I recognized anyone. I saw Artie and we talked a long while and Steve arrived while we were gabbing. No big deal. We did go in pretty much together."

"Rita signed in right after you Artie. You forget that Rita was there Jack."

Jack had no answer. Artie shut down. Mazer returned to his list of names.

"What am I going to find when I go through this list, Jack? Who signed in right before or after you and Steve. I know a lot of these people, fellas. Someone will say something if you guys don't. Someone always does."

Mazer threw the list of names on his desk and folded his arms across his chest. He had a pretty angry look on his face which suddenly changed and he looked confused. He picked up the list and turned the pages rapidly. He saw something and put the pages back down. He started searching through the mess on the table in front of him.

"Where's that info on Winston?" He found it under some town notices. "Says here Paul Winston was convicted of murdering Sylvia Kean, not Rachel Morgan."

"Right Bob, they dropped the Rachel murder charge. There was no body and Paul wasn't talking, they didn't want to risk losing the case by overplaying their hand. Everyone knew Paul killed them both and he was going to get the penalty for killing them both."

"Then you gentlemen, please tell me how a lady murdered 25 years ago attended your party last night."

He tossed the pages at Jack who picked them up and looked at the name jumping off the page … Rachel Morgan.

CHAPTER 15

Grave Consequences

Judy came in the conference room to get Mazer, said he had a private call. Bob left the visitor's list with Jack and went to take the call. Jack held the papers in front of Artie.

"Her name's right here Artie, Rachel Morgan. How can that be? Do you …"

"Shut up, Jack." Artie was whispering as quietly as he could. "That cop's probably listening to us right now. Sit still."

The men didn't move a muscle for 5 minutes until Mazer returned. "I've gotta go to Greenleaf on another matter. You two can head back, but stay put there. I'll see you at the Peaks Hotel Jack. Where can I find you, Artie?"

"I live above my restaurant. I'll be there."

"Okay, get the hell out of here, I'll be in touch." Artie and Jack left the station and Mazer called in Judy to the conference room. "Bag these two cans of coke, mark them Artie P. and Jack S. I'll take them to Greenleaf with me to lift DNA. I don't care for these two."

Jack and Artie stood out front of the police station, their car back at the high school. "Guess we're walking."

"Hang on, Artie. Let's grab a drink at that bar. We need to talk about this mess. We're sinking; we need to get our story straight."

The two of them walked to the bar and Jack ordered a rum and coke for Artie and a straight coke for himself. They took the table furthest from the bartender and pumped the juke box with dollars. Jack looked over his shoulder as if he felt someone's eyes on him. When he felt certain no one could hear them, he had a simple question for Artie, "Now what?"

"Now what, what?" Artie asked. "I don't have a clue about what's going on or how we got pulled into it. I can't lose my business."

"Your business? I make almost a million a year because people trust me with their life savings. Before they give me a penny they check out every little detail of my life on the internet. My name comes out on these murders and my life won't be worth a buck and a half."

"Well poor you, mister high and mighty millionaire, you can buy my restaurant with your buck and half when the crap hits the fan because that's all I'll be worth. Why'd you bring us here? To find peace, I think you said. How's that going?"

The bartender walked over and put another round, same drinks, on the table. "There you go sir."

As soon as he walked out of ear shot Jack started again. "There's no way Rachel's alive, right?"

"How the hell should I know." Artie paused for a second and finished his drink. "What if she helped Paul kill Sylvia and went into hiding?"

"That can't be. Paul was into Sylvia. Rage killing yes, elimination killing? No way." Jack motioned to the bartender for another round, played another 5 songs on juke box to drown out their talk and went back to the table. "She's dead Artie; she has to be."

"You want to go to Bob Mazer with that story? What if Paul was really into Rachel and Rachel killed Sylvia. Then crazy Paul took the blame for his woman? She would have had to go into hiding after that."

"You want to go to Mazer with **that** story?"

"I don't want to go to Mazer with anything. I swear for a nickel I'd kill him."

"He's no dummy Artie. He's been picking our brain without us knowing it from the second he saw Steve's body. I think he believes we killed Steve and I think he knew about the murders 25 years ago. He's laying a trap."

"You told me that Rachel Morgan called you Friday night. Why are you so certain she's dead?"

"I said the voice claimed to be Rachel Morgan."

"And that guy at the party last night said a lady there was looking to shock you. Rachel you think?"

"And someone put that knife in your restaurant Artie. You think Rachel?"

"I guess not, but it could be, right? What I do know is that knife could connect us to the murders and it's probably sitting with Lynn in her room right now. How long before Mazer gets around to Lynn and she gladly hands him the knife with our fingerprints or DNA all over it? Someone's setting us up Jack and I don't want to go to jail for something I had nothing to do with. We gotta get rid of that knife."

"I'll go get the car, it's a bit of a walk. We gotta get to Lynn and get that knife before Mazer does. Have a last drink, I'll call you when I'm out front, should be about 10 minutes."

Jack walked quickly to the high school to get his car, his head spinning from all his wild theories. No matter which way he looked at things, all he saw was his way of life coming to a crashing end. He got to his car and had to call Artie.

"Artie, I'm at my car. They put a boot on my wheel. I called the station and they said that stupid kid cop misunderstood Mazer and he's coming over to remove it. This could take a bit and make it tough to get back to Lynn before Mazer. Be ready to run when I call, but we could be looking at an hour now."

Artie said that Mazer probably planned the whole thing. Jack agreed, hung up the phone, and got into his car and drove north out of town, not even feeling a little guilty about lying about the boot.

Jack continued for about a mile out of town and turned down a gravel road. He followed the road up until he came to a single level white wood house; he got out of his car and took in a deep breath. The air was good, the mountains looked great. The house was surrounded by tall pine trees with a thick forest growing wild just west of the place. In front of him was a barbed wire fence and off in the distance he saw a small herd of cattle. He took a few steps toward the fence when he heard a screen door slam shut on the house. He turned around to see a man a little older than himself walking towards him.

"Can I help you?"

"You know they say it takes a million years to wash a mountain to the sea. I could say in 25 years I don't believe one spec of dust has left those peaks."

"And?"

"I'm sorry, Jack Spencer. I grew up in your house. Raised a few hundred head of cattle where yours are now."

"I can't keep 50. So little rain I usually only get one hay cut a year now.

"There were some years when I was young we actually got three. But always at least two."

"You here to buy hay?"

"No, nothing like that," Jack said with a quiet laugh. "I was at our high school farewell tour and got a little nostalgic for my old home. Thought I'd take a last look around before leaving Pyrite. Think that be okay?"

"Suit yourself. You did good getting out of here. Do yourself a favor and don't get any crazy ideas about moving back. But if you do, make me an offer."

"No chance. Think I'll just take a walk into the woods a bit, see if my old tree house is there. I buried a time capsule up there somewhere. Can I take your shovel with me in case I find the spot? I think I buried some hot wheel cars, may be some cool ones."

"Just put it back when you're done."

"Thanks, Mr ..." Jack paused. "I'm sorry, what's your name?"

"Doesn't matter. See yourself out."

Jack watched the rancher disappear into his home and quickly crouched out of sight next to his car. He opened the back door and took the box with the knife out from under the seat. He pushed the door almost closed being careful not to slam it and headed into the woods. He found the old tree where he built his treehouse but his place was gone. He counted 25 steps, exactly 25, dug a shallow hole and buried the box. He covered it with dirt and rocks and thought it looked perfect. "Once a rancher always a rancher," he said to himself. He put the shovel back where he found it, slammed the car doors, and headed back for Artie, more convinced than ever that he couldn't risk his big city life for anything going on here.

He parked outside the bar and went in for Artie. Artie was drinking a cup of coffee at the bar while watching a Colorado State football game on the TV.

"Ready to go Artie? Can't imagine what's waiting for us in Greenleaf."

"Mazer probably, and a bad talk with the ladies. You get Shelby and Lynn. I'll talk to Rita and Nancy."

"Unless Bill's been flapping his gums. He's only quiet for money you know," Jack added. "You think Bill could've killed Steve? He seemed awfully calm when we found the body. We could tip Mazer."

The men got into the brown Cadillac and blasted the air conditioning.

"Just drive Jack. Mazer isn't going to believe one more thing we say, but he will dig like a badger to find out why we said it. We need to keep quiet."

"Again?"

"Again."

CHAPTER 16

Sharing of the News

A rtie and Jack didn't speak for a while as they raced back to Greenleaf. They didn't know if they were lucky that Bob Mazer got called there, which made him release them, or unlucky because it put Mazer right on their backs. They hoped whatever the call was about it would lessen his focus on them. This was doubtful as they were certain that whatever the Greenleaf call was, it wouldn't rise above murder.

"I got one big problem Jack," Artie said dropping that statement like a bomb out of nowhere. "It's something you said."

"What'd I say?"

"This morning when we left my restaurant you started to go with just me and Shelby. I said we needed to wait for Lynn and Steve. You said that they wouldn't be coming. How'd you know that? Then you stopped and said we should wait, like you were covering your ass. What was that all about?"

"It's no big deal. Steve came to my room last night and said that Lynn was tired of the whole bunch of us and wanted to head back home early this morning. I figured they were gone already by the time we met and even if they weren't, they wouldn't be coming with us. Okay?"

"Fine if you would have said that this morning, but you didn't. Instead you turned off the car and said we should wait for them. Your story has more holes than Swiss cheese."

"I thought it was easier to park the car than go into a long story about Lynn and Steve's feelings. If you really must know, Steve said that Lynn won't let our hiding things during Paul's trial go unreported. She planned on calling authorities or sending a letter as soon as she got home. I didn't want to discuss that in front of Shelby. I have no idea on God's green earth how Steve ended up in Pyrite and God help us when Lynn gets a hold of us. She's bound to tell Mazer that we were at least somehow involved in the murder. You can count on that."

"Yeah, wish we didn't have to share the murder news with Lynn," Artie said, "First thing she's going to do is give Mazer that damn knife, we're good as dead Jack. And I have one more small problem."

"Shoot."

"When we were in high school and you wanted me to do something stupid with you, ring a fire alarm, phone in a bomb scare, crap like that, you always liquored me up. Today you bought me four rums and the bartender told me that you drank straight coke. Why are you trying to liquor me up now?"

"I'm sorry Artie, you're right. I just needed some time to think about everything going on around here. I thought if you had 3 or 4 drinks under your belt, you'd sit tight and let me alone to rack my own brain. It was stupid, I should have known better."

Jack drove into Greenleaf and pulled into the Peaks parking lot across from the hotel. Parked in front of the hotel was Mazer's police car from Pyrite, a Greenleaf police car, and the county coroner's vehicle.

"This ain't good, Jack." Artie spoke quickly; he was visibly nervous. "Drive me home. If I get out here, I think they're going to arrest me. I need to see Rita."

"Pull yourself together. You didn't do anything. You knew they were going to question us again, may as well get it over with. Let's go over this as fast as possible, Mazer may be staring at us through the window. Don't offer any more than they ask."

"I never do, you're the one with the big mouth Jack. But they must have the knife by now and know it came from me."

"Listen, we have to lead them to Bill. Don't think about the knife now, wait until they bring it up. If you or I didn't do this, that leaves the girls or Bill. You want to accuse one of the girls?"

"No way Jack; they couldn't have killed Steve. Lynn may dislike him on the surface, but deep inside, she loves him. Or my wife, oh God Jack, I'm gonna be sick. I can't do this. Take me home. Let Mazer talk to me there if he has to."

Jack drove Artie home so he could calm himself down. Artie could tell Rita about Steve's death now, and they could tell Nancy if Rita thought it wise. After dropping Artie off Jack drove back to the Peaks, ready to face the music. He had to talk to Lynn first and then to Shelby. He hoped he had the opportunity to do that right away. Then Mazer was next. He knew that Mazer was waiting for him and he guessed because he was in the town of Greenleaf, their police would also be in on the questions, or arrest if they grow tired of him. He walked up the front steps, fear running completely through him. Inside the lobby there was commotion. People were standing around in groups of 2 or 3 or 4, talking up a storm. He looked around for Mazer and when he couldn't find him, he thought he had a clear path up the stairs to Lynn's room. Seemingly out of nowhere Shelby threw her arms around him, her face a bit puffy from crying.

"Where have you been Jack, I needed you. Can you believe this happened? Who could have done it."

"They kept me and Artie in Pyrite to question us. I told the officer that I thought Paul Winston did it. Turns out Paul's long dead and I think it made us look guilty. It's all too weird Shel."

"What's Pyrite got to do with this? Why are they getting involved?"

"Just what did Bill tell you on the drive back here?"

"Bill? Surprisingly he didn't say a word. The police came to my room, told me a little about what happened, and asked me a few questions. They seemed really shocked when I said that Lynn was here with Steve."

"Ouch. What did the cop say to that Shel."

"*Interesting.* Yeah, he said *interesting*, that was all. Took my name, told me to stay in my room or the lobby and not to leave the building, and then I heard him pounding on other doors. I came down here. I'm scared Jack."

"Where was the cop from that you told about Lynn and Steve?"

"I don't know. Greenleaf I suppose. What's the difference?"

Shelby was hugging Jack, but Jack was in another place as he studied the faces in the lobby. His dizziness wouldn't allow him to recognize anyone. He walked Shelby to a couple of empty chairs at the far end of the lobby and held her hand as he talked to her.

"Listen Shel, we need to keep as quiet as possible about everything. Answer questions the police might ask, but don't give them anything more. We didn't tell them that you were in Pyrite this morning. Thought that'd be best kept private and then the day got away from us. We can't change our story at this point. Where's Lynn now?"

"So what if they know I went to Pyrite, it doesn't mean anything. And why are you mentioning Lynn so coldly."

"I just want to know how she took the news of the murder."

"Who are you talking about Jack? Whose murder?"

"Steve. Steve Connor was murdered. Who are you talking about?"

"Lynn, Lynn Mitchell is dead, Jack."

Jack turned completely white and his brain went numb. No words, no thoughts, just a sick feeling in every part of his body. He felt the need to flee, probably the most logical impulse he had all day and looked around for all the exits. Shelby was calling his name, but he heard nothing. Then a man's voice got through his wall. It was Officer Bob Mazer.

"Glad to see you finally made it back, Jack. I was worried you got lost and thought I'd have to come looking for you. But you don't get lost, do you Jack?"

"We stopped for a drink at that bar you recommended."

"Bar I recommended? The place I said I could get you a sandwich from if you were hungry? My fault entirely Jack, I see how you took that for a recommendation. I will have to choose my words more carefully with you, won't I?"

"You're in charge, do what you want."

"Thank you for the permission, Jack," Mazer said, "and I guess congratulations of some sort is in order."

"I don't follow."

"You come all this way from New York, alone. Luckily bump into two old friends you never planned on seeing. You find the dead body of one of them and go out celebrating with the other. You're a man of steel ... cold, cold steel. And just how lucky are you that Steve gets murdered and not you? And as if that isn't lucky enough, in the middle of two murders, you somehow manage to meet this pretty lady and stand hugging away in the middle of the mayhem. Celebratory hug?"

Jack's face went from pale white to red. His ears burned and the knot in his stomach almost knocked him down. Mazer was pushing all his buttons now and he damned well knew how to do it. Jack wanted to strangle him and for a quick fleeting moment, he considered it. He looked at Mazer's throat and imagined his hand ringing every last drop of life out of him. He looked at Shelby and chilled a bit, just enough.

"We're old friends. I never said that I didn't have old friends here. I told you that I came for the party, not to meet anyone in particular." Jack was holding back his anger now and seemingly slipping into a game of cat and mouse. "But my fault entirely, BOB, I could see how you misunderstood that. I'll have to choose my words more carefully with you, won't I? Just so you know, this is an old acquaintance from Pyrite, Shelby Runnert."

"Oh we've met. Shelby and I had a short talk this afternoon. It was a wonderful talk that I look forward to continuing. Perhaps tomorrow, Shelby."

Shelby stood motionless beside Jack as the two sparred, she remained polite to Mazer. "Tomorrow's fine Officer. You said that there were two murders. Does that mean that Lynn was murdered too? I assumed it was natural causes. I never heard anyone say murder until just now."

"I'm sorry Shelby. We didn't let word of the murders go public. We want to get a jump on the investigation before too many people know what we're doing. But yes, your friend Lynn was murdered; she was shot in the chest just like her friend and yours, Steve Connor, but I guess Jack could tell you more about Steve's death than me, he found the body. Might be a good idea if there's no more information for me to get here, that I send the press guys your way, Jack. It would be interesting for me to read the papers online and see what story you cook up for them. This damn thing is going to go through the internet and be printed all around the country, including your oasis in New York City. That's not the kind of help you or I need."

"What do you want, Mazer?"

"Walk me to the stairs." Mazer nodded towards the stairs and turned to Shelby, "okay if I call on you tomorrow morning Shelby, not too early, of course."

"Any time's fine, Officer."

"A minute then, Jack." The two walked over to the stairs and Mazer checked out the crowd, he had to be certain nobody was standing too close. He talked in very hushed tone. "You know I don't trust you one bit, but if you're innocent you have no reason to not talk to me. I think you've been lying to me all day and right now I'm exhausted. You wasted my time with your Winston story and you're holding back the names of your little clique that all met here. Before I head back to Pyrite for the night is there anything you want to say to me to put yourself on better footing. I'm eventually going to talk to every single person whose name is on that sign-in list. If I come across one more name that you hid from me, then I am locking you up for obstruction and sending the arrest report to New York."

Jack stood frozen. Mazer thought he had him cornered. Jack wanted to put Mazer onto Bill anyhow, this was perfect, but he had to play it cool. Make Mazer think he got something special here, a solid lead.

"I don't know everyone who came for the party. Whatever I say, you make me look bad. I just don't know that many people. There's no reason to say any of this to the press either. That would only kill me."

"Five seconds. See that guy wearing the green vest, he's the local reporter."

"Okay, okay. I don't think it means anything, but there is one more of our old group staying here in the hotel and he was at the party last night. Please don't mention to Shelby or Artie that I told you this."

"Keep talking."

Jack had to hold back a sarcastic chuckle, he finally had Mazer eating out of his hand. He looked around for effect and walked closer to the front door to be out completely out of Shelby's view.

"You should talk to Bill Addison, biggest failure of our group, never amounted to anything. I'm not saying for one second I believe he could do anything like this, he's just an old punk, but I don't want you to blame me for holding back. And that's all I got Bob. I give you my word."

"What room?"

"No idea, they'll tell you at the front desk. Are we good, Bob?"

"I'll let you know after I talk to this Bill Addison."

Mazer headed to the front desk and Jack smiled to himself and returned to Shelby. He sat back next to Shelby and saw Mazer head up the stairs. He glanced at his watch so he'd know how long Mazer was questioning Bill. 8:15. He knew he'd be sitting here a while and smiled at Shelby.

"How about a glass of wine Shel? I think it will help to calm us down, may even allow us to get a little sleep tonight."

"That could be good, Cabernet for me."

"Two Cabernets. Be right back."

Jack walked over to the bar and ordered the wine. He thought that the crowd in the lobby was dispersing and this horrific day would soon be over. He wondered if any of these folks had also ended up on Mazer's suspect list. The more on there the better, he thought.

"I said 16 dollars."

"Sorry," Jack said as he snapped back to reality. He threw a twenty on the bar and left with his wine.

He said a toast for Shelby, "to better days," and took a large sip.

"To better days," she repeated, "hopefully soon."

They then talked about the weekend, their disbelief in their friends' murder, and how it felt like 1993 all over again. They were interrupted by an incoming call on Shelby's cell phone. She glanced at the name on the screen and exhaled loudly. "I better take this, it's my husband. You can stay."

"Hi Eddie, I was just going to call you."

"I'm not lying. I've been alone in town all day." Shelby was quickly growing uneasy and got up and walked a few feet away from Jack. He could still hear her half of the conversation.

"No, I won't be home tonight, I'm still in Greenleaf."

"I can't say yes to that. There's some things going on here and I probably won't be able to leave here tomorrow either."

"Don't call me that, Eddie."

Shelby took a couple more steps away from Jack until the wall stopped her. Jack could no longer hear her words only the sound of her now unhappy voice. He stared in her direction until the sound of an ambulance pulling up out front captured his focus. Both he and Shelby turned and watched two paramedics come through the front door carrying a stretcher and run right up the stairs. Shelby's phone conversation was over and she returned to Jack. He looked at the tears in her eyes and all the thoughts of the murders for this one moment were forgotten. Shelby brought him back to the now.

"I don't even want to guess what's going on now. Maybe I should head home now."

"This probably has nothing to do with any of us Shel, besides that cop, Mazer, would have you back here in no time. Let him talk to you tomorrow and then if you must, hit the road then. Utah isn't going anywhere and your husband can function without you for a few days."

Shelby was standing next to Jack when Mazer came walking down the stairs backwards directing the paramedics as they moved the stretcher down the last flight of stairs. As soon as they turned the corner, the face of Bill Addison was clearly visible. Shelby shrieked and put her hand over her mouth. Jack put his arm around Shelby. Mazer stayed in front of stretcher and held open the front door for the paramedics. Once outside he helped secure the stretcher into the ambulance and watched as they headed to the hospital, he then bee lined it back inside right for Jack Spencer. Standing nose to nose Mazer didn't mince his words.

"You give two leads today, one of your suspects turns up dead, your second one almost dead. Well bad news for you, the bullet in this guy's chest missed its mark and he may be talking in a day or two. You two stay put here, I'll be back tomorrow. And call your friend Artie, tell him he and Rita better not try leaving town. And just so you know, I'll be spending the night at the hospital so don't try paying your friend a visit." Mazer emphasized his point by poking hard on Jack's chest. He clinched his fist in Jack's face and took his anger with him to look in on Bill Addison.

"What the hell was that all about?" Shelby asked Jack. "What leads did you give him?"

"He was badgering me about who I was here to see, I told him nobody but that I did bump into a couple of old friends. He asked if any of my friends were staying in this hotel and I told him to go talk to Bill. No reason for it Shel, but I did it. And Mazer gets up to Bill's room and turns out Bill's up there with a bullet in his chest. For absolutely no reason Shel, I end up looking suspicious, this is how innocent people get their lives ruined or sent to prison. This is why we should all remain as quiet as possible. We were right being quiet during Paul's trial, look what could happen."

"Being quiet got us here, maybe talking got us here. Maybe it's just hiding the truth that got us here. What's that old saying about weaving lies?"

"Oh what a tangled web we weave, when first we practice to deceive."

"Yeah, that's it."

"Walter Scott wrote it in Marmion. A romantic poem. Marmion lusted for an engaged rich lady and with the help of his own mistress, framed the rich woman's fiancé. Battles and death followed. Lies and love don't work well together Shel."

"You're giving me the creeps. I'm shaking."

"I can't take any more Shel. My hands are shaking and I'm about ready to just scream at everybody. My insides are burning a hole in my gut. I have to go lie down before I pass out. You should turn in too Shel, that cop will be back early tomorrow. This nightmares only going to get worse."

"Someone's hunting us Jack, one by one we're being picked off and you want me to just turn in?"

"I didn't think of us being in danger Shel, I didn't think that clearly, but you're right. If you want you can spend the night with me. I have two beds, and I'll just be there to protect you, nothing out of line. Or we can call Artie and Rita, I'm sure they have room for you."

"No, they have Nancy staying there and a business to run. I guess I'll stay with you. I trust you more than I trust whoever is killing us. Let's go to my room first for some of my stuff. Or you could bring your things down to my room."

"Let's stay in my room, if someone's after you they'll go to your room. We're safer in mine."

They walked up to Shelby's room on the second floor and she got a few of her things. She was packing up so many small items it seemed senseless to leave anything behind. She decided to pack up all of her stuff and leave the room deserted. Outside the door, Jack placed a small piece of paper between the door and the door jamb.

"I saw this in a movie. If somebody opens this door the paper will fall on the floor. We'll see it right away if someone went in."

"And then what?"

"We run like hell, I guess."

Jack carried both of Shelby's bags up to his room and put them on the antique dresser. He let her choose which bed she wanted and grabbed a beer from the minibar while Shelby changed in the bathroom. When she came out she saw that Jack had wedged the desk chair under the door knob.

"Can't be too careful," he said, being awestruck when he saw Shelby in her short nightgown. He was at a loss for words when Shelby's cell phone interrupted his thoughts again.

"You have to be perfectly still now, not a sound. 'Hello Eddie, you calling to say goodnight?'"

Jack sat in the recliner at the end of the room and didn't move an inch. He thought about not breathing if it would make Shelby happy then realized how childish he was acting. He continued to listen to Shelby's half of the conversation.

"I didn't hang up on you, but I should have after what you called me."

"No I'm not too sensitive, just too tired of being treated so badly"

"I doubt I can leave here tomorrow, I'll let you know."

"Oh you'd love that. Be careful of what you say, you may find your threats are more harmful to yourself than they could ever be to me."

"I already told you ... hello, hello. You still there Eddie? Oh what an ass." Shelby turned off her phone and apologized to Jack as she crawled under the covers of her bed. Jack never took his eyes off of her and slid between his sheets, fully dressed."

"Good night Shel."

CHAPTER 17

Sunday, a day for Prayers

Jack was awakened by the sound of the running water in the shower. He felt good for a second and looked around the room. He saw the nightgown on the other bed and slowly started to remember where he was. The death of his friends, the police ordering him to remain in town, his nightmares from yesterday now paled when compared to today's events. The nervous pain in his stomach returned. He crawled out of bed and was blinded when he opened the curtains. Eventually he regained his vision and looked at the mountains toward Pyrite that looked so beautiful on Friday. Now the view seemed foreign, ugly. He felt like a trespasser and wished he had never come back. Shelby came out of the bathroom wearing a bright summer outfit and a wet towel around her hair. She said good morning to Jack and he was suddenly thrilled that he did come back to town. He took a fresh set of clothes into the bathroom and climbed into the shower. Shelby used the room's hair dryer and looked incredible when Jack set eyes on her.

It was almost 8:00 when they headed down for breakfast. They each started with coffee and Jack asked one of the workers to put the local news on the hotel television. He was informed that there was no such thing as local news on Greenleaf TV. He felt really back at home now and turned his thoughts to breakfast, filling up on toast and yogurt. Shelby had the same. After breakfast, they went out in back of the hotel and found a quiet table in the courtyard. It was a bad day yesterday and now seemed like the time to start making some sense of it. Jack was more concerned about Shelby now after hearing her conversation last night than he was about his murdered friends or Bill lying in a hospital bed. He wanted to start there.

"I couldn't help but hear you last night Shel ... you know, when you were talking to your husband. You seemed hurt or aggravated by him. Is everything alright?"

"I should lie here, everyone does right? Say oh everything's fine, minor disagreement, I'm fine, nothing to worry about. But I won't bother with that only to end up way down the road telling you every little problem in my life. I'll just tell you now, life sucks, my husband turned on me some time ago and it's been steadily getting worse. So you asked, I told, now are you going to save me Jack? Do you even know why you asked me if everything's okay? You didn't just want me sitting here feeling sorry myself did you?"

"I asked because I care, not because I have a magic wand. I thought maybe you'd feel better talking about it and if you gave me enough info about your life right now, I wouldn't be afraid to make a suggestion. My life's not perfect Shel, but it's good, damn good, and I guess coming back here was an attempt to bury the bad things from the past, recapture the good things, and leave here with a cleaner slate than I left here with 25 years ago. I hoped that would bring me closer to the perfect life I want. There's a hole in my heart, an emptiness that haunts me. I don't know if it's from Rachel and Sylvia, or if it's all from you. I guess I came home to find out but I never bargained for this mess. I may be a lost cause Shel, but maybe I can help you, if not, I can at least listen to you. Don't shut me out."

"I'm not comfortable having this conversation with you, but I can nutshell my life for you if that's what you want. Put the 25 years since you walked out on me in a few sentences. First go get me a coffee, let me think about what I can tell you."

Jack walked back into the breakfast room for a couple cups of coffee and as he was heading back outside he heard the church bells start ringing and the sound was so beautiful to him that he turned and went out the front door instead. He stood on the stoop listening to the bells and watching the people without a care in the world casually begin their day. The bells completed a short tune and then sounded one ring at a time. Jack counted nine bells and prayed for a better today than yesterday. He went back through the lobby and out the back door to the courtyard. Shelby hadn't moved an inch. Jack put the coffee on the table and sat down a little closer to her than he had before.

"If you don't want to talk Shel, I understand. We can take a walk through town, go see the Paycheks."

"We should do that, but let me tell you a few things first. Eddie and I met at a ski resort in northern Colorado, I got a job there a couple years after high school and moved there in '95. Eddie started there closer to 2000 and we dated and were married in 2004. Over 15 years now, wow. Anyway after 9/11, and I don't think that had anything to do with it, he started pestering me to move to Utah where he was from to live near his folks. Eventually we did it. It really seems to me that from that day on he started to slowly turn on me. He started telling me that I couldn't go out or go back to Colorado to visit people from my old job. He started being rough with me, never hit me, but squeezed and bruised my neck too many times. He pretty much ordered me to not come here this weekend and he's been calling and threatening me to get home before he comes and drags me home. He told me last night that if I'm not home today I can never come home. I haven't turned my phone on today. But I pretty much have made up my mind. When I heard that Lynn died, before I heard she was murdered, I thought she had a heart attack or something. I said to myself that life was too short to put up with what I've been going through. I'm done with Eddie, done with Utah, done with married life. I have some family in Denver, I'm heading there when this mess is over. You ready for that walk now?"

"Sure, I guess that means no questions, I understand." Jack stood up and pushed his seat in. "I'll just say one thing Shel, it's not a question, I just want you to know there's a place for you in New York if you want to try a new start there." He stopped his words right there and stared at Shelby hoping to read something positive in her eyes. He saw only a blank stare and wished he could put his words back in a bottle. "Hey, we better go see what our friends are up to, we don't even know how much of yesterday's nightmares they're aware of."

Before they could leave the table a now too familiar voice ruined their morning; it belonged to Officer Bob Mazer.

"Well how lucky is this ... finding you here, both of you. When there was no answer at your room Shelby, I thought you might be out for the day. I'm so glad you're here."

"We said we'd be here Bob, so we'll be here." Jack was done hiding his displeasure with Mazer. "We just met down here for breakfast, been sitting pining for over an hour, we lost some good friends yesterday and you don't seem to want to acknowledge that."

"I do acknowledge that Jack, I'm sorry if I haven't been sympathetic enough for you, that's on me, one of my many weaknesses. You both lost two near and dear friends, just putting your lives back together will be a challenge. I hope I'm around to see where you go after this. But enough of that for now. You'll be happy to know I spent the night at the hospital and your other dear friend is doing well. He's not awake yet, he took a bad hit on the head, and elsewhere I might add, in addition to the bullet to the chest. More to the shoulder actually or he might have been killed too. But the doctors expect him to come around by tomorrow at the latest."

"Thank you Bob; that is good news."

"Yes, thanks Bob," Shelby added.

"I'm heading over to talk to Artie and Rita now, just a few things to follow up on. After that I'll go through my notes and maybe see you folks later or tomorrow."

"I'm sure we'll see you before we know it."

"Thanks Jack, and before I go, do you know if Artie owns a gun? Most people around here do."

"I have no idea, officer. You're heading there, just ask him."

"I will Jack, I will. You see buddy, we now have the bullet that killed Lynn and the bullet that killed Steve, and doctors removed the bullet from Bill Addison that almost killed him. All three of those bullets are at the local crime lab right now. I know it's impossible that Artie had anything to do with this, but if those three bullets match, and we can find the gun that they match to, then I could get you two back home tomorrow. And while I'm looking for that gun, if I can clear Artie's gun and him at the same time, well … how wonderful would that be?"

"Yeah, wonderful Bob. You should go take care of that."

"You sound bitter, Jack. Do you think I'm not giving you enough attention again? Do you have a gun you'd like me to look at? Clear your name? I could get a warrant if you'd like, Jack."

Bob Mazer was grinning from ear to ear, Jack was biting his lower lip and clenching his fists behind his back. Shelby stood with her mouth half open and her head turned to the side. Her eyes met Jack's and he felt he could read her mind.

"You don't need a god damn warrant Bob," Jack threw his room key and car keys on the table. "I don't own a gun, there's my room key for 301, and my rental car keys, brown 2019 Cadillac parked in the hotel lot across the street. Search to your heart's content and then leave me the hell alone, leave us both alone. Don't make me lawyer up on you, I've done nothing but try to help you from the second we met. Go have your fun."

Mazer picked up the keys and jingled them in Jack's face before walking away.

Jack watched him until he disappeared inside. "Before I came back here I never thought I could kill anybody, but I could kill this Bob Mazer guy and not lose a minute of sleep."

"Jack, please don't talk like that. Words like that can haunt you for the rest of your life."

"I'm sorry Shel, you know I don't mean that, it's just an expression. Forget I said it."

I wish I could, Shelby thought to herself.

"Guess Mazer killed our walk, Shel. We can't go see Artie and Rita with him heading there and no telling how long he'll be rifling through my room. We could go visit Bill, but with my luck he'd probably die while I'm talking to him and Mazer would charge me with murder."

"I thought I was in a dark place, but you've got me beat by a mile. Lighten up Jack; nobody's out to get you."

"I hope you're right, but somebody's for sure out to get us, our friends haven't been shot by accident. I should call Artie, give him a head's up on Mazer heading his way."

Jack walked away from Shelby and called Artie. He told him

that Mazer was heading there soon and not to say too much. Then almost in a whisper he added, "he's going to be looking for your guns, I'm certain he hopes to link you to the shootings, so be careful. Guys like Mazer are more dangerous when they're framing people than actually catching real criminals. Don't let him plant anything in your place. We may want to start thinking about a lawyer too. Let's all lay low today and meet in your restaurant at 9:00 tomorrow morning. Mazer will have to be back in Pyrite, we won't be disturbed."

"You're talking like a guilty man, lawyers, laying low, being framed. It's all too crazy."

"Not a guilty man, a suspected man. Mazer suspects me and you of everything. Wise up Artie or handle this on your own. Mazer doesn't care who he locks up as long as he closes the case. He's a hunter or a fisherman, he's no detective, and we're ruining his fun. He said it himself, we're on his list."

"I guess," a reluctant Artie said. "But someone has killed our friends and they may be coming for us. Mazer has to do something … if not to catch us, then to protect us. I'll show him my gun and make sure that he knows that I know how to use it."

"Be careful Artie, he's no dummy, no detective, but not a dummy either. And you're right on the gun, we'd better be ready to protect ourselves. I have to go, Mazer's coming back, either with an arrest warrant or an apology. You a betting man Artie?" And with that Jack hung up and went to spar with Mazer.

Jack rejoined Shelby at the outdoor table and motioned for her to look in the direction of Mazer walking towards them. He sat down, looking relaxed, almost smug.

"Find anything Officer? You ready to arrest me?"

"I'll tell you a few things, Jack, no, I didn't find anything and I didn't expect to. And yes, I am ready to arrest you just as soon as I have the evidence I need. You'll see just how ready I am. I don't like you Jack, three of your old friends get shot, two of them dead, and you sit here cracking wise with me. Not normal behavior, but you're clean for now. Just be where I can find you. I'm heading over to talk to Artie now. I would call ahead as a courtesy, but I'm sure that call's been made already. Good day folks."

Mazer turned and began to walk away, but stopped and turned to face Jack again, Mazer now looking smug. And congratulations again Jack, for a man travelling alone without any real friendships in Greenleaf or Pyrite you seem to be doing OK. That's a very pretty black nightgown on your bed and interesting feminine luggage on the dresser. Sorry to break that news to you Shelby, I know you folks told me you just met down here. I guess all part of Jack's luck in bumping into people." And finally a laughing Bob Mazer walked away.

"Talk to him Jack," Shelby said loudly. "You're just making him mad and then you get angry at him. He's just confused at the way you're talking and to be honest, so am I. Why does everything have to be a lie, so what if we're staying together for safety reasons. What's eating you?"

"It's him Shel. I feel his accusations in every word. He's trying to push me into saying something incriminating. If I don't keep him off balance, that bastard will frame me, or us Shel. He just wants to be done with this. I know what I'm doing."

"If you say so, what now?"

"You should check out of your room, make sure you emptied it. If someone's looking for you, the front desk will tell them you've checked out already, it'll keep you safe. Here's my room key, go relax there and maybe jam a chair under the doorknob. While Mazer's tied up at Artie's Place, I'm going over to the hospital to see if Bill's come around see what he might know. I have to be careful though, Mazer or one of his henchman might be watching my car. I should take your car Shel, they won't be watching for you."

"Sure, but be careful, and quick. I don't feel very safe and I don't want to be alone very long."

"Understood. Kill as much time as you can here and if you get too nervous just walk over to see Rita and Nancy. You should probably do that anyway, just make sure the Pyrite police car isn't there when you go in. No reason to give Mazer fuel for his dying fire. I'll see you back here as soon as I can."

Jack and Shelby walked together back into the hotel. Shelby took the stairs up to her room and Jack went out the front door. He walked slowly down the street looking around for any cars that looked like they might be spying on him. He saw a new Subaru facing the parking lot and walked over to check it out, empty. He walked to the end of the street in the other direction and didn't see anything suspicious there. He walked back next to the parking lot and at about the halfway point made a quick left into it and hurried to Shelby's Jeep Liberty. In a matter of seconds he was heading out of town in the opposite direction from the hospital.

Nearly 100 miles later, Jack entered the small town of Pinon Bark, Utah and parked in front of the gun shop and club. He hadn't been without a gun for a long time and the feeling was starting to bother him. *Time to level the playing field*, he thought as he entered the store.

Jack was greeted by a rough looking but rather short older lady. He told her that he needed a gun for protection due to his line of work in finance and understood that Utah gun purchasing laws would allow him to buy a gun fairly quickly. The clerk confirmed his understanding, had him fill out a background check form which she quickly input and they discussed Jack's needs.

"I prefer the weight and size of a .22 caliber revolver," Jack said. "It will fit well in whatever clothing I carry it in. I only need a small box of ammo, I'll load the gun as soon as I leave here. I'll pay you an extra 100 if we can wrap this up in less than 30 minutes. In fact I think I see the gun I'd like on the top shelf of this case."

In a matter of minutes, smelling profit, the clerk had good new for Jack.

"Your approval's done, background check passed. You can leave now for that extra 100. I'll get your gun; we don't like to sell the display models, and a box of shells. Why don't you come out back to the firing range and shoot a few rounds. I always find that helpful to buyers even experienced shooters like yourself."

Jack went back with the clerk and his new weapon. He quickly loaded it and put three shots inside the white outline of a human body. Pleased, he reloaded the gun, tossed out all the packaging and receipt and jumped back in the Liberty. He made tracks for Greenleaf, Colorado. With his gun hidden under the passenger seat, he was careful to stay well below the legal speed limit. Hunger replaced anxiety now and Jack thought about a meal but by the time he'd get back, he will have been gone a good five hours. Without a decent town on his route, or a decent restaurant either, he decided to head straight back and worry about food later. He started running stories through his head that would explain a five hour visit with Bill Addison to Shelby.

Jack got back to Greenleaf before 3:00 and pulled into a combo car wash, oil change garage and left the car while he went across the road for a sandwich. The work on the car cost him another hour, but he felt the look of the car and paperwork for the oil change gave him a believable story to tell Shelby if he needed to. He got back to an empty hotel after 4:00 and called Artie.

"Yeah, she's here. Been talking with Rita and Nancy. She said you were at the hospital, but should have been back hours ago. She's really nervous, Jack. Anything new going on?"

"Not really, but I exchanged words with Mazer this morning and add that to Lynn and Steve being murdered and you can see why she's out of sorts. I don't want to pressure her, please tell her I'm at the hotel and to come back when she's ready. I'll call you tonight after she's settled."

Jack hurried down to Shelby's car and got the gun and bullets. He hid the bullets in the trunk of his Cadillac and brought the gun to his room and hid it under the mattress. He figured he was safe from another search and wanted the gun close to him. He took a drink from the minibar and waited for Shelby. His nerves began to settle so he had another. He put on the TV and watched a foreign banker get grilled on *60 Minutes*. This bothered him on too many levels so he settled for a blank screen. He eventually walked to his window and stared out at the distant peaks. "Damn Pyrite."

Shelby entered the room as Jack was cussing out Pyrite. She had a bag of carry-out from the restaurant and suggested they eat downstairs, which they did. Shelby asked where Jack was all afternoon and he had his story ready.

"I was heading to the hospital when the oil light came on in your car so I figured I'd take care of that for you so you didn't get stranded on the road somewhere. I went to see Bill first but he was either sleeping or unconscious when I got there. I waited a bit then figured I better get your car to the shop I used to know in Pyrite. I drove all the way out there and the shop wasn't there anymore. When I got back here, I thought I'd get a sandwich at a place I saw at the south end of town. When I got there I saw a quick oil change place across the road, so I took the car there. The guy looked it over, there's no oil leak anywhere, so you must have just burned it since your last oil change. I had them change it, no more oil light, it's like brand new, so I washed it for you too. I guess my entire day turned out to just be taking care of you."

Shelby looked at him in disinterested confusion. "Most people would have just answered, *odds and ends*, but thanks for taking care of the car. I'll be careful what I ask you from now on."

"How was your day? Good visit with Rita?"

"I guess, but what was really nice was Nancy. She was talkative and seems to have finally found a place of acceptance for her daughter's death. She said, and I'm paraphrasing here, something like she's stopped trying to imagine her daughter slowly aging and just accept that she's in heaven and will forever be her little girl waiting patiently for her mommy. She's comfortable now; not fully at ease or open by any means, but comfortable enough to be able to function in life. May even be able to leave the assisted living home she's staying in."

"Wow, cognizant. That is good. Should we head up to the room, Shel? Couple things we should discuss and I promised to call Artie."

Back in the room Jack peered out the window again at the western peaks and the red sunset above them. "This is very poetic Shel, the sun setting on the dying town of Pyrite."

"Just make sure it doesn't set on us, that's poetry enough for me."

"I've got you covered Shel. You're as safe as you can be."

"Okay tough guy. No more talk tonight. I'm exhausted. Put anything you want on the TV, I just want it to put me asleep."

"Good idea. I'll call Artie on my cell from outside so I don't disturb you. We'll set a time for all of us to meet tomorrow. Figure out how to put Pyrite behind us one last time."

Jack walked downstairs and out to the backyard courtyard once again. The Sunday night air was cooling down Greenleaf as the tourists, as carefree as children, slowly walked the streets. A tale of two towns was about to emerge. The church bells rang nine times and the conversations around town were about to cause a creeping static upsetting many.

* * *

Two supposed hunters staying in a rented house received their call and heard a single word, *status*. They're reply was almost as brief, *strong message given to Bill*. A longer conversation was set

97

for Monday.

A woman got into her Subaru in the hospital parking lot and dialed a burner phone number. She left a clear message. *Left the note at the hospital, nobody saw me. Have newspapers, heading home, let's talk tomorrow.*

Bob Mazer received the call he was waiting for from the Greenleaf investigator. The ballistics report was in his hands. Bob told him to not say a word of it to anyone, not even him. He wanted it read first to everyone at once. He would be at the Greenleaf police station in the morning with his Pyrite officer, the Greenleaf investigator should be there at 10:00 am with the county coroner.

Jack reached Artie and told him that the four of them had to talk before Mazer came around again. He felt Bill and Nancy could only cause more harm than good if they were even capable of sitting in. *We have to figure this all out without those two.*

Like chess pieces on the board, the figures moved back and forth and sideways. The torment in Jack's head made it impossible to distinguish the King and the Queen from the pawns.

CHAPTER 18

Everyone Hates Mondays

Everyone who was due at the Greenleaf police station at 10:00 arrived by 9:00. They had a private investigation office set up for themselves with some loosely arranged chairs, note pads, pens, a table, and big dry erase board in the front of the room. Mazer was busy writing notes and taping pictures on the board while the others studied his work. The county coroner was there (even though he didn't know why) as was Mazer's gofer officer from Pyrite, William Denton, and the lead investigator from Greenleaf, Jeff Tidrow. Tidrow and Mazer had worked a case or two in the past, but nothing like this; the Greenleaf/Pyrite area was normally calm and had very little crime. Tidrow brought in some newspapers that hit the street late last night, very late for a Sunday, but the police had asked the press to hold up the printing so the murder story could contain some bit of calming news about the targets of these or any other potential shootings. Mazer asked everyone to read the news story and then they would begin their discussion. By 9:30, Mazer started things moving.

"I asked the coroner, Mitch Andrews, here for one important question that we'll get to first and then he can leave. Mitch I need to know why Bill Addison is in the hospital and not the morgue?

Was it possible for a good shooter to miss his mark. Do we have two shooters in town?"

"Always possible Bob, but the evidence leans to one. The two dead bodies were shot in the chest, dead center, no struggle, no fight, suggests they may have known the shooter. The man in the hospital was shot in chest, but it looks like he got beaten first. Bruised head and body, it may have been a sneak attack from behind suggesting it was more personal and that he probably knows the shooter too. Following giving a beating like that with adrenaline flowing, the shooter's aim would be off. However, the shooter did go for the chest for a kill shot. If I had to guess, I'd say you have only one shooter."

"Thanks Mitch," Mazer said, "that's a big help. Let's assume for now, were looking for one shooter. Jeff, you got some info on the bullets, fill us in on that."

"Mitch gave me the bullets from our dead victims, one clean through in good shape, one stayed in the heart pretty damaged, and I got the bullet that hit that Bill guy. It went clean through him, just barely scraped bone, and ended up in the floor. It hit a floor nail and got really deformed. Shooter had to be right on top of him. Anyway, I put them under the microscope and had a few talented people take a look. No doubt here gentlemen about the bullets that killed Lynn and Steve, same gun. The third bullet is inconclusive, I'd guess same gun but I sent them to the FBI lab for further confirmation. If I had to guess, same gun."

"I think that's important too Jeff, lets run with that, one shooter, one gun. Did you question most people on the reunion list yesterday?"

"Some. I have a few more names. We know that at least two people were shot in the hotel so I asked questions assuming the shooter is staying at the Peaks. The night clerk told me that the majority of guests passed through the lobby and headed to their rooms between midnight and 1:00 am. He said that Steve Connor came in later than that and came to the front desk for a new keycard after 3:00. Steve said he only had the one keycard with him, the other was in the room, no point in carrying it around. Steve told the night clerk that his old practical joker friends scraped the magnetic strip off the card to lock him out of the room. He offered to pay for a new card, knew it was his fault, and offered

30 bucks. I think the kid took it. Fast, easy thirty bucks. Odd that Steve was locked out of his room and then shot a short time later."

Mazer looked through his file and found the bag with Steve's belongings. "This is odd too. Steve said he didn't see a point in carrying two key cards, but in his pocket when he died, he was carrying two key cards. Anyone else find that odd?"

"Could have wanted to avoid being locked out again," Tidrow said.

"Perhaps. Willy, run these cards over to the hotel, find out when they were encoded. If the night clerk is there, ask him if he took the money. If Steve paid, he wanted the card pretty badly. Oh, and for the record, ask him how he knew it was Steve Connor that was asking for the new card. Get the dead card too, maybe an FBI lab can check the room number on that card. Hurry up, Willy."

Willy took off and Mazer went back to his board. Jeff Tidrow and Bob Mazer were the only two left in the room.

"Here are the names of the people I've linked together and this simple task has been like pulling teeth." He pointed to the names he had written. "You should write these down Jeff, I believe they're old friends, planned on meeting here for some strange reason other than a reunion, and know more than they're telling me now. Lynn and Steve, came down together from Wyoming, business partners, now dead. Both of their rooms were completely overturned. Whoever shot them was looking for something. Bill Addison drove in from New Mexico. I can't verify any current info on him, but he was shot and was about an inch from being dead. His room was messed, but not trashed all that badly. Shelby Runnert, drove here from Utah. Married, pretty, soft spoken, but not soft. Don't underestimate her. Jack Spencer, rich; probably very rich. I keep getting the feeling he's either lying about everything or being just vague enough to cover something up. I checked his car and room yesterday, no gun. I did find Shelby's sleepwear in his room. We need to keep a tight rein on Jack Spencer. Artie and Rita Paychek, owners of Artie's Place. I'm sure you know them Jeff. When I questioned them Rita seemed willing to talk, but kept looking at Artie when she did, and she offered nothing worth a damn. Artie showed me his shotgun. He said he knew how to use it very well and if whoever shot his friends tries anything around him and his wife, it will be the end of the road for them. Last member of this cabal is Nancy Braxton. She lost her husband and daughter in a car accident, I got that from Rita who said that Nancy couldn't talk about any of this because it could cause another breakdown. Nobody mentioned Nancy until I pointed her name out on the guest list right under Rita's. I didn't talk to her much more than a hello. If what they say about her is true, we have to be careful. But if she's delusional and drugged up, she could be causing problems. Seems like a longshot, but let's keep her on our radar."

Tidrow looked unsure of things and had a thought for Mazer, "don't you think we'd be better off bringing the FBI in on this? These multiple shootings may be too much for us."

"I got this Jeff. Listen, what's left of the station in Pyrite will soon be handed over to the state and I'll be looking for a new job. The last thing I need on my resume is that I cried for help on the only major case I ever had. These people aren't going to ruin my life. Trust me Jeff, I got this."

"Okay Bob, what theory should we be looking at the hardest?"

"Keep tracking down people on your guest list. See if anyone heard these eight friends arguing or anything like that. I'll keep badgering this group; someone will crack. If we rule out the three shot people and for the time being rule out Nancy Braxton, we have four solid leads to find one killer. We should be up to the challenge Jeff."

"We'll get 'em, Bob, I'm with you."

Jeff Tidrow went down the hall to his office to review his guest list and put together some new questions. Bob Mazer went upstairs and waited outside for Willy to return. He wanted to go back to Pyrite and run some more detailed background checks on this secretive group that was burrowing under the skin on his neck. Willy turned the corner and stopped in front of where Mazer was standing. He left the car running and shouted to Mazer "Both keys were coded at 3:30 pm on Friday when Steve and Lynn checked in, they were both for room 215. A keycard was coded at 3:10 am, and you're gonna love this. Seems someone coded a master, there's a key card out there that opens every damn door in the hotel. We going back, Chief?"

"Cut the Chief crap Willy. Yeah we're going back. I'll go get Jeff; he's got the keys to the murder scene and we need a better look around. Call the hotel and get the night clerk there right now, I don't care if they have to drag him in. Move it Willy."

Mazer stood silent trying to smooth out the thought wrinkles on his face. It was personal now, his job, his future, his entire life would be dictated by the results of this investigation. No stone would be unturned he thought, and for a brief second he wondered if he could ever manufacture his own stones if need be. He shook his head in a non-committal fashion and went to find Jeff Tidrow. For now he filed his final thought deep inside his head, *making it fit isn't the same thing as making it up*. The bounce returned to his step.

CHAPTER 19

A New Hangman Tightens the Noose

Things were starting to come to life in the trailer park just north of downtown Greenleaf. Situated on the Greenleaf Creek, the trailer park featured cheap homes and rentals with a million dollar view. Sitting in his lawn chair, cup of coffee in hand, sat Sam Spraynor. Walking out of the trailer looking a bit tired came his partner, Donna. "I can't sleep; we need to go over your plan." Sam heard Donna, but made no move. "Now, Sam." They disappeared inside.

At about this same time in town Shelby was just waking up. She finally had a good night's sleep after being totally exhausted. While she was showering, Jack was about to call Artie to set up a meeting time when the hotel phone rang and stopped him. It was Bill Addison calling from the hospital. "They're holding me one more day, you need to get over here. There's something you need to see and get it the hell out of my room. Hurry, Jack."

A couple blocks from Main Street, two supposed hunters paced around their too large of a rented cottage nervously waiting for a call. The call came into the hunter's burner phone at 10:00 am. "Status?"

"He's in pain, took his beating worth every cent of twenty

thousand bucks. We left him in a ball rolled up on the floor. But after we left someone else shot the guy, he caught lead in the shoulder. He's mixed up with a couple murders here."

"In Greenleaf, Colorado?"

"Yeah, and he had a gun, we took it."

"I didn't want him shot yet, someone's going to bring me attention that I don't need. This guy's becoming more trouble than 20 large is worth and Addison's only thought now will be on fleeing. It'll look bad on me if I let this two bit bum run again and nobody will think they ever have to pay their gambling debts. Go get his car. I'll call on this line at noon, your time."

At the hotel, Jack scribbled a note to Shelby and headed for the hospital. When he got down to the hotel lobby's front door he saw Mazer with two more guys who he was sure were additional cops. He pulled a quick u-turn and darted out the back door and hurried to his car. He'd be at the hospital in minutes.

Mazer entered the hotel and checked in with the front desk and told them to send the night clerk up to 215 as soon as he got there, he then went upstairs with Tidrow and Willy.

Minutes after 10:00, Sam and Donna sat at their tiny kitchen table where Donna had put last night's newspapers. "Did you read these yet?" she asked Sam.

"No, I've had a real bad stomach all morning and was too nervous to read the story, I've just been eating crap all morning to settle myself. We can read it now."

The story was short and they read quickly. Sam commented first. "No names, no good theories, just a load of crap about a love triangle not having anything to do with locals. What a stupid bunch of people in this town." Sam got mad and more sarcastic. "Three people shot, but don't worry good citizens of Greenleaf, go out and spend your money and have a good time, the lovers are off the street. Your town police protecting all of you good folks. All dummies Donna, I don't know if this is good or bad for us."

"You've got to quit calling me Donna. If I ever need to use that name again I will, but I buried Donna with Paul Winston. I just want to be Rachel Morgan again."

"I understand", Sam said then added after a short pause, 'Rachel. You've been put through hell and I promise you this, if nothing else, I will put a bullet in the middle of the head of anyone who hurt you."

"What's that beeping, Sam?"

"Wow, my spy tracker, Rachel, it's working. Follow it on our laptop, it's connected to the sensor I put on Jack's Cadillac. If he leaves town, I have to move quick and follow him. I have a remote trailing device in the Subaru too."

"The blinking stopped. What does that mean?" Rachel asked.

"It means he stopped. Look at the location, he must be at the hospital. Your note got him. We might be getting close, we're going to get even, Rachel."

Jack parked in the hospital lot and found Bill's room. He stood between the doorway and Bill's bed so he could keep an eye on anyone that might get close but where he could still hear Bill. "What's the emergency, Bill. There's cops all over the hotel, I probably should get back to Shel soon."

"Here, look at this." Bill reached under his pillow and pulled out a note card. "This was on my table this morning. Read it."

Not as much fun when you're the one being attacked, is it? Rachel Morgan.

"Rachel Morgan? Damn, she's been calling me, Bill. She doesn't say much, but she's been calling. She was at the reunion Friday night too. Her names on the list; Mazer has it."

"I don't know anyone named Mazer."

"He's the Pyrite cop heading this investigation. He had you brought here, he's probably the one keeping you here. He's shifty."

"Get rid of that card Jack. We don't need any cop sniffing around me all day because of it. Tear it into a million pieces and throw it away. Rachel's dead and according to Rita we don't know where the knife that killed her is, unless you have it. You've pulled us all into your mess. Fix it."

"You're wrong on every f'ing level, as usual. I don't have the knife, Rita said she gave it to Lynn and Rachel's probably not dead and this isn't my mess to fix. I wish that bullet did a better job on you; that would fix this so called mess. Suppose when Paul hid Rachel's body she was still alive and has been in hiding, or suppose Rachel killed Sylvia and Paul took the fall for her. That would explain her hiding and coming back after he died. Wise up. Rachel isn't dead and she may be coming for all of us. I'd get out of here as soon as possible if I were you. I'll lose the note, but I have to go take care of Shel; she shouldn't be mixed up in this at all."

Jack ripped the note into tiny pieces and deposited them into three different garbage cans as he walked to his car. He had nothing on his mind but Shelby as he drove back to the hotel; he did not want Mazer harassing her anymore and thought about calling his lawyer in New York.

Sam Spraynor called over to Rachel, "Jack's on the move. Let's see where Bill's sending him." A few minutes later Jack's car came to a stop. "Damn, he's back at the hotel; nothing breaking yet." Then a few minutes later, "this is odd, Bill's car is on the move, I have the second sensor on his Malibu. Jack must be going somewhere with it, somewhere important." After a rather short drive, the car stopped. "Judging by this location he's stopped near the middle of town. I can scope it out tonight after dark. Jack's running us in circles."

The hunters parked the stolen Malibu in the garage as noon was approaching. Suddenly, the one who stole the car burst into the house.

"We got a problem - get up. I scanned the car and found a spy tracer. It's on and we've been tracked. Has to be the police spying on Addison; they'll be here soon, we need to pack up everything and wipe the place down. I'm walking the tracer to the grocery store and putting it on a car with out of state plates. See what the boss wants us to do." The panicked man fled the house with the tracer.

"Bill's car is moving again, Sam." Rachel watched patiently until the tracer stopped again in town. "Now what Sam?"

"I'm taking the remote and see where Bill's car is parked and who's driving it. I'll stay out of sight, but if they head out of town I'll have to follow them. This sensor won't reach us here once they move. Be safe - I'll be back as soon as I can."

The hunter's boss called at noon and he got the news. They stole Bill's car, but there was an active spy tracer on it. Spy tracer is now on a Utah car. Their marching orders were precise; put the Malibu back where it was and get the hell out of Greenleaf. The boss will send in a new team. If the sensor is the cop's sensor, they'll be coming soon or watching. Get rid of the burner phones and head back to Denver. Within minutes all was done.

Sam drove down Main Street into Greenleaf trying to get an exact fix on his GPS tracer. He turned into the grocery store parking lot and drove up and down the aisles. No sign of Bill's car. He parked his car and walked around the parking lot with his tracker in hand. It seemed to be honing in on a minivan with Utah plates. He went back to his car. He watched the minivan and waited. A family of four eventually showed up with a few bags of groceries and drove off. Sam watched his tracker follow the family. He let out a few cuss words and deleted the spy device from his tracker. He next drove to the location where Bill's car first showed up on his device, it looked to be an empty house on a deserted dead end street. Lastly he drove back to the Peaks hotel and saw Bill's car in the parking lot right next to Jack's. He drove to the trailer park; he needed to figure things out with Rachel. He felt he stirred the hornet's nest but was worried he'd be the one to get stung.

Jack called Artie as soon as he got back to the hotel about getting together. Artie said that the set up crew would be in the restaurant in the afternoon and Nancy could walk in on them at any time. They agreed to get together in the hotel courtyard, with the women, at 3:00.

Shelby was sitting next to her dead phone after shutting it down following her latest argument with her husband. Her personal problem was much bigger to her than a few shootings.

Mazer and Tidrow were about to grill the night clerk while Willy stood guard outside room 215.

Bill Addison kept demanding his release until a Greenleaf uniformed officer was posted at his door.

Sam pulled up next to his rented trailer and was ready to run a new plan by Rachel.

The hunters who have never hunted anything other than men who've wronged their boss, were enjoying a leisurely drive back to the casinos in the Denver area. Somewhere along their route they will pass another hunter heading in the opposite direction, heading to the troubled town of Greenleaf.

CHAPTER 20

New Plans for Old Problems

The night clerk was let into room 215 by Willy, "Your boy's here, chief." Mazer gave Willy a stern look at the word *'chief'*. Mazer and Tidrow approached the night clerk and started their questions.

"You keyed a new key to this room Friday night and a short time later, the lady staying in this room was murdered. You're in deep here buddy, so we'd better not get one single false answer out of you. You understand?"

"Yes, sir."

"Can you identify the person you gave the key to?"

"Not without help, sir. I think it was … but you tell me who you want it to be and I'll say so."

Mazer and Tidrow looked at one another and shook their heads.

"How do you know it was Steve Connor you encoded a new key for?" Mazer was asking all the questions now.

"He told me he was Steve from 215. He wouldn't know that if he wasn't Steve and he had the broken card that his friends scratched the magnetic strip away from. I remember that. He said he had two rooms under his name and that checked out too, but he only needed the key to 215. He seemed legit."

"Do you have the old card he gave you somewhere?"

"No, I'm pretty sure I threw it out. I was pretty wasted by that time; that's why I can't identify who asked for the new key. Anyway the key wouldn't read, he was telling the truth. Please don't turn me in, I need this job, and it's easy."

An aggravated Mazer had enough. "Get the hell out of here before I arrest you, you have no idea what you did and how you encoded that card. I may not be done with you yet, but for now you're making me sick. Beat it." As the kid walked away, Mazer added, "and quit drinking on the job. I can arrest you for that too."

Mazer and Tidrow went back in the room leaving Willy standing guard in the hall again. They attempted to recreate the crime while writing all of their ideas down to study again later. They had some good leads now to start from. Except for Lynn's body being out of the room it was exactly as the police found it on Saturday. They got a couple pillows from housekeeping and laid them down where Lynn's body was found and started walking through their case to this point. They knew someone got a key to this room around 3:00 am - definitely not Steve, and broke in. They crept in and kept Lynn quiet when they woke her up. Mazer assumed the perp put tape on her mouth or simply quieted her with the fear of the gun. The shooter had her sit on the edge of the bed and her final minutes began. Mazer asked Tidrow to be Lynn and act out what he believes went down.

"Okay, you sit on the bed and look at me; you're Lynn and I think maybe you have a piece of duct tape over your mouth and you for sure have a gun in your face." Mazer shapes his hand like a gun and points it at Tidrow's face. "We can tell by the way the room's been tossed that he, or she, was looking for something. So he first probably pointed the gun and said 'give me the so and so if you want to live'. She tries to talk so he pulls the tape off and she says something like 'I don't have it now get out of here before I scream'. He knows he can't have that so he panics and eventually shoots her square in the chest. The shot didn't wake anybody so we can assume it had a silencer. Lynn is dead almost instantly and she falls from where you are to right where those pillows are; it lines up perfectly. The bullet was found on the floor next to the body, we thought that odd but it makes sense now. She was shot from point blank range, the bullet went right through her and landed on the bed. The shooter goes around the bed and flips the mattress on top of the body, the bullet flies off the mattress and lands there. The shooter didn't find what he was looking for under the mattress so he then lifts the box spring to look under it; that's why the box spring is out of the frame, he didn't find anything there. Shooter then starts going through everything as quickly as he can. He's throwing clothes, towels, sheets ... every single thing in this room was rifled through and the perp found nothing. That's what I got, Jeff."

"That's about what I got Bob, nothing I could add or subtract from that would change anything. How do you know the shooter didn't find what he was looking for."

"Easy Jeff. Because he then went next door through the adjoining door. Right?"

"Right, Bob. But this one's trickier, more guess work. Let me run my theory by you, see what you think. Keep in mind I'm still putting this together." Tidrow walks over to the adjoining door and starts acting out his theory.

"I'm the shooter now Bob, stay with me. I'm done in Lynn's room and I got nothing. I slowly open this door and Steve's asleep. I creep over to his bed, turn the light on, he jumps and I shove the gun in his face. I give the usual orders, *make one sound and you're dead and then I'll go next door and kill Lynn, are we clear?* He says yes and asks what I want. Maybe I hit him with the gun here, scare him a bit. And I say, you know damn well what I want, where's the so-and-so. Steve says that the thing is hidden - or maybe planted - at the Pyrite school right now - by his partner in all of this. *You'll never find it, but the police will with a helpful phone call tomorrow.* At this point I really hit Steve hard and knock him out. I duct tape around his feet, hands, and mouth and toss this room just like the other one. I get a laundry cart, throw him in, and wheel him out to my car, which I conveniently have parked near the back door. I put Steve in the trunk, drive to Pyrite school and then get Steve, who's now waking up, out of the trunk. I ask him where his partner is and if he's gone, where is the thing he hid. I'm guessing at this point Bob that we're talking about a gun. Anyway, Steve tells the perp where the gun is hidden and takes a bullet to the chest leaving that tiny blood splatter at the front door. The shot was from further away than the shot to Lynn and hit a lot more muscle, so the bullet stayed in Steve's chest.

Shooter puts Steve in the laundry cart and wheels him down to where we found him. Gets the gun right where Steve said it would be and leaves the area. If we look hard enough, we'll find a laundry cart somewhere between here and Pyrite. What do you think, Bob?"

"I could see that. This whole thing might have nothing to do with Greenleaf or Pyrite at all. Steve and Lynn are probably mixed up with something pretty bad in Wyoming and someone followed them down here and administered some western justice. We should call the authorities in their town and see if anything might be going on. This will play good here in the press, people will feel a lot better."

Just as Mazer was starting to feel good about their investigation, he crashed. "Damn it, Jeff; it doesn't work, we got a little problem." Mazer stared at Tidrow, and Tidrow finally got it,

"Bill Addison. Nobody from Wyoming comes here to shoot Bill Addison. Whoever shot these three people wants to find something pretty bad and is hell bent on shutting up anyone that knows he's looking for it. Let's go to my office and compare notes. I got a feeling were on the right track at least up to some point."

"I'll meet you at your office as soon as I can. You go update our case board; I'm going to the hospital to check on Bill Addison because he's the next link in the chain. If we expect to complete the chain and put a lock on it, we go through Bill Addison, I'm sure of that. Take Willy back with you, use him however you want. He can be helpful, sometimes."

As they tried to put the past crimes together from an investigator's viewpoint, Sam Spraynor was putting together a future plan to allow him to be his own investigator. The police were trying to bring more things in the open, Sam was trying to keep things hidden and was now finally ready to share some thoughts with Rachel. He turned off the engine of his Subaru, left its coolness and sat down with Rachel in the heat of the trailer.

"I gotta be honest with you Rachel, I'm a little confused or maybe I should just say a little concerned. Someone found my spy tracker on Bill's car and moved it; they tried to get us to follow a car to Utah. They don't know it's my tracker so who did they think they were sending on a wild goose chase? And I don't know who moved it unless Bill's out of the hospital. Couldn't be Jack or he would have also found the tracker I put on his car. Could have been Artie and Rita - but why? Is someone working with one of these people, an unknown loose cannon? Let's assume it was Bill. He got released, checked his car, maybe had a flat tire and saw the sensor when he was changing the tire, lots of assumptions, but it moves us along."

"Bill wouldn't be out of the hospital this quick after an attempt on his life - and there's no way he's changing a tire."

"I think Bill's doing fine. Someone just went three knee deep on him."

Rachel made a face at Sam, "what the hell is three knee deep?"

"I'm sorry Rachel, remember me telling you about a *backdoor pardon*?"

"Yeah, that was about dying in prison when you're in for a long stretch or life."

"Right. Well a three knee deep is a warning. In prison it's usually a shiv in your side or back, not meant to kill, only to warn. I'm sure someone sent a warning to Bill, he knows what for."

"Talkers seem to die in this town. What's our next step?"

"Talkers will die in this town and we do have a loose cannon out there. We need to get Nancy Braxton; that's our next move. No telling what's in her head and what she could reveal."

"That could be dangerous Sam, this whole town's on alert and she's tucked away at Artie's Place. She's protected."

"BS. Artie couldn't protect a puppy. I'll get her, I'll get her myself. You stay here, but be ready to run. The heat's only going up after this."

"Is this move necessary? It seems too dangerous."

"It is, tr, tr, tr, trust me Rachel."

"Take a breath, you're stuttering again. Be careful."

"Thanks. Okay, I'm heading out. Keep your cell handy, I'll call if I get in a jam, if I can. I'm heading over to the hospital to see if Bill Addison is still there. Then I'm going to park near Artie's Place and try to see what I can get away with there. This could be a while. I may walk around the hotel too, see if I can see what those bastards are up to. Think anyone could recognize me?"

"You serious? They haven't seen you in 25 years when you were a messy haired boy. Now you're a 40 something bald old man with a scraggly beard. Your own mother wouldn't recognize you. Oh, I'm sorry about the mother thing, Sam, I didn't mean anything."

"She's been gone forever Rachel, don't worry about it."

Sam drove down Main Street to the hospital. He slowed as he passed the hotel parking lot and glanced at both Jack's Cadillac and Bill's 20 year old Malibu; both were where they should be. He offered himself a shake of his head and a verbal 'damn' as he continued to the hospital. He parked a good distance from the door and snaked his way around the lot and through the front door. Rachel had given him the room number and a description of the way there. As soon as Sam made the final turn to Bill's room, he saw two police officers talking at Bill's door. He quickly turned into another patient's room and fumbled for words. He finally asked the patient if his dinner card had been turned in already and got a loud cussing for his answer. Sam apologized and sped back to his car.

Once back in town and his heart rate slowing, Sam was able to laugh at his lack of luck. *'Story of my life.'* He continued toward the restaurant and saw Artie and Rita walking towards him. He went down to a side street and turned around to follow the pair. He saw them go into the Peaks Hotel and parked his car in the hotel lot and casually walked into the lobby. He picked up a newspaper that was laying on a lobby chair and sat down pretending to read. Artie and Rita were standing at the back door and in a few minutes were joined by Jack and Shelby. They exchanged a few words and three of them went outside. Jack headed to the bar. Sam saw his chance and rushed back to his car and drove to Artie's Place parking his car as close to the back door as he could without drawing attention to it. The door was being held open by a block of wood on the ground and Sam easily slipped inside. He crouched as low as he could so the workers in the kitchen and restaurant wouldn't see him. He crawled from behind the stacked boxes of supplies over to the stairway leading upstairs to the apartment. Each step creaked as he made his way up.

Once on the second floor, he looked from room to room, his breathing grew louder by the second as he paused outside each door. And there she is. Taking one last deep breath he jumped into the room with arms extended, hand aimed at Nancy's face. Holding her down with his hand over her mouth, he reached under his shirt. *This is for you Nancy!*

CHAPTER 21

The Answers are Multiple Choice; Like Being Back in High School

Mazer went in the room to talk to Bill Addison, leaving the Greenleaf duty officer standing guard right outside the door. Bill was shot two days ago but was feeling good and was antsy to get released. His arm and chest hurt like hell, but there was nothing the hospital was doing that he couldn't do for himself. He made that clear to Mazer and Mazer made things clear to Addison, "I can't protect you out there, but you're losing your guard today anyhow. Answer my questions and you'll be out today."

"Fire away," Bill joked, "sorry about the pun."

Mazer didn't smile; instead, he picked up the newspaper laying on the chair next to the bed. "I see you read the story; you're a celebrity. What do you think of the theory?"

"That I was having an affair with a lady that I haven't seen in 25 years and her jealous boyfriend, who is not even her boyfriend, shot all three of us? Your editor should write pulp fiction."

"It said fling, not affair. Big difference. And it didn't say Jack shot all of you, only a veiled hint at that."

"So I guess it's your story. Don't quit your day job."

"More the Greenleaf Investigator's story; he needs to keep things calm in his town so tourists still come and spend money. He likes calm and I like chaos. What about you?"

"I like organized confusion, officer."

"Like tap dancing, Bill?"

"Only around a fire."

Mazer sat in the empty chair and reread the Sunday murder story. He glanced a few times at Bill but didn't say a word. Bill stayed quiet too and was oddly comfortable in the awkward situation. Mazer next took out his writing pad and started jotting down notes. As he wrote, he would mumble carefully chosen words for Bill's benefit, *"I see now, of course, yes, that makes sense, how did I miss that."* Bill pretended to fall asleep, bored by Mazer. Mazer walked over to the Greenleaf officer standing guard and whispered something in his ear which caused the officer to look at Bill, shake his head, and leave the area. Mazer went back to his chair and started scribbling more notes. A few minutes later the Greenleaf cop poked his head in the door, "I'm sorry Bob, you said a list of things missing from Steve's room, what about his truck?"

"Outside," an angry Mazer shouted at the young cop. Right out the door he spoke softly but firmly, "Don't you ever talk about a case in front of the public again you idiot. Just canvas the rooms; we don't have a warrant for the truck and I don't want to blow the case before we even have one." A not so sleepy Bill Addison heard every word.

Mazer sat for a while and waited for Bill to wake a bit. When he moaned Mazer spoke up. "Can you handle a couple serious questions Bill? Then I'll approve your release. Tell me exactly what you remember happening."

"Fine. I went out for a walk after noon. It was lunch time, but I wasn't hungry so I just walked. I got back to my room and planned on reading the room service menu. I didn't feel like going out again, I didn't care much for Greenleaf, no offence, I was thinking of heading home. I inserted the keycard, pulled it out and opened the door. I got hit in back of my head as soon as I did that. I remember that clearly but then it gets a little hazy. I was getting hit or kicked. Things weren't making any sense and I think I may have lost consciousness. When I started coming to, someone was shaking me or rolling me over and he said something about a bullet. Give me a minute." Bill tried hard to recall the words. "I think it was something like, 'this bullet's probably too easy for you, but I hope you at least suffered enough.' Then he shot me. 'This bullet's too easy for you.' That's what he said. I heard the shot, never felt it, and I woke up here. That's all I got for you."

"Did the voice sound like one of your friends?"

"Some friends if it did. But I don't know; I was pretty out of it by time he spoke."

"One guy?"

"No idea. Could have been ten for all I know, but could have been one, a good size one, every hit still hurts."

"Why didn't you go on the school tour Saturday?"

"I didn't like Friday; it wasn't what I expected. No big hugs, no big kisses. The girls were just as cold to me that day as they were 25 years ago. I shouldn't have come and I was thinking more about leaving than going to some stupid school tour. To tell you the truth officer, if I didn't get shot I'd be in Vegas right now. If Lynn and Steve didn't get shot they'd be in Wyoming right now. Real friendly town you got here."

"Someone wants you dead, Bill. I hate to say this, but I don't want you leaving town just yet. You shouldn't be driving anyway so just stay at the hotel a day or two, I'll get in touch with you there. I'll have the doctor sign you out. Keep the deadbolt in your room locked."

Mazer left word at the nurse's station for the doctor and walked out to the parking lot where the young cop was waiting for him. "Think he bought our act, Bob?"

"No idea, it was a long shot anyhow. But if Bill's the one that tossed those rooms, he'll be heading for the truck soon. Keep an eye on it but stay out of sight."

Back at the hotel Jack was handing out the drinks in the courtyard. Everyone was quiet, not sure exactly what to talk about first or if any of them knew what was going on. Everyone was a little sick and everyone was on edge. The first round of drinks went down quickly and Jack went for another round before the first word was spoken. As Jack put the second round down, the church bells tolled again. It was getting hot and this group felt all the heat in the world was on them. Someone finally asked if they were going to talk or just look at one another. Nobody had a good answer, but everyone knew things had to be discussed. Jack began fidgeting in his chair and readjusting his clothes; he was afraid that the shirt he choose did a poor job of covering his gun. This model was a little bigger than the gun he was used to and his pockets a little smaller. He was thinking about his poor planning when someone asked what his problem was. That momentarily brought him back to earth.

"Let's start at the top guys … the only question that really matters," Jack stopped and looked around the table before finishing his sentence, "is who's trying to kill us and why?"

There was an obvious elephant in the room that no one wanted to address. Jack and Artie touched on it back in Pyrite and ended up in an argument. Someone in this group may well be the shooter. They all agreed that that was a fact they had to accept. They then all denied being that person. The discussion moved to the last night they were all together - the last night they were all alive. They all agreed that the night got tense and when the evening ended, there was disagreement about what the right thing to do was. They recalled that Lynn, Steve, and Bill wanted to let the police know what was never divulged at Sylvia's murder trial and now those three have been shot and two of them are dead. Rita remembered wanting to go to the police too, but anonymously, she was now worried that she was next. Artie tried to calm her. He took her hand, touched her cheek, and swore that he would protect her and that no one would ever get close enough to hurt her. An hour into their talk and not a word that amounted to much of anything was voiced. No one had offered anything of substance, no one mentioned a possible suspect. Tension was getting thick, hands were being wrung, sweat was building on the backs of everyone's necks. Jack snapped.

"To hell with building to a shooter, we're getting nowhere. Let's put the names out there that were too scared or stupid to say. We'll work backward then."

"You love putting names out there Jack, don't you?" Artie said. "You pulled that stunt in Pyrite about Steve and almost got us arrested."

"What did you pull in Pyrite, Jack?" Shelby asked.

"Nothing."

"He blamed Paul Winston for killing Steve," Artie yelled.

"Turns out Paul Winston's been dead for years. He also blamed him for killing Rachel Morgan and the police said that Rachel was at the party Friday night and she was very much alive. Great stories, right Jack. We looked like total assholes trying to cover up something. This from the king of the 'let's all keep quiet' theory. Who you want to blame this go round?"

"Hey, at least I'm trying to protect us by putting out possibilities, not with my big mouth and empty promises."

"You accused Bill of the shootings to that cop too, didn't you?" Shelby asked.

"I explained that to you Shel, I had to. And I was sure that Paul killed Steve when I said that, I was trying to keep me and Artie out of jail and they wanted something. And yes, I do have another suspect to name, and one that makes total sense with all that's happened. Rachel Morgan."

The disbelief on everyone's face was unmistakable; nobody believed Jack again. They looked at each other and then at Jack.

"You don't believe she was murdered with Sylvia? Then where the hell has she been for the past twenty-five years?" Shelby asked.

"I fully believed she was murdered until I got back here. But I've had two phone calls from her and she left a note in Bill's room at the hospital. She signed the guest book at the party and left a message for me with Frank Koonce - more of a warning I think now. I don't know if she escaped her killer or was kidnapped by him. I don't know if she's been in hiding or was being hidden. I think it's even possible she may have even killed Sylvia. But to me one thing is fairly certain ... Rachel Morgan's back and she's settling scores. If anyone has a better theory, let's hear it."

"Too many holes, Jack," Artie said. "There's no way she carried Steve Connor down a flight of stairs at Pyrite High."

"Then she must have an accomplice, a partner. After all these years it makes sense that she would have somebody close to her. Lovers do strange things."

"You're assuming way too much. You want to go to Mazer with this story?"

"Screw Mazer," an angry Jack said. "We've given him all the names, he has to get there on his own. It's the only way we skate. We just have to be on our guard, twenty-four hour guard. Artie, you stay with Rita and Nancy and I'll stay with you Shel if that's ok. If we get something concrete, I guess we go to Mazer. Last resort only, agreed?" They all agreed.

The heat was getting to all of them when the church bells rang at five. The bells rang nine times. "I know it isn't 9 o'clock Artie, what's up with your church?"

"Those bells have been broken for months, repair isn't in the budget. It's always 9 o'clock in Greenleaf."

"Great town. Let's head up, Shel. Too damn hot for 9 o'clock."

The group went their separate ways all agreeing to lay low, stay quiet, and be on their guard for anyone acting suspicious around them. Jack was glad he had a new gun hidden in his pocket, Shelby thought of returning home, but almost preferred a bullet at this point to Eddie. Artie told his wife that he was keeping his shotgun loaded in their bedroom. It was the best they could do with an unseen evil stalking them. While they put their plans together in their heads, a weak, disheveled man slowly dragged himself into the hotel and up to his room. Bill Addison was back.

CHAPTER 22

Hiding in Plain Sight

Sam Spraynor hurried out of town, driving quickly but still careful to not go over the speed limit or push through a yellow light. The cargo he carried was too explosive if seen by the wrong people. He had kept Nancy calm as he led her into his car. His story to her back at Artie's was straight and urgent. He said that he was Sam Spraynor and he was there to protect her.

He handed her a newspaper that he had rolled up under his shirt and told her that it was for her to read, he said that there are people in town coming to kill her and she must leave with him if she wanted to live. Nancy glanced at the paper, nodded a yes to Sam and eagerly left Artie's Place with him. Safely in the car now, Nancy read the whole story.

Death was touching her again and she had no idea why, no idea who this Sam was, no idea where they were going. Nancy had questions but gave up on looking for answers a long time ago. She looked at the mountains in the distance and the store fronts as they drove through town. She'd wait for Sam to tell her what she needed to know. As soon as he got them out of the north end of town, Nancy uttered a single word, not as a question, just an observation;

"Pyrite."

Fifteen minutes out of Greenleaf, Sam turned down a gravel road he knew well and parked out of sight of the highway, about 200 yards in. He told Nancy to wait in the car and he walked back towards the highway, well out of earshot, but keeping Nancy and the car in sight. He called Rachel.

"I've got her, she's alive. I had to get out of town quick. I'm heading to the cabin, I'll have to come back for you later, maybe not until tomorrow."

"Did it go smoothly at Artie's?"

"As smooth as could be, nobody even looked my way and Nancy was ready to run through the walls when I told her she could be killed."

"You don't want to finish it with her tonight?"

"I thought about that, but I think I want to try and drag some things out of her still, maybe there's something in that head that she doesn't even know is buried there." Sam sounded confident if nothing else.

"And you can get in her head?"

"I spent enough time in the Ding Wing to know my way around the mind."

"And just what is the Ding Wing, Sam?" Rachel asked, seeming a bit annoyed.

"Sorry Rachel, it's the psych ward in the pen. I'll find out what's in that head. But listen, things are going to pick up now and we have to speed things up too. Call Jack, Bill, and Artie tonight, make them understand you're running wild out there and not happy. If Bill's not in the hospital, he'll be in the hotel. He's gotta be too weak to drive anywhere. Fear will move Shelby and Rita and they'll make the men panic. Don't give them too much info; we want them reacting to what they don't know, not to what they do know. Okay, I'm flyin. Gotta get to the cabin with Nancy. See you tomorrow around noon."

"You said Nancy used to be the sweetest girl in Pyrite; is this the only thing you can do."

"I gave it a lot of thought Rachel, I'm positive this is necessary - no guilt here. Tomorrow."

Sam raced back to the car and thanked Nancy for waiting as he slid behind the wheel. He was back on the highway in less than ten minutes from when he turned off. Following about thirty more minutes of curves, hills, and dodging deer, Sam entered then quickly exited Pyrite. Ten miles out of town Sam took a right turn and proceeded up a beat up dirt and rock road. Twenty miles on this poor excuse for a road Sam pulled up in front of a cabin that very few people in the world knew existed. He helped Nancy out of the car and into the wooden cabin. He went out back and started the generator. Sam was always hungry when he was nervous and he was starving now. He'd pick Nancy's brain over dinner.

Back in town Shelby went with Jack up to his room. She sat down and appeared very depressed and distant. Her broken marriage weighed heavily on her mind and the unsteady actions of Jack made her question all men in general. She was leery of Jack, yet she felt safe with him. She spoke a few words just barely loud enough for Jack to hear. "I'm scared, Jack."

"I'll take care of you, Shel. That's my only goal from now on. I came back here to bury an ugly past but the more I see you the more I want to give our past another try. Let me show you something." Jack took the gun out of his pocket and put in on the table next to Shelby. "I couldn't buy a gun here in Colorado because of some antiquated resident law so I drove to Utah and got this no questions asked. I even got a permit. I only bought it to protect you. Anyone tries to come in here, I won't miss; I know how to use it. I'll have it with me wherever we go and under my pillow when we're asleep. You're safe, Shel."

Shelby wished she felt as safe as Jack wanted her to feel, but there was too much pain in her stomach. She walked over to her bed, laid down, and curled up into a tiny ball. A light sleep came while Jack sat and watched her breathe. Life could have been so much better he thought as he too drifted off.

A loud banging on the door woke them both. Jack jerked up grabbing his gun. He took a couple quick steps to the door and asked who was there.

"It's Artie, open the F'in door."

Shelby was sitting up in bed and Jack opened the door, hiding the gun in his pants pocket. Artie barged in.

"Nancy's gone. I drove all through town, no sight of her anywhere. No note, her suitcase is still there, she's just gone."

"Calm down, Artie," Jack said. "She probably just went out for a walk or to a store or something. Shel wait here in case she calls or comes by, Artie and I are going to canvas this damn town; we'll find her."

A nervous, shaking Shel sat next to the phone waiting for it to ring just as Rita was doing back at the restaurant. Jack and Artie walked with purpose looking into every building they passed. No sign of Nancy. They blamed one another as they walked, getting angrier and losing confidence in finding her with every step they took.

CHAPTER 23

Mazer and Tidrow take a Deeper Look

M azer met Tidrow back in their conference room. Tidrow was looking over the names and pictures that were on their story board. Mazer walked over to the board too and as hard as they studied it, nothing jumped out. They were sold on their story of Lynn Mitchell. The perp knew Lynn had something he wanted, Lynn refused, Lynn was a threat, Lynn gets shot from up close, bullet goes right through her, room gets tossed, nothing found, move on to Steve Connor. Mazer wanted to look at things assuming Steve got shot at the hotel, they'd get the laundry basket in play that way.

"No good," Tidrow objected. "He was shot from further away so the bullet couldn't go through him. Couldn't happen in his room, too small. And if Steve was killed here, his body would've stayed here. No Bob, he was shot in Pyrite. We figure out why he was there and we'll be circling our killer."

They ran through the crime scenes again in their heads … from hotel to car to school to closet. A new look at a mysterious shooting. They started with a sleeping Steve Connor and tried recreating from his vantage this time, not the shooter's. Tidrow played Steve.

"I'm asleep and someone wakes me up with a gun to my face. They tell me to keep quiet or they'll shoot me and then they'll go next door and shoot my girlfriend. I ask what they want and they tell me that they want the gun from the holdup, let's say. I'm worried for my life, but moreso about Lynn. I need to get this guy out of my room and the hotel and buy as much time as possible to protect Lynn. I need to keep this guy away from here until daylight. So I say that the gun is being planted by my partner in Pyrite and it will be found during the school tour. The shooter tells me to call my partner's cell which I say he didn't take because he didn't want to be tracked. I'm the only one that can get the gun now. He holds his gun on me and makes me drive us to Pyrite High School. Once there, I tell him what a fool he is; that he was standing 3 feet from the gun in my room in Greenleaf. He paces, thinks about it, and smiles. He says to me, 'I guess I don't need you anymore' and shoots me in the chest. He hides my body to buy himself more time, goes back to Greenleaf, and tosses my room looking for the gun. It's not there which I, of course, knew all along so our perp moves to the next victim, Bill Addison. Now Bill could be right person, wrong time. Our perp leaves room 217 and heads for the stairs as Bill is entering his room, 211 right down the hall. Perp sees him and whacks him good; his anger is now out of control and he kicks Bill a few times, cusses him out, hears commotion outside, and he goes to the door to listen. Bill tries to get up but he's pretty badly beaten up. Shooter sees him on his knees and fires from the doorway. His shot is off from that far away and it hits bone between his heart and shoulder, passes through him and lodges right there in the floor. Bill passes out and as soon as things get quiet in the hallway our shooter flees. There's no time to search Bill's room now. With Bill in the hospital, the perp comes back and has plenty of time to search the room without tossing it. Assuming he still hasn't found whatever it is he needs, we can be certain that someone else will be attacked soon."

"That could fit Jeff, probably other scenarios work too, but that could fit. If someone else gets shot, we're on the right track. If not, we'll be starting over."

"We won't have to start from scratch, Bob, this shooter is looking for something, we need to figure out what that is, I think our lives will get a whole lot easier at that point."

"When I had Jack and Artie in the squad room after Steve's shooting, they said this all has to do with the murders 25 years ago. Hang on, let me check my notes."

Mazer pulled his note pad from his uniform pocket and ran through the pages, stopping when he found his interview notes.

"Here it is Jeff. *J & A try to link murder to another murder twenty-five years ago. Blamed Paul Winston who's long dead. Said Paul murdered Steve and previously, twenty-five years ago, he murdered a Sylvia and a Rachel Morgan. Guest sign in sheets show Rachel Morgan was at the party Friday. Story full of BS. J & A at odds about everything. Old murders a smoke screen??? A & J involved if not downright guilty. Only suspects so far. Lean on them. Bad feeling about them.* That's all I wrote. The file on Sylvia's murder was pretty empty. I asked Judy to dig a little deeper, but after the Addison shooting, I kind of put it on my back burner. Let's move it up Jeff."

"Okay, if we assume that the murder of this Sylvia led to the murder of Steve, are we looking for a murderer or a weapon? Could we, *and* the murderer, be looking for a weapon … the same weapon? Could this Rachel be looking for this weapon? Or could she be using it."

"At least it fits, for right now anyhow," a cautious Mazer said, "I'm heading home to Pyrite for the night, I need to see what Judy found out. I'll touch base with you in the morning. Those two clowns may have given us the break we need. I have a feeling that when we find this weapon, we'll learn everything we need to know about Rachel Morgan. See you tomorrow."

The hour was late for Mazer, but the night was young for Jack and Artie as they tried to search every inch of downtown Greenleaf. Nancy would never have wandered far on her own. When they reached the grocery store they split up for a while; Artie walked the aisles inside, Jack continued up the street and stopped to read the decorative street signs. One sign said 'library' and had an arrow pointing east, Jack had hopes as he headed up the hill.

No luck at the library; the quiet played opposite the inner turmoil he felt. No Nancy at the car rental office, the coffee shop, no luck in ice cream shops, candy stores, and no Nancy in the city park. He caught up with Artie again on Main Street near the hotel.

Artie had the same result as Jack and they were both sick to their stomachs. Jack said the obvious, "Someone's got Nancy; we may already be too late. Go get Rita, come up to my room, 301. I have to run, Shelby's alone and I'm afraid not safe."

Jack and Artie hurried along Main Street and Jack sprinted up the stairs inside the Peaks. He got to the room and found that Shelby hadn't moved an inch. He reported to Shelby all the places they looked, all the buildings, parks, stores, no sign of Nancy anywhere. Shelby said that there wasn't a single peep around the hotel. They sat fidgeting when the hotel phone rang startling them both. Jack answered quickly hoping to hear Nancy's voice. His hello was followed by a woman's voice, but not the woman he was hoping for.

"Did you think ignoring me Friday night, just like you did 25 years ago, was fair?"

"Rachel," Jack screamed into the phone, "you've got to stop this."

"I left something, or should I say someone, where you thought you left me. We're halfway home." And the line went dead.

"Rachel," Jack screamed into the phone and then again and again, "Rachel .... Rachel .... damn you Rachel."

"What did she say Jack? Are you sure it's Rachel? Talk to me."

Jack went and took a bottle of booze out of the minibar, whatever was in front. "She said I ignored her Friday night and we're halfway home. I guess that means she's got 4 of us, and 4 to go. I'm only guessing Shel, let's wait for the Paycheks."

One floor down, Bill Addison was awakened from a deep sleep. It hurt like hell to roll over and reach for the phone. The drugs were supposed to help with the pain, but they were only as good as a mild sleeping pill. He moaned into the phone. "What?"

"It's Rachel. It's been 25 years and I'm finally close to ending it, if not for everyone then for you. You're going to pay, Bill."

Bill slammed the phone down. "This isn't happening. Bitch." No amount of sleeping pills could help Bill find rest now. He struggled to the bathroom and got dressed. He limped upstairs and banged on the door of room 301. After he knocked, he leaned against the door to hold himself up, when Jack opened it, Bill staggered into the room and fell into the first chair he saw. A few minutes later Artie and Rita got to the room. All Artie could say when he saw Bill was "what the hell is he doing here."

"We don't know, he just got here and kind of collapsed." Jack then turned to Bill, "why are you here Bill, you look half dead."

"I told you all before, I want to get out of here, now, I need money. Jack, you and Artie are loaded. 25 grand and I'm gone. Nobody will ever find me."

"I thought it was 20," Artie said, "and we aren't giving you a penny anyway."

"Looks like I'm calling the police and talking to the press tomorrow. You four criminals better talk it over, I'll call in the morning."

Bill struggled back to his room and threw the deadbolt. He knew that his so called friends didn't want him talking to the police, but he didn't know if they would buy his silence or cause it. He was in no mood to get shot again.

"It would be worth a 100 grand to just get that bum out of our lives," Jack said. "If one of you shot him keep it to yourself, but thank you, and have better aim next time. Now what do we do about Nancy?"

"We're out of time here Jack," Artie said, "and keeping quiet hasn't done anything for us. We need to call Mazer and let him know that Nancy's disappeared. We don't know anything else so we won't be saying anything else. I say call him now."

Both girls agreed and a nervous Jack found Mazer's card on his nightstand and dialed the officer's number. The friends listened in.

"Officer Mazer? Jack Spencer here. We have an emergency in Greenleaf. You in town? ... No, not everything is an emergency, but this is. ... Our friend Nancy is missing; we've looked everywhere in Greenleaf, she's not here ... I would take offense at that, but we're desperate ... We didn't want you talking to her about her friends being murdered because she's still dealing with her own personal tragedies. In hindsight, maybe ... Come on Mazer what can you do?" Jack listened a long time and finally disconnected with Mazer. "He's going to call Jeff Tidrow, his counterpart here in Greenleaf, and have the police here keep an eye out. He'll be back here tomorrow and come here first. I'm sure he'll want to talk to all of us. He hinted that if we would have let Nancy talk to him this may have been prevented, but he's wrong on that. We've done nothing wrong, being quiet isn't a crime. Are we done until tomorrow? It's about time I started tossing and turning for the next 8 hours. Sleep would be nice, but I'm not that optimistic anymore."

Before the group went their separate ways for the night, Artie whispered a final bit of news to Jack, "Rachel called me right before we came over. She said my nice guy act is about to come crashing down, that old crimes demand new payment. She's coming Jack, we better be ready." Jack hung his head low and felt his insides turning over. It felt like a fist had a hold of his stomach from the inside. He looked to Shelby who was already under the covers not bothering to even change clothes. He turned the deadbolt, put his loaded gun under his pillow and called it a day. Another beautiful day in Greenleaf, he thought to himself.

CHAPTER 24

All the Cards on the Table, Face Down

Sam Spraynor was up before the sun came up. He was sitting at his folding table going through Nancy's purse while she slept on the sofa. The purse was small and relatively empty. A couple IDs, old family photos, and a couple bottles of medicine. Sam read the labels and looked at the pictures. A couple photos of a young girl standing alone, one of her holding a bike and smiling from ear to ear. Another picture, very weather beaten of a man holding this child, in this picture the man is smiling ear to ear. Sam knew the story; he knew these two were killed in a car accident. He looked over at Nancy and for the first time in a long time almost felt human. But the clock was ticking and he had a lot to do today. He gently shook Nancy and it was enough to awaken her. She did her morning routine as best she could in the cabin and sat down at the table.

"I wanted to talk to you last night Nancy," Sam started, "but you fell asleep. I thought you needed sleep more than talk, so I just let you rest. You probably don't remember me do you?"

"Of course I do, you got me out of Rita's place before the killer came. You saved me, but I don't why."

"I mean before that Nancy, we went to high school together, but

I wasn't part of your group. You hung around with Rita, Sylvia, and Rachel. You remember all of them?"

"Rita of course, she's a good friend. Sylvia and Rachel? Maybe. I have a hard time now with memory. Doctors say I don't want to remember. I say I can't. My father died when I was in high school. Did you know him?"

"No, no I didn't. Did Jack know your father, and Sylvia and Rachel?"

"My mother took me away from Pyrite after my dad died. Did you know my mother?"

"We said hi, that was about it. Did Artie know your mother? Did he know Sylvia and Rachel?"

"My mother died after we left Pyrite. We shouldn't have left. Death always finds you."

"Any other death find you Nancy?"

This last question beat Nancy badly, she started crying and moaning. Sam got her a glass of water and gave her one of each of her pills. He gave up on getting into Nancy's head. As soon as Nancy calmed down, Sam helped her into the car. He gave her a pillow and blanket and had her lay down in the back seat. The sun was casting its rays just over the mountains; it was time to move. Nancy was asleep by the time Sam pulled away from the cabin. He drove slowly with lights off down the deserted back road.

In Greenleaf, Jack was up early and called Artie to ask about Nancy. Still no sign of her, but Rita and Artie were safe and having breakfast without a word exchanged between them. Jack got Shelby moving. He wanted to be down at breakfast and not in his room when Mazer arrived. Jack and Shelby also sat speechless in front of a couple of lone cups of coffee - no words, no food. They waited for Mazer and called Artie when he got there. Mazer, Jack, Shelby, Artie, and Rita went out back to be away from any other people. They carried a table even further away from the other tables and sat down – each with a look of distrust on their face. Mazer took out his note pad and was expecting Jack's cat and mouse game when he asked his first question.

"Has Nancy returned by chance?"

"No Bob, and we spent hours yesterday walking the streets looking in just about every building in town." Artie felt Bob Mazer was a good cop in a bad situation, he wanted to show respect.

"What's her full name?"

"Nancy Braxton." With that they all stated talking at once.

"Braxton was her maiden name."

"What was her married name?'

"Doesn't matter the doctor's changed it back. Thought it would help her."

"Help how?"

"She wouldn't have the constant reminder of her husband and daughter."

Mazer finally had enough. "Enough!" he shouted. Everyone stopped talking and looked at each other. "One at a time, when I ask you something. She was staying with you Artie, I guess that means you know her best, give me her background."

"We told you just about all we know already."

"Hardly, and if you think you did then give it to me again."

"She left Pyrite after graduation and moved with her mother to Pine Square, small town a couple hours east of here. She was married there and had a kid and I'm sure they all lived with her mother until she passed. After that, the daughter and husband got killed in a car accident and Nancy has been fighting brain issues ever since. She's been in the assisted living home in Pine Square for some time - maybe 10 years now. She could maybe function on her own now, what with new meds and her needing less help, but it wouldn't be ideal. She was where she belonged. I signed her out for the reunion weekend. Her doctor thought it would be good for her and I was going to have her back by this coming weekend. They didn't want her away much longer than a week, I'll have to call them."

"I'll call them, I might have some questions for them when we're done here. Go ahead."

"Well yesterday," Artie continued, "she was sleeping, I guess about 3:00, Rita and I came over for a couple drinks and a short visit. When we got back home, Nancy was gone. We had the restaurant staff downstairs and we asked each of them if they saw or heard anything from upstairs. They all said no. I came here, got Jack, and we searched the town. Not finding a trace of Nancy, we called you."

Mazer wrote feverishly as he tried to get everything and then asked a few questions of the group with every answer being 'no'.

Does anyone have a picture of her?

Do you know what she was wearing?

Does she have other friends in town she could be visiting?

Has she wandered away before when she was alone?

And then he asked the question that got a different response.

"Did she know this Sylvia and Rachel that Jack says are the cause of all my troubles with you people?"

"She knew them as well as we did Bob," Jack said.

"Come on Jack," Artie spoke up, "she treated them a lot better than we ever did. She talked nice to Crazy Paul too. Nancy was better than the rest of us Bob - and that's the plain truth."

"Screw you Artie, I know I treated them well, I don't know about you. Speak for yourself."

"Be careful who you speak for. You're treating these crimes as a game show, bouncing from guess to guess throwing each one of us under the bus as you go, so just shut the hell up."

Mazer was holding back his smile, "every time I have you two old friends together a fight almost breaks out. I have a feeling that if I locked you two in a room for half an hour I would either have my murderer or one of you would be dead. Nothing solid yet or I just might do that. You folks go about your business, in Greenleaf. The police here are looking for Nancy, watching for anything strange. I'm meeting with Tidrow at the station. I'll be in touch."

Mazer shoved his note pad back in his pocket and took off for the station. The air slowly left the balloon that Jack and Artie filled up. It once again came close to exploding and no one really knew why. Overused and fake apologies were offered then Artie and Rita headed back home. Artie turned and left Jack with a cryptic message, "we have to give Mazer more." Jack went with Shelby inside for breakfast, she chewed on a piece of dry toast, Jack chewed on his lower lip. He was a million miles away.

CHAPTER 25

Who's on Whose Side

Sam pulled up to Rachel's trailer well before noon. Rachel was anxious to hear how things went and if he learned anything new from Nancy. In Sam's opinion, Nancy was lost in another world and maybe at peace now. They both felt she was best forgotten and time for them to move on to more urgent business. They debated cleaning up the trailer and moving to the cabin. Sam was worried that his spy tracker wouldn't work that far or that well out in the back country. They packed up everything they could for a quick getaway but decided to keep the trailer as their home base. Something was bound to break soon.

In the hotel Shelby and Jack returned to their room and sat like a couple in mourning; a few days late, but the mourning emotion was finally hitting them. A dark cloud hung overhead as Shelby fought a losing battle to hold back her tears.

"I'm not going back home Jack. I'm done with Utah, I'm done with my marriage. Eddie and I aren't on the same team any more. I should be able to call him now, cry on his shoulder, lean on him for strength. I'm hurting now and if I call him he'll only threaten me, call me names, accuse me of things. We've become complete opposites, I'd have to be crazy to go back."

"I think that's good Shel, I really do. Where will you go?" Jack took his thumb and gently wiped away the tears beneath Shelby's eyes. If he were being honest with himself now he would admit that this move felt good for him, he didn't really know or care how it was for Shelby. "Have you thought about New York? I know you wouldn't want to live with me right away, but I could help you get your new life started and maybe see what we could be together."

"No. No New York, Jack. I have to make my own life. Besides, I don't feel like we're always on the same side either. You're always saying we all need to keep quiet and then you're spewing story after story to the authorities around here. I think you're only interested in yourself."

"You're wrong, Shel. It's all about you now, I give you my word."

"Really? Then tell me, what did Artie mean when he said *'we have to give Mazer more'*?"

Jack struggled to take a couple deep breaths, he was getting light headed and exhaled loudly. He tried to look into Shelby's eyes but it was growing increasingly difficult to focus. He got up and walked to the front window, the sight of the peaks beyond Pyrite only made him sicker. Shelby was staring at him now as he paced around the room. He finally sat down again, right next to Shelby, and tried to do something he was pretty poor at, tell the truth. He went back to their first night in Greenleaf, the conversation in Artie's Place. He recalled the night and spoke slowly. He started his story from the time Shelby left the restaurant.

"We continued arguing after you left. Bill told us that he owed big dollars on a gambling bet he lost. He threatened us that if we didn't pay the debt he would have to go to the police and the local press about everything we did to Paul and how we covered it up at his trial. We never agreed to pay him off, none of us believed we did that much wrong, but in hindsight I guess it was pretty bad what we did and then on top of that we clammed up about it. While we were having that argument with Bill, Steve left with Lynn. Sometime around then Rita told us that she knew Artie got a package with a knife inside and that knife must be the murder weapon that killed Rachel Morgan. She said that she gave the package to Lynn so that she and Steve could give it to the police in Pyrite after the school tour. Well Shel, Artie went nuts and started screaming at Rita about her ruining them and he left the restaurant. I walked back to the hotel with Bill and we saw Artie's truck parked right across the street. I told Bill to go send him home and I came up here to my room. When I got here Steve was waiting for me at the door and he had the package. He came in and we talked a bit more. Now it was after 3:00 Shel and I was cashed, I'm sure Steve was too. We talked about the girl's murders and got a little emotional, it really hit home that we didn't do anything to see that Paul got a fair trial, we were as bad as those TV shows where they don't care who they convict as long as they convict somebody. And you know what Shel, even though we were emotional and even though 25 years had taken us from boys to men, we still didn't want to stand up and say we were wrong. Steve told me that he and Lynn were heading back to Wyoming first thing in the morning as long as I promised to get the knife to the Pyrite police. I didn't know how I was going to do it but I promised that I would. Steve left and I never saw him alive again. I had the knife in the car when we found Steve dead and I didn't know what to do. Mazer was sweating us and I wasn't sure how deep in Artie might be, I was scared too Shel. I tried to get Artie drunk so I could hide the knife somewhere safe in Pyrite, I kind of did both, but Artie didn't get as drunk as I had hoped. But the knife's safely hidden and when Artie said that we need to give Mazer more, he meant the knife, he wants me to get the knife Shel and I guess it's time to do that. I can't do this anymore, I'm scared every second that one more of us is going to get killed, I'm petrified it might be you. If I lose my career so be it, we've somehow fallen into a black hole and it's time we get out."

"Where's the knife from and how did Rita get it?" Shelby asked.

"We think it's from Rachel's murder, or alleged murder since I think she's still alive. The knife went missing after Paul's trial and since he was found guilty it wasn't needed anymore, so it just fell off the radar. Whoever found it must have done some research and figured the only people tied to Paul still in this area were Artie and Rita. Not wanting to get involved himself, he planted the knife in the restaurant where Artie or Rita would see it. He figured he did his good deed and it was up to Artie now. Could be a cop or admin person, I don't know, and it's all a guess anyhow. I can't take another guess to Mazer, he's dying to lock me up already, I have to get the knife and give him that. I guess I'll do that tomorrow."

"I'm going with you Jack, I need to know you're telling the truth, for a lot of reasons. It's still early, we should go get it now. We'll be in Pyrite before 4:00. How long to get to where you hid it?"

"Half hour from the highway Shel, there and back. It'll be easier with a shovel, we'll buy one on the way."

As Jack and Shelby made their way to Pyrite, with shovel and gun in hand, Mazer was meeting with Tidrow. He ran through everything he learned about Nancy from her old friends and added 'missing' to her name on the crime story board. Tidrow reported no sightings of Nancy or any other lone woman walking the streets of Greenleaf. Mazer reported that his assistant found an inspector Anderson's notes in the file on Sylvia's murder and Rachel's disappearance. Rachel's classified as a 'cold case', Sylvia as a solved homicide. They decided to go up to Tidrow's office and pull up the trial notes on his computer, and compare those to Anderson's notes. First Mazer had the unenviable task of calling Nancy's hospital home and reporting her missing. Tidrow watched Mazer turn red with anger while he was talking to a hospital doctor. Whatever Mazer was asking he was not getting the answers he needed. Mazer finally hung up the phone, nearly breaking it, and held back a tantrum.

"That goddamn Jack got me again, and this is the last time, maybe that F'n Artie too. We must be close, it has to be them. I get Nancy's doctor on the line, tell him I want to talk to him about Nancy Braxton. Now get this Jeff, he says, all I can say is the trip didn't do her any harm, she seems to be exactly as she left. He tells me that she came walking through the front door this morning seeming very happy. Jack or Artie must have driven her home early this morning while were running around looking for her. They ushered her out of town for some reason, she knows something and they know there's no way I can head there until I know more about what's happening here. They got me again Jeff, they're playing us for fools buddy."

In the trailer park the spy beeper went off on Sam's laptop. He told Rachel that it looked like Jack was heading to the store, that's what the location light showed him. It stopped moving for about 10 minutes and started again. Sam almost turned the tracker off when the light showed Jack moving north. He grabbed his shotgun and called for Rachel.

"He's heading to Pyrite, Rachel. You got him, we, we, we, got him."

"Calm down, breathe. The car's all loaded, gimme the laptop, only one road to where he's going, we'll catch up, stay far enough behind."

"It, it, it, it's been 25 years." Sam struggled to get the words out.

"Are you crying?" Rachel asked.

CHAPTER 26

Some Things Should Stay Buried

The sun was starting to pour into Jack's side window while at the same time casting long shadows across the highway in front of him. It was still hot enough to need the air conditioning, but both Jack and Shelby preferred the fresh air blowing in through the slightly opened windows. The further out of Greenleaf they drove, the greener and denser the trees grew. Jack felt better than he had in days, maybe even years.

Once he handed Mazer the knife and Mazer had it checked for every ounce of detail with modern technology, he knew he would finally find peace. If it cost him his position in the New York firm but brought Shelby back to him, the whole fiasco would be worth it. In spite of his best intentions to give Mazer everything he had and let the police handle things, as they should have all along, Jack still ran his own theories all through his head. He believed, for the moment as he told himself, that Paul Winston, with help from Rachel Morgan, killed Sylvia Kean. Rachel fled that night when she saw Paul get arrested and established a new life for herself somewhere safe.

Paul kept quiet during his trial to protect Rachel, and the two of them stayed in touch while Paul was locked up. When he died in prison, Rachel began plotting her revenge and this so called Pyrite High reunion gave her every chance she needed to do so, even though she was the guilty party. Jack believed that new evidence on the knife would somehow show Rachel played a different role in Sylvia's murder than previously thought and that threat has Rachel doing everything in her power, including murder, to get that knife and disappear again.

He knew he shouldn't bother giving Mazer yet another theory on the murders, but the only thing he really knew was himself, and he knew he had to tell his latest story, and tell it soon. He was busting once again.

Jack pulled down the back road that led to his old home's long driveway. He parked at the entrance and not wanting the current owner to see him there again, got out of the car and grabbed the shovel from the trunk. He told Shelby that he was heading into the woods for the package and she should drive around, maybe get some gas or waste time in the park, but be back right there in 40 minutes. Jack disappeared into the woods and Shelby made a u-turn almost hitting the blue Subaru, which just dropped off its passenger.

Jack made the long walk uphill, it was much more strenuous today than he remembered it being so many years ago. He didn't want to get disoriented on his former property but knew that was always a possibility in this terrain. He chose to walk parallel to the driveway until he reached a direct path to his old tree house route. As soon as he reached his old walking trail, he turned left and stopped for a few breaths. Being on this land for this reason allowed for no happy flashbacks. He was on a rather sordid mission and wanted to get out of here as badly right now as he did 25 years ago. He got to the marked plot and tossed away the rocks he placed on top. A few shovels full of dried dirt tossed to the side and he hit the package. He dropped to his knees and brushed aside the remaining dirt and pulled the package from the ground. His feelings of success were short lived.

Both barrels of a double barrel shotgun were planted on the back of Jack's neck, his entire body went numb. The all too familiar sound of the cocking of the shotgun followed. Jack threw up violently in the now empty hole in the ground. *Was the blast next, he wondered.*

"Don't turn around, hands behind your back. I got a hair trigger on this gun, if you die right here, it'll be your own fault."

Jack did as he was told and was soon handcuffed, hands behind his back. "Are you the police? I'm not doing anything wrong here, I just came to pick this package up for Mazer. Call him, I'm Jack Spencer. He'll tell you I'm alright. Please."

A cloth bag was placed over Jack's head and his package taken from him.

"I know you didn't come here for this. Why don't you tell me why you're really here." There was anger in this man's voice and the fear inside of Jack was growing by the second.

"It's the only reason I'm here. Tell me what you want or who you are and I can help. You can have the package if that's what you want, no point in killing me, I'll leave Colorado tonight if you let me go. No reason to make more trouble for yourself."

"How will your partner feel about that?"

"She'll leave with me, we've already talked about it."

"When and where is she meeting you?"

"At the front of the driveway that leads up here. She'll be there in 20 minutes."

"I'm going to take the cover off of your head, you turn around and you won't see tomorrow much less me. My partner's following your Caddy around. If your partner comes back you better hope she's in a cooperative mood. Leaving you and your partner dead in your car just may be the best way out of here for me. Stay away from the driveway, head down through the trees, stop when I tell you to. Now get going."

The walk down went way too quickly for Jack and he stopped the instant he was ordered to. He was told to kneel and the bag was put back over his head and tied tightly. Shelby was sitting in the Cadillac waiting for Jack to return. Rachel was parked alongside the back road that passed by the driveway. When Rachel spotted Sam waving from the woods, she approached the Cadillac. Sam told Jack to stay right where he was or it would be an unfortunate ending for him and his lady friend. While Rachel held Shelby's attention, Sam got to the car completely unnoticed and pointed his shotgun directly in Shelby's face. They put a cloth bag over her head, handcuffed her, and put her in the back of the Subaru. Sam had final instructions.

"You stay on the floor in here. I'll be following you Shelby. If I see so much as a hair from your head, your friend Jack takes a bullet, right before you do. I'll follow you Rachel, as soon as I get Jack in the car we can leave. We have another problem however, we'll talk about it tonight, when we're alone."

It was quick ride through Pyrite and then Rachel, with Sam right behind her, turned off onto a rock filled dirt road that they followed for a number of miles. Well into the middle of nowhere, they parked beside the cabin where Sam and Nancy Braxton spent the previous night. Rachel was worried about the new problem and couldn't wait any longer to hear about it. Sam opened the trunk of the Cadillac and loosened Jack's head cover to give him some air. Sam talked openly to Rachel, it didn't seem to matter anymore what Jack heard.

"I have the knife back. It may be all Jack was going after. I might have jumped the gu, gu, gu, gun Rachel."

The stuttering, the knife, and most of all, Rachel. It all made sense to Jack now. He trembled at his realization that his captor was none other than the cause of his 25 years of nightmares and Sylvia's murderer, Paul Winston. He and Shelby are being held by Paul Winston and Rachel Morgan. But how do two dead people kidnap anyone?

"Let's get these two in the 4x4; the old cabin's ready and we can hold them as long as we need to. Nobody will ever find them back there, but I may have to get rid of the Caddy. Take the knife inside and get our stuff out of the Subaru. I'll be back as soon as I can."

Paul buckled Shelby into the front seat and put Jack in the storage rack in back. They covered the mile or so to the old cabin in a few minutes. Paul had spent a lot of time the past few years readying this place for today. A 6 inch deep cement block was laid against the back wall, heavy iron rivets were bound deep into the block, chains ran through the eyelet of the rivets, shackles, handcuffs, and a handgun hung on the wall. Paul's design ideas were simple, if I bring you in, I'm your only way out. He brought Shelby and Jack in one at a time and chained them to the cement floor before removing their head covers.

"My great-grandfather built this place over a hundred years ago, Jack. There's a creek right out back, almost dry now, where him and my grandfather panned for gold. To hear my dad tell of it, the water roared through here in those days. They never hit the big strike that they were after, but made enough to sustain them. When the water slowed and the gold washed out, my grandfather moved to town and worked the company mines. My Dad worked there too. He was hard as nails on me Jack, but you already knew that. We lived in that cold building that you knew me from, near the mine, until they took me away." Paul paused here and then screamed at the top of his lungs.

"THEY TOOK ME AWAY JACK! YOU REMEMBER THAT THEY TOOK ME AWAY DON'T YOU. FOR WHAT JACK? FOR NOTHING!"

Paul left the two alone and went back down the mountain slope to talk to Rachel. Jack started looking for a way out of his cuffs and chains. Shelby was not nearly as panicked as Jack as she observed the shack.

"Look at this shack Jack, he's no killer."

"What? The gun on the wall? These handcuffs and chains? The shotgun he shoved in my face?"

"No," Shelby countered, "we got water and cups right behind us, an air mattress we can sleep on, some energy bars, blankets. Paul doesn't want to kill us, he wants something from us. He's no killer Jack."

"Maybe Rachel's the killer. I rather not be here when either of them come back."

CHAPTER 27

Beware Visitors Bearing Questions

Mazer wanted to go through the investigator's notes from 25 years ago as well as the court transcripts, but he had his own current Pyrite murder to solve as well as Tidrow's Greenleaf murder. He left Tidrow to study the old case and went to investigate the new one … his first stop, Jack Spencer.

He parked his squad car in the hotel parking lot and didn't see Jack's Cadillac anywhere. He radioed Mitch who was doing surveillance on Steve's Silverado and asked for an update on his watch. Mitch said that no one's been near the truck and when asked about Jack's Cadillac, was told that Jack and a woman, probably Shelby, took off in it some time ago. A very aggravated Mazer took off for Artie's Place and sat down upstairs with Artie while Rita ran the restaurant. The questions caught Artie off guard beginning with "where the hell are Jack and Shelby?"

Artie told Mazer that he thought Jack was in his room at the hotel, with Shelby. Mazer asked Artie if he had gotten into any more disputes with Jack about his theories and if Jack could be out chasing down one of his self-created leads. Artie played dumb about every question and suggested that Mazer go find Jack and ask him. Mazer sarcastically thanked him for his cooperation and took three steps toward the door when he turned to try and get under Artie's skin.

"Oh, you forgot to ask me about your close missing friend, Nancy. Seems she walked through the front door of her hospital home this morning without a care in the world. Now you don't suppose she walked all the way home, over a hundred miles from Greenleaf, do you?" Before Artie could say a word Mazer held up his hand to stop him, "oh, no answer necessary, I'll be talking with Nancy soon enough, you can let Jack know that too as soon as you talk to him. Well I'd better get going. I imagine there's a lot of calls a busy restauranteur like yourself has to make."

Mazer then drove to the Peaks hotel and on a lark knocked on Jack's door. When no one answered, Mazer was worried that Jack and Shelby skipped town. He knew they wouldn't be hard to find but he was growing restless with having no hard suspect for the two murders. He felt the town folk and his bosses in Pyrite wouldn't tolerate much more inaction. He rubbed his chin and walked down a flight of stairs and knocked on Bill Addison's door. A weak, hunched over Bill Addison invited him in. As soon as both men were seated, Bill fired off the first question, "you catch my assassin yet?"

Mazer took the gibe in stride, "I think you have to be dead to have been assassinated Bill, you don't really want me to be hunting an assassin do you? I much rather help keep you alive, I like you Bill, you're much more down to earth than your friends. They all act like they think they're better than you, I don't know why you put up with them."

"Tell me about it. One's worse than he next. I get shot and I don't get one visit from any of them. Maybe one of them shot me Bob."

"You could be right Bill, and if one of them shot you, then that same person must have shot Lynn and Steve. What's their motive Bill? Best guess of course."

"No idea. It sure had nothing to do with money seeing as they shot me."

"Did Lynn and Steve have money?"

"They said that they didn't, but I think they were loaded. So I guess it could be about money."

"But wouldn't that make your shooting unrelated? If it was

about money I mean."

"No, no, no. They're related. Have to be. So it isn't about money. You need a better motive Bob."

"True enough buddy, thanks for the help. I need to get back to the station. Is it alright if I stay in touch? You're not in too much pain are you?"

"I'll be fine. Call me when you need me."

"Oh and you'll be glad to know we found Nancy."

"Found her?" Bill said, "I had no idea she was lost."

Following the exchange Bob Mazer headed back to the station to check out his crime board with Tidrow. He knew he got something important from Bill, but he didn't know exactly what. He radioed Mitch on his way back and told him to keep a distant eye on the Silverado until the end of his shift and pick it up again tomorrow. It's a longshot, but it's our best shot for now. Mazer found Tidrow at the board looking very confused. Mazer stood next to Tidrow and wore a similar look.

"We have to rework this board," Mazer began, "something Bill Addison said to me didn't make sense but turned a light on. He said he was in a different financial boat than Lynn and Steve so the motive couldn't be money, which we never thought it was to begin with. But we always assumed that there is only one thing driving all these shootings, the way Lynn's and Steve's rooms were tossed, our shooter is looking for something, a gun perhaps. Well look at Bill's room, it wasn't tossed, just maybe Bill was shot for a different reason, and since he's still alive I think we have to look at that. And here's a new twist that we better add as we rework this thing, Jack and Shelby aren't at the hotel, we have to consider them missing. Maybe they'll just drop out of the sky like Nancy did. Now before we start on this board again, let's look at the info from the Sylvia Kean murder. Let's move ahead from the assumption that that murder is square one. The file's in your office and we'll need your computer, we should work there. Plus it will be good to research that without all the current stuff we have on the board. These people threw a lot of obstacles in our way, we have to figure out what we need to throw out. Best to start at day one, 25 years ago."

Mazer and Tidrow walked up to Tidrow's office and he had one of his assistants make an extra copy of Ken Anderson's original investigation report from the Sylvia/Rachel murders. The report was thin and they both read through it, twice, very quickly. From Anderson's personal notes, they could tell a few things right off. Number one was that Anderson assumed Paul Winston was guilty from minute one and the little investigating he did was only to put a bow around the case. The report mentioned the broken door, the bloody knife, Paul's shovel in Sylvia's car, and the eye witness to Paul stalking Sylvia. To Anderson, the case was cut and dry. They pulled up the trial notes on the computer next and those notes told the same story. Motive, opportunity, blood - the jury was out about two hours according to the Greenleaf notes. Paul was found guilty and was sent away. Sylvia had a small town funeral, but Rachel's body was never found. Anderson retired and died a few months later and most of the Pyrite graduating class of 1993 moved away as soon as they could. Armed with this new information Mazer and Tidrow, Bob and Jeff to one another, reassembled their crime board. The top line was the names of the murdered and shot, Bill Addison, Lynn and Steve, Sylvia and Rachel. The second line was the names of those who were or are missing, Rachel, Jack and Shelby, Nancy Braxton. The third line of names under the names they corresponded to were the likely suspects, Rachel under Bill Addison, Rachel and everyone else under Lynn and Steve, and Rachel again under Sylvia Kean.

"Well there it is Jeff," Mazer said, "any one of these people had the opportunity to kill Lynn and Steve and we need to keep looking hard into that, but the one person who could have killed them and Sylvia, and shot Addison is Rachel Morgan. We have to arrest her before she kills anybody else and we don't know the first thing about her. And to be complete Jeff, there's one more suspect we need to be looking at, we may have a killer in town, then and now, that is completely unknown to us, a rogue murderer."

As the sun went down behind the Pyrite cliffs, the cool air drifted down from the north. Jack and Shelby were shivering until they covered themselves with the blankets and laid down to try to sleep. Paul Winston and Rachel Morgan built a fire and burned the box and packing that the knife was hidden in. Bob Mazer and Jeff Tidrow called it a day and went to their respective homes. Artie and Rita turned in early with a loaded shotgun under their bed. Bill filled up with pain pills and bottles of booze until he passed out.

And two hours away, finally free of the pain of Pyrite, Nancy Braxton softly sang a child's lullaby to her daughter's favorite doll. It was the only love given by this group in a long long time, and it was given to a toy.

CHAPTER 28

Bad Bait Springs the Wrong Trap

Rachel and Paul were up early, neither slept very well. Paul did not expect Jack to lead him to the knife that he himself had planted, but felt that since the knife was that important to Jack, he must have the right man. Now he had to figure out how to close the trap even though Jack didn't step completely in it. And what's Shelby's role here? Is she in this with Jack or merely into Jack? Paul recommended to Rachel that she leave Colorado now and let him finish things for better or worse. Rachel refused. She reiterated that she was in until the bitter end and toasted up half a loaf of bread for their prisoners. Paul wanted to keep Rachel away from Jack and Shelby until he had a better feel for what to do. He took the toast from Rachel and headed to the shack to press Jack further. He felt defeated for now and his goal was changing as he rode, he now only thought about getting Rachel out of Pyrite undetected.

The pair looked none the worse for wear when Paul arrived and were grateful for some food to go with the water they'd been drinking all morning. Paul began his attack immediately.

"I had a feeling it was you all along Jack, but to be honest I never thought for a second that Shelby was in it with you."

"In what?" Jack asked. What are you talking about?"

"Stabbing Rachel and murdering my girlfriend, the only girl in Pyrite that ever gave me the time of day. I don't know why Sylvia liked me Jack, but she did, and you ended that. You know that knife's going to convict you, that's why you came for it. Sad thing is Jack, you never had to stab Rachel to have your way with her. She liked you a lot and never understood why you didn't ask her out on a real date. You hanging around with the three of us confused us all. What was your game?"

"No game Paul. I liked all of you and had fun whenever we went driving and drinking. I'll be honest with you, I didn't want anyone to know that we were friends, everyone thought that they were better than you and I wasn't man enough to handle the ribbing, I was stupid. I'm sorry Paul. As for Rachel, I couldn't date her because I was dating Shelby and that's all I ever wanted. I liked Rachel, I liked being with her. We talked serious stuff, we laughed at silly stuff. She was my friend and when I've looked back over the years, I've realized she was my best friend. I hid her too. Maybe peer pressure, maybe I just believed that Shelby wouldn't understand. It drove me crazy and I couldn't wait to get out of Pyrite after graduation. I felt responsible when I thought you killed Rachel. I thought that by me keeping my relationship with the two of you secret, I kept you guys on the bottom of the ladder. I was a crappy friend to everyone, I know that now, and I'm truly sorry. I'm sorry to you too Shel, I'm sorry I never told you I loved you and I never treated you well enough that you could feel it. When I left here I knew you could do so much better than me and that's what I wanted for you. I made the decision to stay out of your life forever and I've regretted that decision every day of my life ever since. I'm sorry Shel."

Jack sat on the mattress next to Shelby. He was a broken man and had only one question for Paul. "You going to kill us Paul?"

"If I was certain you killed Sylvia you'd probably be dead already. Are you claiming you're innocent Jack?"

"Of course I'm innocent, I just told you Rachel was my friend, my best friend. I would never ever have hurt her or Sylvia. Go ask Rachel how close we were."

"Why'd you want the knife so bad?"

"Shelby and I talked about that, we decided that we were going to give it to the cop investigating Lynn's and Steve's murder. If that's the knife from Sylvia's murder there could be more DNA or blood on it than they could get 25 years ago. We thought that there might be some holes in their case against you. We all had secrets from back then and it was time to open up. Even though we believed that you were dead, we were doing it for you too. For you, for Rachel, for ourselves. It's been 25 years of hell, enough already. If you kill me Paul, please don't hurt Shelby, let her go home, she won't say a word, will you Shel?"

"I'm not going home and I have no idea what I'll do. I won't lie for my life Paul."

"You two need to get your story together and confess your crimes to me, then we'll talk about who's going home. Rachel wants to hear it from you too, but I won't put her through anything until I know that you're finally going to be truthful. I'll be back in a couple hours, I expect to hear something worth hearing when I get back."

Paul drove his 4x4 down the mountain side and had a talk with Rachel. He told her that there was a good possibility that Jack and Shelby were innocent in everything from the past and present. He went to check out Jack's car for any evidence of what these two might have planned. He came back in the cabin carrying a loaded .22 caliber handgun. "You don't have to believe in Jack Spencer very long before your hopes get shattered."

CHAPTER 29

Looking for a Needle in a Haystack

Mazer arrived in Greenleaf along with his young aide, William Denton. He explained his next step to Tidrow that Denton was going to search the entire town for Rachel Morgan. He was going to start at the hotel, going through the registration log and call on the rental agencies, trailer parks, campgrounds, any place where an out of towner could stay. Denton also had a picture of Jack and Shelby, so he could include them in his search. He wanted Tidrow to wait at the Greenleaf station to do whatever follow ups and leads Denton phones in. He wasn't overly confident of results, but he was confident that this was the best course of action. While Denton headed to the Peaks to start his search, Mazer headed to Artie's Place in hopes of getting some new info on Jack. There were too many loose ends right now, but Mazer felt that he was holding the end of each string. Tying them all together was the task at hand. He walked right in to Artie's through the main door. Artie sat at his bar in front of a cold cup of coffee. Mazer wasted no time and while he was adjusting himself into the seat next to Artie he fired away, "Any word yet from Jack?"

"Something always seems to be going on with him Bob. I don't have any idea where he is. I could try calling him if you like. You know when this whole Pyrite school get together started I thought that it would be fun. Then Jack started working real hard to get our group back here. I began trying to remember how and why we all went separate ways and I was actually looking forward to our own reunion. Now all I can think about is getting all of these people out of Rita's and my life once and for all. It's like Sylvia and Rachel were murdered yesterday, it's like Nancy's family was killed yesterday. You know the old saying Bob, you can't go home again? Well who the hell would want to? I'll call Jack."

"Going right to message. Sorry. He's probably out for a drive with Shelby. If you wait for them at the hotel I'm sure they'll be back soon. I was just going to pour some cheap whiskey into my cup to improve my coffee. Any reason I need a clear head this morning Bob?"

"No one goes out for a two day drive Artie. He should be easy enough to locate if I send out an emergency bulletin, but if I want him back here I'll have to swear out a warrant. I can do that, but it's best for him to just get back here so I can talk to him. Keep trying to reach him. And drunk or sober is up to you. You haven't helped me in whatever shape you've been in. Find him Artie. If I have to get a warrant, they'll be one for you too."

Mazer went back to the station to wait with Tidrow. He expected word soon from Denton on possible locations to check. Sitting across from their crime scene board they went over things again and again. He tapped his pencil on the desk, paced the room, cursed under his breath. He poured himself a cup of coffee and knew why Artie wanted to add whiskey to his. The station phone finally rang.

Tidrow picked up and handed the phone to Mazer, "it's Denton."

"What do you have kid?"

"There's over 80 rooms in the Peaks and only two single woman were checked in this past week, and one of those is not really single."

"I don't have time for games Denton, what do you mean."

"Sorry boss, I was trying to be positive. One single was Lynn Mitchell but she checked in with Steve Connor, so not really a single."

"And dead Denton. What about the other one?"

"That was Shelby, but she checked out Sunday."

"And we know her and she's gone missing. You're done at the hotel for now. Too many couples to question. What's next?"

"Vacation rental place next to the super market, we've got a ton of rental properties in Greenleaf that they handle. Maybe won't be as many couples, I'm not expecting any single women though. I'll be in touch."

CHAPTER 30

Last Chances, We Don't All Get One

Paul and Rachel knew the clock was ticking; they had to continue to push. Jack was a growing aggravation to Paul and he worried about keeping cool enough to not explode at his prisoner.

They decided to lean on Bill Addison and Artie Paychek a little more, they hoped they were getting through, causing a bit of panic. Rachel called Bill first and watered the seed she planted yesterday.

He picked up on the first ring and Rachel was ready. "I shouldn't have run when you tried to kill me, I should have come right back from that hole you put me in and got even. I didn't, but I warned you, it's time to pay now."

Rachel's message to Artie had to be different in case he talked to Bill but it had to light a fuse. She dialed him up. A tipsy Artie eventually answered. Rachel's words went a long way towards sobering him up. "Everyone's going to see your evil side now. I already got Jack and Shelby and they both said that you attacked me alone. You screwed that up and I'm done hiding."

Rachel never gave either of them a chance to say a word. She and Paul figured that they were pacing, scared, trying to figure out what to do. The fuse was indeed lit; they hoped the next call would cause the explosion they've dreamed of. Paul got back on his 4x4 near noon and went to give Jack one last chance to confess; it seemed last rites were more likely.

Paul entered the shack carrying his shotgun and cocked it. The very sound of it instilled fear. He checked the chains and handcuffs on Jack and Shelby and was satisfied that nothing had been pried loose. He pulled a folding chair closer to the couple and tried once more to get his answers. It felt like the last hand he could play with Jack and he told him just that. Paul was ready to push in all of his chips.

"You two ready to talk about class night 1993? I know you didn't go home together because you called me that night Jack." Paul got up and walked over to the far wall. He hung the shotgun in the gun rack and walked back to his chair. "I don't want to lose my temper and blow both of your brains out. I'm close to doing just that so the gun's better out of my hands for now. But you can see how close it is. Don't make me want it." It remained quiet for a while and then Paul spoke again. "Either of you feel free to talk, but one of you better start talking soon." Silence followed again, Paul exhaled and got out of chair, knocking it completely to the ground with a startling noise. He moved for his gun. His steps loosened Jack's tongue.

"I took Shelby to the café and left her there. We argued about something stupid so I took off. If I remember correctly I drove around for a real short time and went home. I never called you. I swear, I went home."

"He's telling the truth Paul, he left me there with a coke that I didn't have money for and the owner of the café drove me home."

"You pretended I was your friend Jack, but when you were with your idiot friends you treated me like a dog. Why didn't you tell the police that you bastards locked me in that closet. It was pitch black in there and I thought I was gonna die. I broke the door down, got kicked out of school, and labeled a crazy maniac that goes around kicking in doors. Everyone loved that story ... the judge, the jury, the prosecutor. Everyone but me, old friend. And you didn't say one word, and my county provided lawyer never brought it up. Why the quiet treatment? You framed me Jack."

Paul went over to a rusted cabinet standing in the corner. He took out a rope with a noose tied to the end of it and pulled it over

Shelby's head followed by the cloth bag. Shelby lost her last few ounces of bravery and started crying uncontrollably. She cried the words, *'I didn't do anything, I didn't do anything'*, again and again. Jack pulled as hard as he could on his chains to no avail. He was near tears himself and begged Paul to stop the madness, finally asking one more time, "what do you want from me?"

"I want to know why you killed Sylvia and framed me for it."

"I didn't kill anyone, I didn't go to Sylvia's and Rachel's home that night. I didn't even know Rachel was moving in with Sylvia, I thought you were going to live there. Go ask Rachel, I wasn't ever there. Bring her here, she'll tell you. Why hasn't she told you it wasn't me?"

"She never saw her attacker, she can't say anything for sure and that's why she's been in hiding for all these years, waiting in fear for a murderer to return. Waiting for you Jack, your game is over, your time is up. Last chance before I leave here with Shelby."

As Jack screamed his innocence, Paul led Shelby out of the shack by the rope. All they could hear before Paul started up the 4x4 was Jack's threat to kill Paul. Paul drove down the mountain and parked behind the cabin. He helped Shelby out and removed the head cover and rope, offering her an apology for having submitted her to such an ordeal. Shelby felt sick, all cried out and angry with the world. She wanted to know what was going on. Paul said that they needed to go inside and talk with Rachel.

CHAPTER 31

A Town Full of Strangers, Some Too Strange

It was afternoon when Bill finally felt strong enough to leave his room. He thought it was time to renew his demands for money from Jack and Artie so he could get the hell out of not only Greenleaf and Pyrite, but Colorado altogether. He was no more than one step out his door when his face was met by a powerful fist knocking him back inside and down on the floor. The intruder stepped inside and closed the door behind him. Bill knew this visit was due and his voice contained no sound of surprise.

"Where's the other two henchman? Am I too boring for them?"

"I'm the night shift, I handle last call. You owe my boss 22 thousand and I need something today."

"Well you're in luck, as I told the other two when they made their house calls, my old friends were more than happy to pay me off and get me out of town. Your guys were far too impatient, but the money's here now in my new truck. The cops have been watching me, there's probably a cop in the lobby right now, so I had to leave the money bag in the truck and the keys by the gas cap. There's 25 grand in there, it's safer if you get it for me. Bring me back my keys and my 3 grand and we're done with each other. I can't hardly walk, so I'll wait here, but I'm disappearing two seconds after you're done with me."

"I'll tell you when you're disappearing. Where's the truck?"

"Hotel parking lot. You can see it from the window. Black Silverado."

The gunman walked over to the window and took a look, a smile came across his face. "Big day for you Bill, if the money's there this is the best day of the rest of your life, if it isn't, then just the opposite."

"First day," Bill corrected him, "first day of the rest of my life. The money's there, I'll wait."

The gunman left Bill's room and Bill uttered, "stupid ass," as he walked to the Silverado. He kept looking all around and behind himself as he neared the vehicle. Bill had his bag packed and was ready to hit the road. He watched from his hotel window as his assailant reached the truck. "Open it up dummy," Bill said out loud. The gunman looked in the driver side window and under the car and stepped back. He scanned the streets and walked around the parking lot then returned to the Silverado and looked in the passenger side window. He couldn't see anything of value from his vantage point and walked around the truck again to see where the gas tank was located. He stood at the back of the truck and was about to call his boss when the police pulled up in a hurry and slammed on the brakes of the squad car. Mitch, who had been watching the truck for 2 days on orders from Mazer, knew he had his man.

"Hands up," Mitch ordered. His orders followed Mitch then patted the stranger down and removed a 357 handgun from the man's holster. "Guess we got you now, we knew you'd show up." Mitch phoned the arrest in on the police radio and took the man to the Greenleaf station. A couple Greenleaf reporters beat Mitch to the station and were in front of the building blurting out questions to Mitch as he pushed the man inside. All Mitch offered the reporters was one comment, "this is him guys."

Mitch took the gunman downstairs to the investigation room dedicated to the recent murders and turned him over to Mazer and Tidrow. He handed the 357 to Mazer who refused to touch it, so he put it down on the table and had his prisoner take a seat. "He was all over the Silverado, Bob; I watched everything."

Mazer turned to the perp, "that truck interest you?"

"Yes, very much," the gunman replied. "I'm thinking of buying one and I wanted to see what the interior layout looked like. I don't know what your problem is with people looking in car windows around here, but I never so much as put a finger on it, I'm very respectful of other people's property. Now if you could call my lawyer, here's his card, and here's my gun permit, I am done talking."

Mitch got irate and the young officer laid into his prisoner. "The reporters are running to the press room right now, your story will be plastered in every paper within a thousand miles of here in a few hours, you need a better story."

"You didn't call the press did you?" Mazer asked. "How dumb can you be?"

"Of course not Bob, they picked it up on the scanner from my radio."

"Damn you Mitch," Tidrow added, "go up and wait in my office, I'll call you if I need you. And don't talk to anybody."

Mazer picked up the cards that the stranger tossed at him, and talked to the man by the name on the gun permit, Hunter Tracy. "Well Mr. Tracy, I don't know what the rookie said to you, but we haven't placed you under arrest, not yet anyhow, we just need an answer or two to a couple questions and you can leave. Or you can play your lawyer game and we could be here forever. So let's get this wrapped up. What are you doing in town Mr. Tracy?"

"I like you officer, so I'm going to be a nice guy and really help you out. I don't know how much of the law you know but just for your information you are breaking it in a real bad way right now and it could cost you more than just your job. You see once I say, or anyone else for that matter, that I want my lawyer, you are not allowed to even ask me what day of the week it is. But you have ignored my request and have kept grilling me unmercifully. This will sadly be very bad for you. Now please go call my lawyer, arrest me, or let me leave."

Tidrow and Mazer looked at one another and told Tracy to sit tight. They went upstairs to check this guy out and talk to Mitch. He may have just bungled a case that was in the crapper already. They gave the lawyer's card to Tidrow's assistant and asked her to check on this law firm with her Denver contacts. They then went in to talk to Mitch.

Mitch confirmed Tracy's story, he never touched the car, never opened a door, never went inside. He looked at the interior through the windows. Mazer sat down, momentarily a beaten man, they waited for the background check on Tracy and the law firm.

Tidrow's assistant reached her contacts in Denver Crime and they knew of the law firm, they only represented one company, a big casino holder in the Denver area as well as Vegas, Reno, and online. She said that the people working in this company also do loans and work with broken bones, and not a doctor or banker among them.

"Hunter Tracy's connected?" Mazer asked, using his complete dictionary of mob speak.

"Very much so if this is his lawyer."

Mazer told Tidrow to go straighten out his understudy about how and when they can arrest people and when not to use a police open channel radio. He told Tidrow to call his people at the press and get their story stopped. He was going downstairs to make peace with Tracy. He held out hope for a lead. He brought a couple cans of Coke in the room and offered one to Tracy. His apologies on behalf of the department and Mitch were given. He said that Tracy was free to go, there were no charges and there wouldn't be any. He told Tracy he had two murders on his hands, a shooting victim, and two missing people. Any help would be appreciated.

Hunter was generous. "I'll give you two things. The guy who sent me to that truck set me up, so he must have known you were watching it, you must know who that is."

"And the second tip?" Mazer asked.

"There's no way I'm touching that Coke can."

Hunter Tracy was released and walked back to the Peaks Hotel, Bill Addison's Malibu was gone, Tracy knew he was in the wind. While Tracy was phoning it in to his boss, Mazer pulled up to the hotel. He knew instantly that Bill Addison was Mazer's target also. Hunter Tracy's boss believed he had a kind of immunity now and the police would leave him alone so Tracy got new orders, Bill Addison was a problem he couldn't afford anymore. Bill crossed the line and was now worth more dead than alive. As soon as Hunter Tracy had the shot, he was to take it. '*Make it ugly*,' was the final order.

Across the road, at the hotel, Mazer went to Bill's room but no one answered the door. He tried Jack's room but again got no answer. He phoned Denton to get an update on the house to house search for a single woman or any type of out of place couple. Denton told him that he was getting nowhere on the single woman and talked to quite a few couples. Nothing seemed out of place. He had a few house rentals to try, a couple trailer parks, and he thought he would cruise through the campgrounds. Mazer thought about stopping at Artie's Place again, if only to see someone's face that's mixed up with this, but he had no new questions or any excuse to be there. He went back to the Greenleaf station to make new plans with Tidrow.

Mazer reiterated that they had three lead suspects now to the murders - Rachel held the key to Sylvia's murder in '93 and Bill Addison and Jack Spencer held the key to last week's murders. He also felt that Artie should be thrown into the mix but he didn't know which murder he was more likely to be linked to. With nothing existing about Rachel, he would keep Denton on the door to door, the other two, Jack and Bill, he believed would be easy to find. He had Tidrow put out an APB on the two including everything he had in his notes. Now knowing that Bill was wanted by the mob, Jack became Mazer's number one suspect. Bill could just be in the wrong place when his life started to catch up with him. Mazer may have been moving Bill down his list, but there was no way he was taking Bill off. With a few hours of daylight left, he still hoped Denton would find something.

CHAPTER 32

Trading Trust for Truth

Deep into the woods beyond Pyrite, Paul led Shelby into the cabin. He explained that he would have to leave her handcuffed until she heard the truth and trusted him. He reintroduced Shelby to Rachel Morgan with an introduction of, 'here's someone that you thought you'd never see again.' Shelby stared at Rachel, trying to recall her face in high school. Her mind was more focused on her own life then and she was only able to say how happy she was that Rachel was alive. Nothing made any sense to Shelby now and Paul had her sit down to hear his story.

Paul told Shelby that one of three people killed Sylvia, tried to kill Rachel, and killed Lynn and Steve. The killer could be one person, two, or even all three of them. He explained that he and Rachel have been setting this up for years and now feel that they're getting close, but still have no solid idea or facts. Paul believed that the whole case was going to bust wide open all of a sudden and he didn't want to be on the receiving end when it does. Paul had one undying belief, either Jack, Bill, or Artie is a cold blooded murderer.

Paul trusted Shelby just enough to tell her the part of his plan he needed her for. Paul knew he could only catch Sylvia's and

Rachel's attacker by getting him to go to Rachel's grave, he would be the only one on the planet that knows where that is. He had Shelby read a message to a phone number that he dialed from his phone. Shelby did as instructed and Paul went back to the shack to bring Jack down. Paul told Jack that he was going to get one chance to save Shelby, he had better sit still on the ride down and be ready to move like hell once he gets his instructions. Paul pulled up in front of the cabin and ordered Jack out of the 4x4 and onto his knees next to his Cadillac. Paul took out another phone and gave Jack his instructions.

"I'm going to give you and Shelby a chance that you never gave to me and Sylvia," Paul said to Jack. He then looked at his watch and continued. "The clock's ticking now and you may have enough time to save Shelby once I unchain you. She's buried right where you buried Rachel with about one hour's worth of oxygen, except those tanks are a little unpredictable. I'm out of here the second you leave, I have others to get even with, but you won't see me again. If you save Shelby, maybe you can each enjoy what's left of your life, if not, then you'll know what I've been living with for 25 years now. Stay right where you are, I'll get the guys to release you and the keys to your car. Listen to this message in case you think I'm kidding." Paul went into the messages on the phone and hit play before putting the phone down next to Jack, he went inside the cabin as Jack listened to Shelby's stammering voice.

"Jack they tell me that you're my only chance. Paul's driven me up a mountain somewhere, I couldn't see where and he's got a coffin half buried. He said he's going to put me in and bury me alive Jack. Please, please help me. I don't want to die in there. He says you have an hour. Please hurry Jack, if you care at all, please hurry." The call ended right there.

Paul returned with gun in hand and the keys for the chains, cuffs, and car. He undid the handcuffs and threw the rest of the keys on the ground. He stepped back, training the gun on Jack's head. "You better hurry boy, you're well under your hour now."

"Hurry to where," a shaking Jack asked. "Tell me where Shelby's buried."

"Right where you buried Rachel, same hole."

"I told you I didn't try to kill Rachel. You're crazy Paul. Take me there before you go up for murder again. I've got over a million dollars in the bank, it's all yours if we save Shelby. Get in the back seat," Jack said as he climbed behind the wheel, "keep your gun on me and tell me where to go." Paul stared at Jack and didn't say a word. Jack began banging on the dashboard with both hands and screaming hysterically at Paul. "Tell me where she is, don't let her die." Jack finally leaped out of the car and grabbed Paul by the throat, he was choking him to death and screaming, "tell me, tell me, tell me." Paul had his hand gun against Jack's stomach. A gun blast split the air and the fight stopped instantly. Another gun blast fired and Rachel spoke up, "get off of him Jack or the next shot's for you."

"He's killing my friend, don't let him do this." Jack said as he struggled to stand up. Before he could get up he fell again and rolled up into a ball crying into the dirt. "I'm sorry Shel, I'm sorry."

Paul put the handcuffs back on Jack and pulled him up, he pushed him into the cabin where his eyes instantly saw Shelby, handcuffed to a chair. He stopped his sobbing and looked at Paul and the lady with the rifle. "What the hell game you playing on us Paul, and who's your partner?"

Jack listened intently as Paul poured out his story. The twenty-five year old story of death and murder was coming back to life.

"I was home the evening of class night because of you guys. It was shortly after the day that you guys locked me in that dark closet. I panicked and felt around for something anything to bust out of there. When I did the school admin heard the commotion and I ended up getting tossed out of school, for nothing once again. I wasn't allowed at class night and late that night I got a call, it was from one of you guys, I always thought you Jack, but in all honesty I didn't know who called. All the voice said was that Sylvia's in trouble at her new house and needs you right away. I flew over there and the house was dark. I walked around the house and saw that the back door was opened. I walked as quickly and as quietly as I could. When I went in the back door I kicked something that was on the ground, I felt around and picked up the knife that was lying there. I came to a closed door and turned the knob slowly, the door was locked. I took a deep breath, held it in, and smashed through the door. I landed on the knife I was holding and I think I passed out for a while. I was bleeding pretty much when I came to and I still couldn't see anything. I felt around for the light switch and when I turned on the lights I saw Sylvia lying on the floor. I lifted her head up and tried to revive her but she wasn't moving. I lifted her up, I was going to take her to my car right out front and drive her to the hospital. As soon as I walked out the front door with Sylvia's lifeless body in my arms, I saw the police. They started yelling at me, the words never registered only the noise, they shined lights in my eyes, their guns were drawn, and they took Sylvia from me. They took her to hospital, knocked me down, beat the living hell out of me, and eventually arrested me for murder. A few days later they added Rachel Morgan's murder to my charges. Sometime during my trial, they dropped those charges but kept threatening me with refiling them. The inspector never questioned me. I was his patsy and that's all he wanted. I was found guilty and sentenced to 25 to life. My lawyer, some law school grad doing pro bono, told me that it may have just as well been life because they would never let me out of prison unless I told where Rachel's body was. I've had over 25 years to think about those murders and I'm not resting until I get the murdering bastard or bastards who did it. I know it was your little clique that was responsible. Now that Steve's dead, and if I believe your meltdown was real, I'm left with Bill and Artie. I have to follow them to Rachel's grave, that's the only way. The murderer's the only person, or people who know where Rachel's remains are."

Shelby was starting to understand things, at least a little, and added some thoughts. "That's why you don't look at all like Rachel, she really was murdered 25 years ago. Have you been pretending to be her?"

"Yes she has," Paul told Shelby. "She's agreed to help me with my search."

"That Pyrite cop, Bob Mazer, told us that you were dead." Jack said.

"I was, or should I say I am. Rachel's husband, I guess we should drop the Rachel now, this wonderful lady is Donna Spraynor. Donna's husband, Sam Spraynor, was my cell mate in the Pen. He was framed for bank fraud and robbery in Oklahoma, crooked bankers did him in, but that payday is down the road. He got sentenced to 7 years, but he confided in me that he had cancer and wouldn't make three. We switched identities in prison. We looked enough alike, and the guards didn't care all that much anyhow. I started wearing large dark rimmed glasses, shaved my head, wore a hat, switched uniforms, Sam worked in admin and was able to switch our dental records, and as many things as we could think of. When Sam started feeling sick and knew his cancer was taking over, we switched everything. He wore the glasses, shaved his head, I let my hair grow, he became me. Donna was in on it and just wants to get even with the guy that framed her husband. When Sam died, they thought he was me, and when they checked the dental records they knew that Paul Winston was dead. The will left his body and personal belongings to Donna, she got to bury her husband without any fanfare in Oklahoma and came back for me. I got paroled as Sam after 5 years of his sentence and Donna and I have been waiting for our opportunity to catch you guys. The reunion was a perfect opportunity, I figured you bastards would return. I planted the knife with Artie to push you guys. Donna made some calls as Rachel to get you to the grave. When I followed you into the woods Jack, I thought sure you were going to check for Rachel's bones. When you only wanted that stupid knife my plan backfired. I'm winging it now."

"It's not a stupid knife Paul," Jack told him. "They can lift a lot more DNA and fingerprints today than they could in 1993. You need to turn the knife in, like I was going to do. Mazer is your best bet right now."

"I planted that knife Jack because I bought it in a hardware store. I bought it about 2 months ago. It's useless. If I turn over a knife they'll only arrest me again and send me back to the pen. I can't do it until I have a better case, the whole case."

"You can't turn in a fake murder weapon anyhow."

"We don't have to do that, we have the actual knife." Paul walked over to the fireplace and took a package off of the mantle. "When Donna got my personal belongings they gave her this box. Read the address label."

Jack read aloud, "Paul Winston's Package, Pyrite Court House, Pyrite, Colorado."

"After the FBI ran their tests they sent the knife back to the courthouse for the trial. Whoever got it thought it was my package and filed it away. When Donna picked up my body, they gave her this, said it was all of my personal belongings. I knew I didn't have anything of value at all in prison so we didn't even look in the box for months. When we did, it pushed us. We thought we may have some evidence and we started working on our plan. It's not going well however. I guess I just don't have a criminal mind"

Paul walked over to Jack and Shelby and removed their handcuffs. "I suppose you'll have to turn us in now. Can you give us a couple hours? We have a plan to get out, but could use the time. We'll figure out what to do about Artie and Bill down the road."

"We have nothing to turn you in for. Paul Winston's dead and Sam Spraynor did his time. We want to catch anyone involved in Sylvia's and Rachel's murder too. I never dated Rachel because I was with Shelby, I loved you Shel, always have, and I realized this week I always will. But Rachel was my friend, I owe it to her. I'll help you Paul. Shel, do you want to get out of here?"

"Almost as much as anything, but more than leaving I want to start living my life, and I have nowhere to go right now. I can't start life over until I come to grips we these murders. I owe the girls that much, I didn't treat them well, I resented Rachel for seeing you and didn't know until today that you were only friends. If I would have trusted both of you, maybe we'd all be here today. One of our so called friends ruined all of our lives. If we solve this now, we salvage whatever time we have left. I'll help however I can. We owe it to Lynn and Steve too, why were they shot, what did they know that we didn't?"

"I saw that in the paper that they were shot, I guess I somehow caused that with my crazy plan. I figured Nancy was in danger then too and that's why I kidnapped her, it was the only way to save her. I took her home, to that damn assisted living place, at least she's safe now. That's more than I can say for us. We don't know who we're chasing, but he knows us. You need to take over Jack, I messed up everything."

Jack sat frozen, his head spinning. He looked at the three people staring at him and oddly felt alone. He lightly nodded his head yes, without the vaguest idea what to do next. He looked deep into Shelby's eyes, he knew he would do something.

CHAPTER 33

Rounding Up the Lost Causes

Mazer was about to call it a day in Greenleaf when Tidrow answered a call for him, "it's Denton."

"No single woman, boss, but I just saw a single man pull into the Mountain View Trailer Rentals that you may be interested in. Bill Addison drove in here with that beat up Malibu. He backed in and parked as out of sight as he could. He's hiding from somebody. I just got lucky, I was leaving the place when he drove right by me. If your theory is that he's one of the most unlucky guys in world, I guess he just confirmed that. What should I do, boss?"

"Keep an eye on him and stay out of sight. I'll be there in 15 minutes. And quit calling me boss."

This was Mazer's best lead, he needed to get something. He almost ran out of the station and took his personal car so as not to be identified. He parked near the entrance and walked until he found Denton and got into the squad car. They made small talk for a good 20 minutes then Mazer's impatience got the best of him. He walked over to the unit that Bill was apparently renting and pounded on the door. A surprised Bill Addison let him in. "What you gonna blame me for this time, Bob? You told me to stay in

Greenleaf, I'm staying in Greenleaf. I can't afford another day at the Peaks."

"Who you hiding from Bill? Your good high-school friends?"

"I'm not hiding, I'm surviving. My good friends either abandoned me in the hospital or put me there, and you don't seem to be able to help me. You ever catch a criminal Bob? I bet you're curious how that must feel."

"I'm probably going for a warrant today to arrest you, make it all real official, we'll have that "captured criminal" feeling to share then. For now, I just want to know where Jack and Shelby are. Tell me that and buy yourself some time."

"If they're not at the hotel then I have no idea. I left there in a hurry when the Greenleaf police were arresting some poor slob in the parking lot. In my haste I didn't think to look around for Jack's car for you, I guess I thought you were the cop. I'm going to lay down Bob, let yourself out when you're done here, and don't tell my friends you saw me. I'm planning on leaving here as soon as you give me the okay. Probably leaving in a day or two without it. And as far as I can tell Bob, you don't have a damn thing to hold me on." Bill went into the tiny trailer bedroom and stared at the ceiling, when he heard the door close he looked out the window and saw Mazer get in the cop car with Denton. He turned on his cell phone and punched in Jack Spencer's number.

No answer. The message he left was brief. "I need my money. I'm leaving. Mazer's all over me, he thinks I have what he wants. I left the Peaks. Without money, I tell all. Call me now."

He searched his phone for Artie's number and punched that in. Artie picked up on the first ring and Bill hurried through his message. "Mazer's close to arresting all of us. Jack and Shelby must be in hiding. I want out, I have to have my money or I'm talking to someone. You try to find Jack. Call me when you do. And before you blow me off again, remember, I saw your truck where it shouldn't have been, more than once."

Artie tried to reach Jack, but Jack's phone was still off. He left a message saying it was time to pay off Bill. He said that Bill saw his truck outside of the Peaks the night that Lynn and Steve got murdered. He said that he was there to talk to Jack and saw Bill walking towards his truck but he turned and went back to the hotel. He said that if Bill mentioned this to Mazer along with the missing knife, there would for sure be trouble. His last words to Jack were to call him. Trouble was brewing.

Mazer went back to the Greenleaf station to talk with Tidrow. He called Mitch and Denton back with him and the four sat downstairs as the sun went down in Greenleaf. Mazer said they had nothing for an arrest and Tidrow said that there was no way they could bring in any of these guys again without some new evidence. Mazer said that they should at least be happy to have just three or four suspects and not the whole damn town. Mazer wanted Denton to conduct a house to house check in Pyrite tomorrow morning to see if anybody has seen anyone new in town; someone must have seen someone. Mazer and Denton headed home to Pyrite, disappointed in their blank slate in Greenleaf, but hopeful in their plan for Pyrite. A few minutes out of Greenleaf, shots hit the Pyrite squad car and the sound of gunfire filled the air. One, two, three shots. Two hits to the front of the car and a third in the front tire. The squad car swerved, but Denton held it on the road and brought it to a stop facing the wrong direction. They both drew their gun and crouched behind the car. They couldn't see anyone moving around and figured whoever shot at them knows the area a lot better than they do and was long gone. They changed the tire and continued on their way home.

"One things for certain now Denton," Mazer told his officer, "were getting close, we may not know to what, but were getting close. This was just a warning."

CHAPTER 34

A Good Day for Bad Ideas

Everyone was up early in the cabin and Paul made as good a breakfast for them as he could. They sat around the small table drinking coffee and hoping Jack, or anyone else for that matter, had some sort of plan. Jack turned on his phone and saw that he had a slew of messages. Maybe the plan would find them instead of the other way around. As far as ideas went, this was as bad as any that Paul had laid out. Paul had one more odd idea up his sleeve. He offered to get Bill and Artie at gun point and kill whoever doesn't speak up. He was outnumbered, three to one. Jack played his messages. Mazer, Bill, Artie, had all called. Mazer wanted info, Bill wanted money, Artie wanted the knife and to get Bill out of town. Jack had an idea for a starting point.

"Forget Mazer for now, let him keep chasing his tail, I don't think he has a clue. I think Bill's our key, he's wanted out of here from the minute he got here, he only came for money and he's been using the girls' murders to scare us. He knew that Artie and I had the most to lose by things coming out. And I'm sorry again Paul, I should have stayed in town for you and the girls. But Bill used that. If we dangle money and the knife in front of Bill, I'm sure he'll bite. If not, we come back for Artie and Rita. They aren't going anywhere. One of us has to call Bill, either me or you Donna. Are you up for being Rachel one more time?"

Jack dialed up Bill and whispered into the phone. "Bill, can you hear me? Just listen, they got me chained up in some shack, I have no idea where I am. They killed Shelby right in front of me. They blamed me for killing Sylvia. It's all Rachel's doing and she's got some mean partner. I finally got my phone out, they didn't know I had it, they only frisked me for a gun. Rachel found your money and the knife that I had in the Cadillac. I was going to help you get away from here and then give the knife to Mazer. Rachel told me I was next, right after she buried the money and knife in the ditch that I tried to bury her in 25 years ago. I heard her talking to her partner. She said Artie and Rita were going to be killed and then she'd call the police and lay it all on you. She must hate you. I think I'm a goner Bill, but get her for me and Shelby. The 20 grand is there; get her and you get it. Oh shit, I hear her car. I can't hide my phone. Do something right for once."

Bill could hear Rachel open and slam a door shut. He heard her yell at Jack, "why you laying like that, sick I hope. The money and that knife are buried now, real easy to find, about as deep as you buried me 25 years ago, and this time your friend, not mine, will take the fall. I guess I don't need you anymore Jack, say hello to Shelby for us." A loud gun blast echoed in the cabin from Paul's shot, the sound from Bill's phone was deafening. He heard Rachel's voice again, "this bastard had a phone back here. It's connected to someone." Bill's phone then lost the connection and he hurried outside and got his gun from his Malibu. He checked the bullets to make sure he was fully loaded. He had to get to Pyrite now and keep Mazer busy in Greenleaf. His head was spinning as he tried to come up with a plan.

Bill decided to call Artie first. He told him that he heard from Jack who just got away from Rachel and some maniac guy she's working with. He's hiding in the woods beyond Pyrite and he's scared out of his mind and needs help. Bill tried a moment of honesty and told Artie that Rachel has his 20 grand and that's all he's really interested in, a matter of life and death for himself. He also mentioned the knife as an added bonus if they could get that back. Artie agreed to go with Bill to Pyrite. He went to his gun locker hidden in the back of his closet and grabbed his rifle and .22

caliber handgun. His nervousness turned to anxiety as he practiced balancing and aiming his handgun. For good measure he aimed his rifle and looked through the rifle's sight picturing Rachel on the other end. The church bells rang nine as he walked outside to wait for Bill. Artie thought it was the wrong time from the wrong church in a messed up town. He didn't know what was real any more.

Bill was ready now to go to Artie's Place but he first needed to tie up Mazer. He called the Pyrite police station and got hold of him immediately.

"Bob, it's Bill Addison," he told the officer, "you'll never guess who's staking me out, our mutual friend Jack Spencer. I saw him creep by my place a few minutes ago and then took off for his car. He thinks he's well hidden by the homes behind me, but I can see enough of his pretentious Cadillac sticking out like a sore thumb. If you hurry you'll get him."

"I'm in Pyrite on official business, I'd never make it in time. Call me when he leaves. I'll call Greenleaf police and send them out, they got enough to hold him on."

He's up to something Bob, he's watching me for some reason. I don't want to be one of his victims. If you head here now you'll see him on the highway if he heads to Pyrite. I dumped him in your lap, it's all on you now."

"All right, all right. I'll get there as soon as I can. You stay put."

"Of course", were the last words Bill uttered as he left the trailer and headed into town. He parked in the grocery store lot and walked over to Artie's. He told Artie that they couldn't use his Malibu because Mazer was looking for it. Artie put his rifle in the bed of his pick-up and got behind the wheel. Bill jumped in the backseat of the cab and told Artie he could hide back there if they passed a police car. Artie pulled out onto Main Street and sped off towards Pyrite. He asked Bill what the plan was and where exactly he should head. Bill gave it to him as cold as possible.

With his .357 resting against Artie's head, the barrel touching his skull right behind his ear, he gave Artie the news. "Jack and Shelby are dead, I'm guessing Nancy too. Rachel is tightening the noose and I'm getting my money and running like hell. You're free to do whatever you want, or can, after I'm gone. I don't want to hear one peep out of you."

Bill cocked the hammer of his gun and pushed it harder against Artie's head. "Probably not a good idea to hit any big potholes, this gun could go off at any moment and most of you will be on the windshield. Rachel buried my money and the knife where she was buried before she escaped that ditch and made her way out of town. We're heading there. And I know you don't mind me frisking you." Bill patted Artie down and found the .22. "Nice pea shooter, this may come in handy. If I blow your brains out with this it won't be quite as messy. Hope that's a comfort to you." Bill shoved the gun under his belt. Artie continued his drive to Pyrite, palms sweating, throat dry, tears of fear behind his eyes.

CHAPTER 35

Follow the Leader

Bob Mazer was about to head to Greenleaf when he got a call from Denton who was out doing his door to door in Pyrite. Denton planned on starting his morning with the old homes of his suspects. He got no answer at Shelby's place and headed to Jack's. He heard enough in 30 seconds to call Mazer. Mazer heard enough to change his plans. He called and put Tidrow and his Greenleaf force on the trailer park to follow up on Bill Addison's lead and headed out to Jack's old place. Denton and the new owner were waiting for him as he parked along the fence. He asked the owner to tell everything he knew from the top, he wanted it first hand and not from Denton.

The surly rancher repeated what he told Denton. A man who said that he used to live here and raise cattle was walking around his property. He came out and asked what he wanted and the stranger said that he was just looking around. He asked if he could go into the woods and look for his old tree house. Then he asked to borrow a shovel, that one sitting against the fence, so he could dig for some old toys. The rancher explained that he went inside and watched the guy from his window. The stranger crouched down on the far side of his car and took out a small box or package and took it into the woods. He returned in 20, 30 minutes, without it and left and he hasn't seen him since. Mazer asked what day that was and the rancher told him it was last Saturday, that the guy told him he was in town for the high school get together. That was everything he had to offer and went inside. Mazer remained to talk with Denton. He told Denton that that means that Jack came up here after he was released from the police station. Mazer's head was spinning and working, trying to put together a scenario that would explain Jack's trip to his old home.

"Check this out Denton. Jack kills Lynn and Steve, gets caught where he shouldn't be, has to call the Pyrite police. Stashes the gun in his car and gives me nothing but attitude during questioning. I get called to Greenleaf on Lynn's murder and this bastard comes up here, the one place he knows inside out in Pyrite, and hides his weapon. That weapon is buried in the woods, right under our nose. We'll find it. The old timer said he was gone 30 minutes or so. He walks in 10, buries for 10, walks out in 10. Let's spread out a little, check your watch and start walking. We should see signs of fresh digging within 15 minutes. Put your gloves on and grab that shovel. We may need it and it may have Jack's fingerprints on it." The pair walked into the woods and sure enough found a fresh dig. They had one problem however, something was dug up and not buried, only a hole was left.

"This was it Denton. That branch is shoved into the ground, a marker. Jack walked to here, buried his gun, marked it with this branch and left. He came back this week to get it. Why?" Mazer was thinking out loud now, his words barely audible. "What are you up to Jack? Protection? Not another killing is it? We have to move Denton, someone else is about to be murdered. Take the shovel to the station, lock it up. I'll tell Tidrow to hurry to the trailer park and arrest Jack Spencer. I'm heading there now. If Jack gets out of Greenleaf and heads here, I'll see his car. It's the surest way to catch him. You cruise town in case he's here already, find that brown Caddie. Call the second you see anything. Don't try to take this psycho alone. I'll be in touch."

Not yet knowing that he had become prey, Jack took on a deeper role as predator. He and Paul left the women in the cabin and drove the Cadillac a few miles south of Pyrite. They parked well back of the highway but where they had a good view of all highway traffic, either coming up from Greenleaf or leaving Pyrite. Paul gave Jack his binoculars and had him watch for the Malibu. They made small talk while Jack kept his eyes on the road. It was the first normal conversation either of them had in days. For a split second, they could almost imagine that life was normal. A squad car from Pyrite heading to Greenleaf brought them back to reality. A small game changer for now, but a short time later, the game not only changed in a big way but blew them right out of the water.

"That's Artie's pick-up truck," Jack said. "What the hell is he doing here? Could he be working with Bill? In cahoots?"

"Maybe," answered Paul, "but as we called it in the pen, one of them is probably the shot caller. That's our man. Can you follow them and stay out of sight? This nightmare may be finally coming to an end."

Jack stayed well behind Artie's truck but kept him in sight. After a couple miles, Jack noticed a long black car a short distance behind him. He didn't say anything and he couldn't pull over for fear of losing Artie. They made it to Pyrite and Jack and Paul watched Artie turn down Mineral Road. The black car made the turn also and this time Jack did pull over.

"That car's been following us for a while now. Not much further to go, the road ends right up ahead." Jack got back on the road and slowly drove further along. They were right next to the house where Sylvia and Rachel were murdered. "I'm sorry we're here Paul, I guess it makes sense now. Rachel's buried somewhere in the wild after the road ends. There's a road up to that old church, we'll be able to see what Artie and Bill are up to from there. Maybe catch a glimpse of where that black car headed. I guess you know this area as well as I do." Jack turned left at a steep dirt road and put the Subaru in low.

"Not really," Paul finally answered, his gaze fixed on Sylvia's old home. I was only up here twice. First time with Sylvia, she was so excited about moving in with Rachel. We talked about us moving in together but Sylvia thought some independent time after high school would be the best thing for all of us. She wanted to make the house look pretty, so we dug up a bunch of irises from her parent's house and replanted them along the front of this place. She was going to dig up some more for under the bedroom windows. I never got to see them bloom Jack, neither did she."

"That's why she had your shovel in her car."

"Yeah, and my free lawyer never mentioned it, he said it sounded made up and would take the jury in the wrong direction. Free lawyer, I guess you only get what you pay for."

The Subaru made it to the top of the hill and Jack parked it behind the church. They walked over to the edge of the cliff and looked down through the binoculars at Artie and Bill. Bill had a handgun trained on Artie and took a shovel out of the back of the pick-up and threw it at Artie.

"Look at this Paul," Jack said as he handed the binoculars to Paul.

Artie's truck was well past the end of the road and Artie was being forced at gunpoint into the woods. Bill had a gun in each hand and walked with complete confidence.

"So it was Bill all along. I should have known Jack, and I spent all those years blaming you. We got him Sylvia", Paul said to his long gone friend, "I didn't lie to you honey, we got him." Paul collapsed on the ground crying uncontrollably. Jack tried awkwardly to pat him on the back but his efforts were useless. Paul was letting 25 years of anger, fear, hate, vengeance, and every other bad emotion he has ever had pour out of him. He eventually did his best to get it under control.

"There's no bag of money in those woods Jack, Artie may be in big trouble. We better get down there."

As if on cue, Artie stumbled out of the woods first, Bill was close behind and when he caught up to Artie he gave him a hard shove sending Artie to the ground. Bill took aim with his gun at Artie's head and it was clear from Jack's vantage point that Bill was talking.

The sound of a gunshot split the air. Jack's eyes were locked on Bill and they never wavered. He saw Bill's head literally get blown to pieces. Another shot rang out and Artie ran back into the woods for cover. Jack scanned the surrounding area and caught a glimpse of a large man standing in the tall wild grass, rifle in hand, run towards and jump into the black car and high tail it out of the area.

Jack and Paul looked at each with fear in their eyes and their minds dealing with shock. Neither could quite understand exactly what just happened or even if it was all real. Jack's mind searched its emptiness for an answer. Finding nothing concrete, he turned to

Paul.

"I guess it's over, finally over. The man who cost you most of your life just paid the price. If you know who pulled the trigger don't ever tell me. I hate how much I know already. I guess you're finally happy."

"Bill couldn't steal enough of my soul to make me happy seeing this; prison couldn't do it either, but they did steal enough to make me appreciate it. Can I live a normal life now Jack? It just doesn't seem possible."

The depression within Jack continued to grow as he explained to Paul why he would never have a normal life, his life, back again.

"You must wait here Paul, nobody knows you're alive. Hide in the church, I'll come back for you. I have to go check on Artie and call the police. If they figure out who you are, you'll be back in prison. They'll still blame you for Sylvia, and probably Rachel now, maybe even Bill. You have to hide. I'll be back as soon as I can."

"Do what you have to Jack. I can't stay here. I'm walking back to the cabin through the back country it's not much more than 4 or 5 miles. I can handle that. I'll be safe at the cabin for now. We may have just seen the last piece of our puzzle snapped into place but be careful, that maniac in the black car is playing a whole other game."

The old acquaintances were becoming renewed friends, they firmly shook hands and went in separate directions. Jack sped down the hill and to the end of Mineral Road as fast as possible. The car bounced high as Jack left the road and sped over the rough field, he pulled next to Artie's truck and jumped out of the car with the engine still running.

"Artie, he yelled, "Artie it's Jack."

Artie peeked out from behind the trees and saw Jack standing there. He walked out further, visibly shaken up. "I was afraid you were dead Jack, if you wouldn't have shot Bill, I'd be dead right now."

"No, he didn't get around to killing me yet, but I didn't shoot Bill. Some guy in a black car shot him and took off. I was up at the church watching."

"Watching. Watching what? And whose goddamn car is that?"

"New rental, no big deal. I was up at the church to watch Bill, I had no idea you'd be here. I called Bill and told him that Rachel was burying his 20 grand where she was buried 25 years ago and that she was going to call the police and turn him in. The money was his if he could get to it before Mazer. I was expecting Bill, alone, not you. What happened?"

Artie was still a bit shaken but was calming quickly while gaining an understanding of Bill's play. "Bill called me and said that you were in trouble and if we hurried we could save you. He said that Shelby was probably dead and that Rita and I were next. He blamed Rachel and some thug partner of hers. He walked over to my place and told me to drive because Mazer was on his tail. On the way to Pyrite, he told me that you and Shelby were dead and he shoved a gun in my head and made me drive up here. He took me into the woods and had me digging for that bag of money. We didn't find it and he got real mad and threatened to kill me out in the open. I was saying my prayers when the gun went off. I really thought I was dead and was waiting to fccl thc bullet, feel the pain. Nothing came. I heard another shot and then I realized the shooter was further away and not Bill. I turned and saw Bill, right where he lays now, and I ran into the woods for cover. When I saw you drive up I thought that you for sure saw Bill aiming a gun at me and took him out. I don't know what's happening anymore, I don't know what's true. Should we run again Jack?"

"Running's over Artie; it's a long story and maybe someday we'll talk about it. But it ends here. Bill's been running for 25 years and we didn't know it. I guess this is how it had to end."

"What are you talking about?" Artie, still shaken from the gunshot and the sight of Bill's ghastly head wound, couldn't settle his mind. What's Bill been running from?"

"Come on Artie, Bill killed Sylvia and Rachel and has been looking over his shoulder for 25 years."

"So Rachel is dead? Then who the hell has been calling me?"

"Not important now. Just know that it was all part of Bill's sick crimes. But you, me, Shelby, and Rita are alive and free now to live the rest of our lives. And you'll be glad to know Nancy is fine too, she's back at her home."

"What do you think his plan was?"

"Well I have to tell you this quickly cause we need to call Mazer. Best I can figure, Bill came here last weekend for money and saw that his crime was not only still open but it was gaining on him. All of us being here gave him the opportunity to shut all of us up. I'm certain that he killed Lynn and Steve, you and Rita were next, and once he had his money, Shelby and I would be killed. After that he'd be free and with more money than I bet he's had in years. No telling where he wanted to go then. Remember how many times he told us that if we paid him he would disappear to where nobody could find him? Well, he had a plan, probably a bad one, but he had a plan. We need to call Mazer. Get him and his team out here. They need to wrap this mess up too."

"Shouldn't we clean up the crime scene Jack? I got a rifle in the back of my truck and there's a bag of money and a knife buried in the woods, isn't there?"

"No, no, buddy. There's nothing buried in there. I told Bill that story to get him out here. No money, and as for the knife, I have it hidden. I'll give it to Mazer when things settle. If I mention it now he'll probably arrest me, or us. Let him keep his head on this place and Bill. We could use a break. I'll come clean though, I promise."

"Makes sense. Mazer won't be happy until he locks you up. He told me that much. Call him. Try to hide my rifle in the back of my truck first please. Nothing illegal, if he finds it, he finds it. I just can't take any more questions now either."

Jack walked to the back of Artie's truck and sat down on the tailgate. He reached into the truck bed and moved the rifle under some old tarps. He called the Pyrite station and was told to sit tight, Mazer would call him back.

As Jack sat waiting for his call, Artie nosed around Bill's body. He wanted things to look as sown up as imaginable for Mazer but was careful to not put his fingerprints on anything. He saw his gun next to Bill and entertained thoughts of grabbing it, but he suspected that Jack saw Bill with two handguns and had to let this one be. He long ago filed the serial number off his gun so he had no worries about it coming back to him. He walked back to his truck and saw that Jack was still waiting. As soon as the cell phone rang Jack jumped off the tailgate and walked away for privacy. Artie took a rag from his truck and soaked it in the tiny creek running into the dying field. He wiped his sweating head down and studied Bill's body one last time before throwing the rag back in his truck. He felt a little cooler now and wondered how long before

Jack would be done talking to Mazer. His answer came immediately as Jack walked back to him with his cell phone now in his pocket.

"Mazer was in Greenleaf; he's calling his station and getting Denton and a couple more uniforms here, he'll be here as soon as he can. He wants us to wait, but I'm sure you figured that already. Weird sitting by a dead body. Great reunion, wasn't it Artie?"

"You know death never really left me after Sylvia and Rachel died, and it was so soon after Nancy's dad passed. Then her daughter and husband. If I didn't believe we were cursed before, I sure do now. Hope Mazer doesn't keep us long like he did last time. I have a wife to look out for."

"No idea. We're at his mercy now. I'd like to get back to Shelby. She's hiding out in a cabin we found a few miles from here."

"Back on government wilderness land? There's nothing supposed to be up there. Be funny if after all this you get arrested for trespassing."

"There's some old mining claims northwest of town on old Goldpan Road. One or two cabins survived. Teens probably sneak up there today for you know what. I don't think the cops know about it, no reason to go up there even if they did. I used to hunt up there with my dad and was just recalling the old days with Shelby when we spotted the place. The cabin's actually fairly new, I don't know who would have built something in such a useless, dying place, but it gave me and Shelby a night of rest. And before you ask, nothing happened, were just old friends but I hope to change that for the better. I really like her buddy, in fact she's the only girl I ever loved, and I want to keep it that way."

"I guess you're crazy Jack, but who am I to talk, I've been with Rita longer than memory. Here comes a squad car. I'm gonna throw up, I hate this."

A Pyrite squad car pulled to a stop and Denton and two cops that Jack hadn't seen before got out. They each took a deep a breath and looked around. They said that Mazer told them to secure the crime scene and have everyone wait until he gets here. They of course checked Bill's body and with most of his head blown away confirmed he was dead. Jack and Artie watched the cops look over the crime scene, it was done out of curiosity, not duty, and then the cops got together. Jack looked at Bill's body and asked Artie if the gun was always in Bill's hand or if the cops planted it there. Artie was sure it was always there. He remembered Bill aiming it at him every second that they were here. Mazer came flying up in another Pyrite squad car and parked and walked over to Jack and Artie who were still sitting on the tailgate of Artie's red Dodge truck. "I knew from the moment I met you two that things would end in this scene. I didn't know the place, I didn't foresee Bill or your truck, but I saw me standing in front of you two as well as I've ever seen anything in my life."

"Hey, hang on Bob," Jack said, "we had nothing to do with this. Bill was shot from a good distance as he was about to shoot Artie. We have no idea who did it but thank God he did."

"You seem at peace Jack. Does anything ever bother you? A man's head blown off? A puddle of blood? Good friends murdered one after another? No, not you. You look like you're ready to go to a show at a comedy club. Mr. Cool." Mazer walked over to the body and knelt beside it. He looked at the giant hole where the back of his head used to be. "High powered rifle, dead center of the head, bullet exploded on entry. You gents are clear on this one." He took out his note pad and made some notes and then gave orders to one of his subordinates. "Phone in an APB on Hunter Tracy. Only the mob gets even like this. Bill asked for it but I still can't let it go, I have to look for the guy. And now you two clowns, who make every day harder for me than the day before, what the hell are you doing here."

Jack retold the story he just told Artie, all the way up to where Mazer came speeding over the rocks and dying weeds.

Mazer then turned to Artie and asked what he was doing there.

Artie told his story about literally being kidnapped and made to dig for money in the woods. He said that his life was within seconds of coming to an end because they couldn't find anything or even dig too deep in the rock hard dirt. He said that Bill pushed him down on his knees and he was sure that he himself got shot when the bullet struck Bill. He said that he was the most surprised man in the world that he was still alive.

"Can we leave now Bob? You got your body, you know who the shooter is, there's nothing else here for anybody."

"Slow down Artie. Why did Bill make you dig here? Jack said

he was looking for money by a buried body. Isn't that right Jack."

"I made up the story about the money. No way was I, or anyone else, going to give that bum any money."

"Show my officers where Bill had you digging Artie."

I'll try to find it but we walked all over the place in there and didn't get far in the little I dug. I think that Bill saw that the ground wasn't disturbed, nothing was buried anywhere in there and he got really pissed."

"This girl that you think might be buried around here, she wear a lot of jewelry in high school, you know, rings, necklace, watch, stuff like that?"

"Junk jewelry if anything Bob," Jack told him, "she didn't have money. I think she used to wear 2 or three rings all on the same hand, left, no, right, she wore them on her right hand. Why"?

"Just a hunch." Mazer went over to the trunk of his squad car and took out a shovel and metal detector and handed it to Denton. "Take one of these officers and Artic and scour where Bill had him digging. If anything's buried there we'll find it. Dig carefully, go slow."

"It's way too hot to dig fast boss. Let's go boys."

Mazer sat on the tailgate next to Jack and soon started tapping his keys on the metal, *tap, tap, tap*. Very rhythmic, very aggravating to Jack. *Tap, tap, tap*, he continued. Jack wiped the sweat from the back of his neck and jumped down from the truck and began pacing around the field. Mazer took out his notebook and made some more notes. When his thoughts were all recorded on paper he continued to doodle and scribble away, talking just loud enough to be heard, "of course that's it," and "why didn't I see that before." Jack stared at Mazer and shook his head. If Mazer could read minds Jack would now be under arrest. Finally a shout came from the woods, it was Denton, "we got something boss. We're coming out."

Denton walked out of the woods with Artie and the uniformed officer. Denton was carrying the metal detector and a shovel, the other officer was carrying a shovel that Bill and Artie left behind. All three men appeared pale and they were as silent as they could be as they walked. Denton had a hard time getting enough air and walked up to Mazer and shook his head, it looked like he was going to be sick.

"Give it to me from the beginning Denton," Mazer told Denton, "that's important."

Denton held his hand up to ask for a minute and tried to recall his steps. He spoke slowly. "We followed Artie back and forth and deeper into the woods. He said that nothing looked familiar, everything looked the same. Then luckily I saw this shovel that they left back there. There was a small hole started near there but not much. I used the metal detector, right there boss and got a ping right away. I figured if it was a body then I was probably pinging a ring. So I started digging a couple feet above the ping, slow and careful like you said. It was tough digging, the ground hasn't seen much rain since spring. But it got easier as I dug. About a foot down I hit something and I switched to digging with my knife around whatever it was. I got it free boss. I pulled a human skull out of the ground. I dropped it right back down sir. We need some better equipment to get the whole body. Something bad happened here sir, this is what all our problems are about. We're standing on desecrated land."

"Calm down Denton. I'll get equipment and a crew up here. Pyrite Electric and their emergency team has all the equipment we need, call them now and tell them this is top priority. I'll bag the guns by Bill's body and get them to the Greenleaf lab. We need the Coroner from Greenleaf also, I'll let Tidrow know what we have here and he can send all the right people. We have enough daylight left to get a good start on this. You and the uniforms stay here. This area's off limits. Work with the crews when they get here. I'm taking these guns to Greenleaf after I pick some things up at my office. I'll call who I need to on my way there. Make sure those bones got treated with some respect, whoever it is, or was, has been through enough."

"What about these two guys?" Denton asked pointing to Jack and Artie.

"We can't arrest them for just being here but I still think Jack's guilty of something. They can leave here but they have to stay in Pyrite or Greenleaf. I think I need one more day with them just to wrap this up. If that body is Rachel Morgan, who the hell was at the reunion and who's been calling these guys? I just need a day Denton, one more day."

Mazer took off for the station to get his file on the

Sylvia/Rachel case. Denton told Jack and Artie that they had to leave the crime scene but remain reachable and go no further than Greenleaf. Jack and Artie had a quick talk in Artie's truck before heading out.

"Listen Jack, we're done here, it's finally over. If we opened our mouths 25 years ago I guess this would have been solved then, but we didn't and we can't change that now. Paul paid for what Bill did, we have to live with that. No point in ruining our lives any further, Paul's dead, let him rest in peace. If you could talk to him he'd tell you that's all he wants. And we can get Rachel buried by Sylvia. I suppose he'd want that too. Time to really shut-up. I'll keep my restaurant, you keep your million dollar a year job, and let's go our separate ways. Take Shelby with you, start a better life. But don't give Mazer that knife, it can only hurt us at this point."

"I have to think about that. I'm a little tired of looking over my shoulder for 25 years. I'll let you know."

"Be careful. You know your fingerprints are on that knife too."

"No they're not Artie, yours either. That knife someone sent you was a prop, just a gimmick. Someone used it to get the killer here and it worked, we got Bill. I have the actual knife hidden. They can do a lot better testing on it today than they did back then. It will have Bill's DNA all over it, hell they're pulling DNA now from the days of Julius Caesar. May be best to turn it over."

At this Artie flew off and got in Jack's face. "What do you mean a prop? What the hell are you talking about? Someone's setting you up Jack. Get rid of that damn knife already, give it to me if you have to before we both end up like Caesar. I'm telling you things can only go south from here, leave well enough alone. I just want my normal life back, can't you see that?"

"Calm down, I understand what you're saying but every time we tried to leave well enough alone we got dragged in deeper. Let me think about it."

"You staying at the Peaks tonight?"

"Yeah, probably. I still have my room there and it'll be where Mazer can find me. I'll talk to you later."

The men drove off and went in separate directions from Main Street Pyrite. Only one thing that Artie said made any sense to Jack, *'if you could talk to Paul,'* that's exactly what he intended to do.

CHAPTER 36

On the Road Again

Jack got back to the cabin and found an exhausted Paul, the walk was longer and harder than he thought it would be, and Donna and Shelby shaking in fear. While fighting for air, Paul struggled through the story of following Bill Addison to Rachel's grave and the gunshot that hopefully ends the nightmare. They needed Jack to tell them everything that happened after Paul left the church. Jack picked up the story where Mazer reached the crime scene of Bill's murder and explained in as great a detail as he could Bill's head wound, the finding of a body in the woods, Artie's anger, and Mazer ordering him to stay put near Pyrite. He said that it wasn't completely over but close enough to breathe easy. He felt that they'd all be cleared now and it was time to look forward to the beginning of the next phase of their lives. He took in a deep breath and tried to read the look in everyone's eyes.

Paul felt good inside even though his face said otherwise. The man who framed him was dead and Rachel would get a better final resting place than what she was shoved into and slowly rotting away in for the past 25 years. He finally felt some peace and was thinking about turning himself in. The others who also finally felt a small of amount of peace, were in complete disagreement with this and knew that that would be a huge mistake. They felt that no matter what the knife showed or what Rachel's remaining bones showed, Paul would be sent back to the Pen for Sylvia's murder and have to continue serving his sentence.

Jack spoke for Shelby and himself. "We know this isn't fair Paul, but whatever plan you have for you and Donna getting away, you have to do it now. I don't want to hear one word of what you have up your sleeve and I don't want to hear one word from you when you're gone. Just disappear. You have no choice. I'll get Rachel's remains and try to find her family to give them to. If I can't do that I'll have her remains cremated, buy a nice urn and bury her with Sylvia. That's sadly the best we can do. It's better than what Bill got. He's burning in hell already."

"You're right Jack", Paul said while staring at the cabin floor, "everyone believes I'm dead now, let's leave it at that. Take the box with the murder weapon and do what you think best with it. Me and Donna always wore gloves in here so we wouldn't leave any prints. You and Shelby leave first, we have a plan. My emotions can't handle much more, but I think I have a lot of life left. Maybe tomorrow things will start to be better. If not, I guess we can always come back."

Leaving Paul and Donna with a half-smile, Jack took Shelby by the hand and walked her to the car. They talked about maybe having a normal evening before wrapping thinks up with Mazer tomorrow. About 30 minutes after they left the cabin, they heard an explosion come from that direction. Paul's new lease on life started with a bang.

"You know Shel, when Mazer gets this box and sees Paul's name on it, he's going to have questions that we'll have a hard time answering. I think we should hide it for a few days so Paul can put some distance between him and Pyrite. What do you think?"

"I guess. Do what you think is best."

Jack turned around and drove back to his old property and walked from the bottom of the drive to where he buried the other knife. He put this box in the hole and covered it pretty well. He was definitely nervous, but felt he was doing the right thing. He and Shelby were both silent for the rest of their ride back to Greenleaf. They both were anxious to get on the road to New York but with every step they made to get away, there seemed to be too much holding them back. Finally being closer than ever, the worries and fears were almost overwhelming. Up in the room Shelby hit the shower, Jack hit the minibar and the bourbon. The church bells rang and as it had before when they rang, everything seemed so wrong.

As the day finally wound down for Jack and Shelby, things were still heating up in the Greenleaf station. Mazer gave the lab technician the two guns taken from Bill and had him dust for prints. He wanted the prints run through the Greenleaf software and also sent to FBI lab for additional comparisons with their database. While this was happening, Mazer sat down with Jeff Tidrow and brought him up to speed on the Bill Addison murder. Mazer said the last thing that he needed now was another case as the Lynn and Steve murders were all but wrapped up. He knew it was it was his job though and knew the shooter was Hunter Tracy. He had Tidrow bring him the file and he called Tracy's lawyer. He got a secretary and asked to speak with Harold Frick, the name on the lawyer's card in the file. It took a while, but in about 10 minutes Frick picked up. Mazer started right in.

"Mr. Frick I need you to put me in touch with one of your clients. It's about a murder so don't play coy with me. I'm the police chief in Pyrite, Colorado, Bob Mazer, and I'm working hand in hand with the Greenleaf police department. We had your boy Hunter Tracy in here recently on another matter and have every reason to believe he gunned down one of our citizens. If you don't want to get in deep into this killing tell me where I can find him."

"Oh hell, I'm sorry Bob, is it alright I call you Bob?"

"Go ahead."

"I should have told you right off that I was recording our conversation, I record all incoming calls. But all's well I guess, you didn't really threaten me. Saying you're going to pull me deep into a murder unless I give you something, I guess some judge somewhere could find that innocent enough. But continue Bob now that you know you're being recorded."

Bob let out a gasp and shook his head, he didn't want to appear weak or nervous, he tried to sound unshaken. "I don't care about your goddamn recording, just tell me where to find Hunter Tracy."

"Slow down Bobby. Can I call you Bobby?"

"Bob."

"Slow down Bob, I didn't realize you were such a tough guy. For the record, I don't now, nor have I ever, as best as I can recollect, represented or known, any Hunter Tracy. Send your arrest record to my office and I'll have a look at it, for legal reasons. Always happy to help small town police. You sound so frazzled Bob, you must be quite understaffed."

And with that Harold Frick ended the call. Mazer had nothing and he knew it. No picture, no prints, not even a real name. He knew he was not much of a detective and longed to return to his simple police duties. He felt that everyone connected to the murders were always a step ahead of him and then they disappeared. As he said to a bewildered Tidrow, "It's always the wrong people who disappear," and then he called it a night. "See you in the morning."

CHAPTER 37

The End of a Long Week

Promptly at 8:00 am, the church bells rang 9 o'clock. In step with the time if not the bells, the phone in Jack and Shelby's room also rang. Artie had spent a sleepless night thinking about bringing the week and the murders to an end. Deep in his gut he knew that he would have to convince Jack what was right if he ever hoped to move past things. He dialed up the hotel early hoping to shake Jack out of his sleep.

"You up and about?" Artie asked.

"Up, not about. I couldn't sleep last night. It will be like this for the rest of my life if I don't do something."

"I agree, I was up all night too. We have to get the knife to Mazer and tell him about the closet and how we stole Paul's car. Since Paul's long dead, maybe Mazer drops the case or gets Paul's sentence overturned. As for last weekend's murders, this woman pretending to be Rachel and her partner are the ones who killed our friends, Mazer has to know that. You give me the knife Jack and I'll get Mazer off of your back, you and Shelby can put this town behind you and I can go back to my holier than thou wife and restaurant life."

"Okay," Jack answered, "it's the only thing we can do. Let me wake Shelby and get her some breakfast. I'll walk over when we're done and we can go get the knife. I wonder if they got Rachel out of that hole last night. Maybe her ghost kept us awake all night."

"Ghosts only live in our heads, what we're doing will drive them away. Get here as soon as you can."

As promised, Mazer was back at the Greenleaf station early. The lab worked most of the night testing for prints on Bill's guns and uploading the information into their computers. Their new software could read and trace a lot in a few hours. Additional help was sought from the FBI lab in Denver. All info uploaded in the Greenleaf computers was sent there. If any valuable info was buried deep, the FBI would have it. Mazer and Tidrow hoped that the info that their computers had access to would tell them something, anything, to help wrap up the case. They were more interested in last weekend's murders than long forgotten murders from 25 years ago. But if one case helped solve another, they were all for it. While their computers were spinning and searching files, the Medical Examiner phoned from the hospital where the morgue and exam room were located. Tidrow put the M.E. on speaker.

"Got your body a while ago. She was put in a couple of garbage bags and then wrapped in some clear plastic, nothing special, something like the cleaners would put your clothes in. But all that plastic that seems to take a thousand years to decompose and our past years of dry weather preserved a fair amount of bone. Your boy Denton ripped through the garbage bag and encountered that skull. I have a lot of careful clean up to do but I see a bad cut through the left side of her sternum. Looks like a knife went in there, sliced the sternum and got buried deep in her heart. She never had a chance. Female, probably about 20 years old at time of death, homicide. I can't say how long she's been buried but it's been a while. She wasn't buried very deep, whoever did it was in a hurry. I'm guessing that with what's left of her, that's about all the useful info you're going to get."

The call was ended and Mazer and Tidrow discussed Rachel Morgan. They figured this had to be her missing body and that means that someone else in town is impersonating her. They suspected Shelby or Rita, but couldn't make any motive for either of them to perpetrate that hoax. They figured that whoever made those calls was working with the murderer, Bill Addison, and that made no sense to them.

"You know Jeff," Mazer said to Tidrow, "the only person who I've heard mention Rachel is that Jack Spencer guy. He keeps giving me leads and then the rug gets pulled out from under me."

"Isn't he the one that organized this entire reunion with his old so called friends? He's the one that got them all here and then they started getting killed. Do you trust him?"

"Not for one damn second. He rubbed me the wrong way from the second I met him, hovering over the dead body of Steve Connor without a care in the world. I have to check my notes but I think he first mentioned Rachel that day, I know he tried to blame Paul Winston then too, but we learned that Winston was dead. That may have thrown his plan, whatever his stupid plan is, into chaos."

"And then he shows up hovering over the body of Bill Addison," Tidrow noted.

"Yeah, dammit. And he's the one, the only one, who saw a man in a black car fire the shot that killed Bill. Did that son of a bitch set me up again?"

As Mazer's blood pressure was about to make his head explode, they got a call from the downstairs Greenleaf lab. "We got something, get down here."

Tidrow and Mazer hurried downstairs to the lab, the technician was looking through his microscope and immediately left his seat when the officers entered the room. He had a point he wanted to make. He asked Mazer to take his pistol out of his holster and tuck it behind him in his belt. Mazer followed the instructions.

"I trust the safety is on," he said to Mazer, who nodded. "Now pull the gun out and pretend to use it to make me walk across the room."

Again Mazer followed the request and they walked across the room.

"I see you withdrew your firearm with your left hand, moved it to your right. Held it near me and changed hands again to get your gun feeling right in your hand."

"Of course, I can't draw a gun from a belt and be in shooting position. It has to be right if I'm going to use it. What's your point?"

"My point is that you probably just put 4, maybe 5 sets of fingerprints on your gun."

"And?" Mazer asked.

"The gun in your dead man's hand had one. One set that shows his gun was very loosely held in his hand. Not the print we should see if a gun was quickly grabbed from the man's belt."

"It was planted? That damn Jack was alone with the body."

"We could never prove that it was planted, all conjecture at this point. But it made me look further."

"Where else could you look?"

"The bullets Bob. I dusted the bullets for prints and sent those to the FBI also. Their discovery and full report will be here any second on my e-mail. I print their attachment and you got your man."

"Can they match them to the bullets we got from last weekend's shootings?"

"Not the bullets that were still in the gun Bob, they can only match bullets that have been fired."

"Damnit," Mazer said.

"Don't despair Bob. We have a chamber for this very purpose. I fired a couple bullets from the .22 you gave me and sent them on to Denver. They should have them soon and if this is your guy you'll have solved this case and probably the murders from 25 years ago. A good job Bob."

The beep the lab tech was waiting for sounded. "The report's here. I'll print the attachment."

Mazer and Tidrow followed the tech to his printer.

"What's your murderer's name Bob?" The tech asked while smiling at his report.

"Bill Addison. God Damn Bill Addison."

The smile left the tech's face as he handed the report to Mazer. "You got a big problem Bob."

"We gotta run Tidrow," Mazer said as he ran toward the stairs. He yelled across the room at Denton who was sitting at the oversized window. "Get your squad car and follow me."

"Where we heading?"

"Peaks Hotel, Room 301."

With his siren blaring, Mazer sped to the Peaks. He had Tidrow call the front desk from his cell phone and order them to program a key for room 301. Mazer and Denton pulled in front of the hotel and charged up the front stairs. Tidrow got the key from the hotel manager who informed him he didn't hear what room key he needed so he coded him a master. The trio ran up the hotel's main stairway. Mazer pounded on the door and yelled police as he inserted the key card. They were in the room before a stunned Shelby knew what was happening. She threw her hands in the air and a look of fear covered her face.

"Where's Jack?" Mazer shouted.

"He went to Artie's place," she answered as well as she could with three guns trained on her.

"Dammit," Mazer said under his breath, "what's his plan there?"

"He said that now that Bill's been identified as the murderer that he and Artie want to give you the knife from Sylvia's and Rachel's murders. They're going to get it and bring it to the Pyrite station, they thought you'd be there Bob."

"They got a big head start on us Tidrow, we may be too late. Denton, take Shelby over to the restaurant and grab Rita. Don't let either of them near a phone. Arrest them if you have to and put them in a holding cell."

"Arrest them for what Boss?"

"I don't give a damn, think of something. Littering if you need a crime."

"Take me with you Bob," Shelby pleaded, "I know where the knife is, I can take you there."

"In the woods behind Jack's old home?"

"Yes."

"I know exactly where the knife is. You're going with Denton. Get moving. We gotta fly Tidrow, let's move."

Denton took Shelby's cell phone and drove her to the restaurant. He went in alone and got Rita to come outside to supposedly talk to Shelby. Once there, he took Rita's phone and put her in the back seat of the squad car with Shelby. He locked them together in a holding cell on suspicion of aiding in committing a crime. He didn't bother with any paperwork. He walked back to the window where he started his morning and prayed that there wouldn't be any more dead bodies in Pyrite or Greenleaf. His view down Main Street looked as peaceful as any town in the world. The scenes whirling around his head told a much different story.

Jack and Artie reached Jack's old ranch and parked well below the house at the bottom of the driveway. Jack led the way to where he buried the knife and talked a bit about getting this incredibly bad nightmare behind them. He spoke a bit about Lynn and Steve and said he believed they were just two unlucky people dragged where they didn't belong. Artie wasn't listening too intently and kept a close eye on Jack. He wasn't about to trust anybody at this point in the game. Jack stopped walking and knelt down in the dirt.

"It's right here buddy. I'll dig it up and we can take it right to the Pyrite station." Jack brushed the dirt away and slowly reached into the ground. Artie's eyes were on him and he pulled a gun out from under his belt and hid it behind his back. Jack jumped up and turned quickly to face Artie, he had in his hands what he came for and looked into Artie's eyes. Artie swung his arms out from behind him and pointed his silver .22 between Jack's eyes. "Drop it right there, old friend."

CHAPTER 38

The Nightmare Ends

Jack threw the package with the knife in it on the ground. He had no idea what Artie was up to and he let him know it.

"What the hell's wrong with you? We agreed this has to be turned in to the Pyrite police. Give it right to Bob Mazer if we can. Tell the whole story and then we walk away."

"I can't let you do that. It would end my life. My fingerprints and DNA have to be all over that knife. When I got the knife someone left in the restaurant I panicked. I figured it came from a cop on the inside and had to be the real murder weapon. Destroying it wouldn't be enough if they had test results on it so I got you to put your fingerprints on it and I thought that would settle things until that stupid wife of mine gave it to Lynn. I couldn't let it go any further, but it did. I end it here."

"Killing me won't do you any good. Shelby knows I left Greenleaf with you. You're probably looking at the death penalty already, but if you kill me too, you for sure will be."

"Interesting take buddy but that's not how this is going down." Artie cocked his gun and waved it at Jack. "Sit down right there and listen." Artie put some hotel stationery and a pen on the knife package and pushed it in front of Jack with his foot, never taking his gun's aim away from him. "Before I shoot you Jack, I'd like you to write your final goodbye in a suicide note. Be sure to confess to killing Sylvia, Rachel, Lynn, and Steve. Make it sound convincing."

"There's no way I'm doing that, shoot me if you think you have to, but all the murders are landing right on you. You'll spend your life in prison until the day they strap you on your gurney with a needle in your arm. I guess it's over for both of us."

"Hey Jack, I wouldn't ask you to write that note that will keep me in the clear without giving you something of equal or greater value. You can tell Shelby that you love her in your note and apologize for everything that went so wrong."

"You are so out of touch Artie. There will be no note. Your offer is rejected."

"You didn't hear it all yet. With no note, and I can live with that, as soon as I shoot you I'm heading to Greenleaf and having my way with Shelby before I put a bullet in her head and let her know that it was done with your blessing."

At this, Jack screamed at Artie and tried to get up off of the ground. He was met with the butt of the gun crashing into his skull and a kick to his face. He laid flat on his face in the dirt with blood running from his head and mouth. His mind was in a cloud and he thought for a minute he was dreaming until he heard Artie's voice again.

"That was stupid Jack. Now listen, I have no reason to kill Shelby and I don't want to. You write that note and I'll tell her how much you loved her and that you just had some issues that we can't even begin to guess at. She leaves here confused but she leaves here alive and not in a box. It's all up to you now."

Jack's senses were starting to return to near normal and saving Shelby with his last act in life seemed to be all he had left. "Okay, I'll write it. But I have to know why you did everything. What happened to you Artie?"

"Start writing Jack, I don't want to be here all day. You want to know what happened? I'll tell you. My deeply religious wife Rita happened. Always telling me I had to wait until we were married before we had sex. I didn't understand it and it got the best of me that night. I was pretty liquored up at the class night celebration and kept sipping from my flask all night. I drove Rita home, her folks weren't home and I wanted her so bad. She cussed me out, threw her religion in my face, and ran inside. I sat there like a fool until I decided to get another pint of whiskey. I went to the liquor store, Reef's, where Louie worked, he always served us guys, and Sylvia was outside the place and she told me that Louie wouldn't serve girls. She asked me to get her a bottle of wine. I told her I would and bring it to her house because Louie didn't serve the boys either if girls were with them. She went to her new place on Mineral Road and I joined her about 15 minutes later. I gave her a bottle of cheap as crap red wine and drank quite a bit more of my whiskey. She said that she wanted to show me her bedroom but I knew she wanted a lot more than that. It should have been good Jack, but when I tried to kiss her, she started fighting and screaming, we fought like hell and I guess at some point I had her by the throat and covered her mouth. I thought she calmed down and I let her go, but she never moved. I never meant to hurt her, but in my drunken fury, I accidently killed her. Then I heard that bitch Rachel screaming at me and yelling about calling the police, I didn't even know she was in the house. I ran after her and she ran into the back bedroom. I picked a knife up from their kitchen table and caught up with her. She was staring at me and reaching for her phone, I knocked her onto the bed and drove the knife into her chest. She made some sounds but not for very long, it felt like I mentally blacked out for a while. When I came around I saw Rachel laying in a pool of blood. I found some large plastic garbage bags and wrapped her in them. When I went outside with her body I saw a huge sheet of plastic covering some plants in front of the house. I spread that out and rolled Rachel in that too. Then I drove well off the road as far as I could and dragged her as far back as I could and buried her and covered her with rocks. I knew the place and the plastic would keep her hidden. I started believing I could get away with this. How's that note coming?"

Jack was trying to write a cryptic note that only Shelby would understand without risking her life. "It's coming. And you still had a problem with Sylvia's body didn't you?"

"Yeah, that could have been a problem. I drove back to Sylvia's house and parked a ways down the road. I called Paul Winston and told him that Sylvia needed him right away at her new place. He asked who I was and I told him to just hurry, Sylvia's in trouble.

He showed up in a few minutes and was creeping all around the house, he finally went in and I called the police. I told them I lived on Mineral Road and I just heard some screaming and fighting coming form that address and it sounded real bad. The cops were there in seconds and set up in front of the house with their guns drawn. Seconds later that stupid ass Paul Winston comes staggering out, covered in blood carrying a dead Sylvia Kean. Idiot walked right into a murder charge. It got real hectic after that with more squad cars pulling up and cops pushing Paul around, an ambulance sped in with siren blaring, some press people showed up just getting in the way. It was insane. I headed home and tried to sober up. It was all an accident that just got out of hand."

"Paul Winston was no accident. You framed the poor guy instead of taking your medicine. No wonder you sat like a statue at his trial and kept your mouth shut."

"Yeah, and when they introduced that knife as evidence I almost died. I thought I buried it with Rachel, it must have fallen off of her on my way out and I thought it would bury me. Turns out they probably didn't run all the tests they should have on it, they only wanted to link it to Paul, and somehow they did. My big gaffe actually saved me and got Paul convicted. When they lost the knife, I almost started crying in the court room. I knew I beat it. I beat it until that knife showed up and you mentioned Rachel calling you. It started all over again, that 25 year old nightmare seemed like it happened a day ago. My mind stopped working again and I had no idea what to do. My first thought was to pick everyone's brain at the reunion, maybe we were all in agreement to keep our mouths shut. But not you righteous bastards, you all wanted to hang somebody. The get together was a bad idea, you caused all this Jack. You're the one who has to pay. Let me see that note."

Jack hesitated as he still had questions about his other friends. "I know you killed Lynn and Steve to get the knife, but you really messed up with Bill. No knife and he was still alive to identify you."

"Bill's a whole different story. I took a quick look around his room when we got back from Pyrite but I was pretty sure that you had the knife by that time. Steve and Lynn never trusted Bill, you were all that was left. I was doing a quick look, I didn't even know

Bill was in the room. When I went to look under his mattress for the knife I caught sight of a badly beaten Bill Addison laying on the floor. Before I could get out of his room he started to come to. He sat up and scared the hell out of me. I shot from impulse. He never saw me. It was more his fault than mine."

"Always someone else's fault with you isn't it?" Jack said as he handed his note to Artie.

Artie read it while keeping one eye on Jack. "Nice touch Jack, finally telling Shelby you love her. I like this part here, '*if Paul were alive today Shel, I'm sure he would understand what I had to do, I hope you can find some understanding for me. I love you.*' Very sweet. You covered all the murders, Shelby will live a long life now, rest assured of that." Artie handed the note back to Jack. "Put this in your pocket, it's time to end this."

"I hope this whole thing blows up in your face and you're facing death just like this someday, only strapped to a prison gurney. But it won't come from me, I'm gladly trading you my life for Shelby's. I'm actually getting the better part of the deal."

"You've finally changed Jack, but it's too late."

Artie held the gun against Jack's head. Jack shook and waved his hands in the air. "Hang on a second, give me a last request. I built a treehouse in that tree right in front of us when I was about 10. Hell Artie, you played with me here hundreds of times when we were kids. Let me kneel there and say my prayers before you shoot. Finding me dead there will fit with your sick note."

Artie obliged his ex-friend and followed him to his tree, the one with a ring of painted rocks hidden beneath 30 plus years of weeds and dirt. Jack knelt with his back to Artie and instantly found a good size rock. He hung his head and began reciting the Lord's Prayer, Artie listened impatiently and took a quick glance at his watch. Before he knew what happened Jack was on his feet and the rock crashed hard through his head. Artie fell backwards and saw the entire forest spinning around him. Jack raced past him and zigged and zagged his way towards the highway. He ran downhill between trees and cut back in the direction he came from, but well below where he left Artie. He was near exhaustion but fear kept him running. He felt he was beyond Artie and made his way back uphill heading for his old house. Each step he took was burning his legs and he crouched behind a thick pine tree and tried to catch his breath, he didn't recognize his surroundings and wasn't sure if he was heading to his old home or back to the old treehouse. He thought a bullet in his back would ruin Artie's plan but he couldn't be sure. A bullet in his back would probably mean a bullet for Shelby, he had to get out alive. A gun went off and Jack heard Artie call his name. Jack couldn't tell where the voice came from so he continued running uphill. When he heard Artie call again he thought the sound was deeper in the woods. He turned to his right and was now running downhill again. He was crying now and kept repeating Shelby's name to himself. He believed the driveway was just a short distance ahead and he felt a last spark of optimism and hope when he was suddenly tackled from behind and felt a gun pressed against his face. He heard the voice in spite of his panic and his heart was beating too fast to last much longer. The voice spoke again, "don't move, stay quiet." It wasn't Artie.

"Mazer?" Jack whispered.

Mazer got off of Jack. "Yeah. Keep quiet. Tidrow's moving up from the highway. I'm going up higher and coming down on Artie from the house level. You need to stay out of the way. Keep low."

"How'd you figure it out."

Time was critical now and Mazer couldn't waste any of it in long stories about police work. He did give Jack a quick explanation. 'We matched the gun to Artie and all the shootings. Now lay low."

"Let me go with you Bob. I know these woods better than anyone. I have my bearings now. I can get you to Artie without him seeing us. Maybe you won't have to shoot him."

Mazer agreed and the pair walked a bit uphill before turning left and heading deeper into the woods. They walked in an awkward crouch using the wider trees for cover. As they got closer they could hear Artie's voice calling Jack in an almost casual way. They caught sight of Artie behind some narrow cottonwoods. Mazer told Jack to call out and let Artie know that he was surrounded. Jack did as he was told but Artie laughed him off. Mazer fired a shot into the air. They had Artie's attention now.

"There's more cops coming up the hill from below you too Artie. Put your gun down, end this. Make your peace with Rita. Don't go out like this."

Jack could see Artie sitting low with his back against a tree. He found the compassion to feel bad for his former friend now facing the last important decision of his life. Artie finally spoke.

"Rita put me in this hole, I have no peace to make with her. Come on down Jack. Borrow a gun, we'll iron things out."

Mazer took over the standoff. "Bob Mazer here Artie. It's over. You got one minute to toss your gun out and lay flat on your stomach. In one minute, we're coming in firing."

In exactly one minute shots came from below. Tidrow was firing in Artie's direction. Fear now filled Artie way more than he ever imagined. Death stood taller when it stood next to him. Artie screamed out.

"Hold your fire. I give up." His gun came flying out from behind the trees and Artie followed. He took 2 steps and collapsed in the dirt. Mazer ran in first and kicked the gun further away. Tidrow came up right after Mazer and picked up the gun in his gloved hand. Jack sat near his old favorite tree and held back all of his emotions. Mazer cuffed Artie and pulled him to his feet. He frisked him and found nothing more than his truck keys. Mazer and Tidrow walked Artie up to Jack. Artie's eyes were distant and he didn't say a word. Mazer tossed the truck keys to Jack.

"Get his truck off the road and drive it back to the Greenleaf station. We're holding Shelby and Rita there now so they didn't call and get word to Artie that we were coming. I want to hold Rita for questioning. She may be involved or at least have known more about Artie's doings than we realized. We'll release Shelby to you and I trust you two can walk to the hotel from there. I want you at the Pyrite station by 9:00 tomorrow morning. We wrap this up and you and Shelby can be on your way. The sooner the better."

"You asked me once if anything ever bothered me Bob, does being completely dead inside count? Guess I'll see you in the morning."

EPILOGUE

Jack and Shelby spent a long quiet night at the Peaks. They brought in some take-out for dinner which neither of them really touched along with a bottle of wine which they completely polished off. They were both certain that Rita was innocent of any wrongdoing and that she'll be crushed to learn of her husband's heinous crimes. They reminded themselves that they too were fooled by Artie up to this point. They still had questions about what led Mazer to Artie, but Jack knew he'd get more info tomorrow. He also knew that Mazer probably had a few more questions for him, but felt that he had no more to tell. In the middle of their talk, Shelby's phone rang and for the first time in days she answered the call from her husband Eddie. It appeared to Jack that Eddie was trying to be decent to Shelby and this hit Jack hard. Soon the controlling monster that Eddie had become returned and Jack could feel his own anger rise.

With tears in her eyes, Shelby wrapped up her conversation as she wrapped up this phase of her life.

"I'm packing up and heading east. You'll get divorce papers in the mail. Goodbye Edward." She ended the call and turned off her phone. The mix of depression and joy wasn't anything new to her, but she felt that this was a good step to at least limit the bad days. Jack watched her pace around the room and look out the windows at the mountains around Pyrite. She returned to the nightstand where her plastic cup filled with red wine stood waiting. She finished it in one tilt of the cup and locked herself in the bathroom seeking darkness and a quiet place to cry. Over an hour later, she left the bathroom wearing her black lingerie and looking as beautiful to Jack as any woman ever could.

"I never did anything wrong Jack and still I got thrown into one bad world after the next. I have to put myself first from now on. It won't be easy, but it starts now. I'm leaving with you when we get finished in Pyrite. Goodnight Jack."

And seconds after crawling into bed Shelby was sound asleep. Jack's thoughts on how things would have been different if he just would have treated Shelby better from day one. Maybe all of their friends would still be here, and maybe Pyrite wouldn't be dying such a sad death. It was too much to put on his shoulders, but as he crawled into bed, the thoughts kept him up for hours. He had to learn to put Shelby first from now on also. And as Shelby had just told him, it won't be easy, but it starts now.

The next morning Jack was out of bed early only because he got tired of lying there without sleep. He dressed and told Shelby that he would be back as soon as Mazer was through with him. On his entire ride to Pyrite, he thought of a future spent with Shelby. Time passed quickly on his drive and he pulled in front of the Pyrite station without a single memory of the drive there. Mazer brought him into his office, an office that gave Jack a bad feeling, and the two spoke to one another in civil terms. Mazer explained that the Greenleaf inspector suspected right off that the gun was planted in Bill's hand. The gun had a covering of mud on it as if it was wiped down with a wet dirty rag. Mazer explained that that would get rid of most fingerprints and as you would expect the gun then only had one weak print. Mazer continued that any gun handled in a shooting and then carried around would have to have many more prints on it, so the inspector ran prints on the bullets. Mazer was happy to report that most shooters never think of leaving prints on the bullets and sure enough the only prints on these were Artie's. The inspector then shot a couple rounds in his lab and expressed the bullets to Denver. The FBI called yesterday and said that the bullets were fired from the same gun that was used to shoot Lynn, Steve, and Bill. We had Artie cold and needed to stop him from killing you. Mazer then wanted Jack to tie up loose ends.

"Artie confessed to everything last night and we have his written statement. He claimed killing Sylvia was an accident and things just got away from him after that. We told him that we were pretty sure Rita pretended to be Rachel and we would throw the book at her if he didn't confess everything. He crumbled. We won't bother Rita. You agree with that Jack?"

"Yeah, I doubt Rita knew anything and sometimes when you have a solid ending it's best to leave it go. Whoever made those calls solved a 25 year old double murder. You're going to clear Paul's name aren't you?"

"Of course. I'll turn everything over to the county DA. They can't convict Artie for killing Sylvia if the conviction on Paul still stands. They'll fix it. A little late I guess. We got the knife from where we arrested Artie yesterday too. Artie said that his prints and DNA should be all over it. That should make it easy to clear Paul's name."

"Shelby and I would like to leave here, forever, as soon as I get back. Sound good Bob?"

"Good idea, one last question. We had an explosion and a bad fire out on the edge of public lands north of town. Cabin blew up."

"That's too bad Bob. I didn't hear anything about it."

"No, I guess you wouldn't. Odd thing Jack, the cabin that blew up and then burned down was on property that once belonged to the Winston family."

"That is odd, Paul always lived in town while I knew him."

"We tried to find the current owner. The land was purchased about 5 years ago for back taxes by someone named Morgan Kean."

"I don't know any Morgan Kean, Bob, I'm afraid I can't help you."

"Just an unusual name Jack. I'll keep a file on it but it's nothing I want to look into unless I ever see you in this town again."

"I'd love to stay and visit Bob, but it sounds like I better get moving. By the way, thanks for saving my life yesterday, good police work, you won't be forgotten."

Jack took a last detour as he headed out of town, a short drive up the road towards his old home. He stopped and walked in the woods where his life nearly came to an end. He looked out to the pasture where a handful of cattle ate the last remaining blades of grass and recalled the happier days in Pyrite when they numbered in the thousands. He wished for the moment that he could reach out to Paul Winston and finally end his suffering with the cold truth. Just an idle thought now. He had no idea where Paul and Donna headed and Pyrite was soon to be nothing more than dust and rubble. Shelby was his priority now and all he wanted was to take her to places in her heart and mind where she wanted to go.

He left Pyrite with sadness, but also with hope. He drove in complete silence.

Jack got back to Greenleaf and loaded his and Shelby's things into her Jeep Liberty and left the keys for his rental with the manager of the Peaks. He then opened the door for Shelby and the two settled in for a long journey. Their only plan now was to drive up to Interstate 80 and head for New York.

The quiet was soon interrupted by the beeping of Jack's cell phone. Shelby read the message.

"Found the guy in Oklahoma that framed Donna's husband. Could use your help."

"What do you think Shel?"

"I've always wanted to see Oklahoma."

ABOUT THE AUTHOR

John Schraub was born and lived his early years in and around Chicago. Seeking a change of pace from city life, John relocated to a quiet corner of Colorado. He found the peace he sought amongst the mountains and rivers while hiking serene wilderness trails. He believes anyone who travels this world with a giving heart and eyes wide open can also find their place in it. John says his life can be understood best in the two words he said to himself when he sat alone on a high peak in the Rocky Mountains so many years ago, "I'm home."